"Mr. Chekov,
Please Take Us Down
Close to the Ground,"

Spock said. As Chekov pitched the joystick forward and eased back on the power, he asked, "Vhat are ve looking for, Mr. Spock?"

"Some indication of the location of the Centaurus Medical Complex," the Vulcan answered. "Dr. McCoy's daughter was a medical student there. I would like to be able to tell the doctor something of her fate."

At last, they noticed the stumps of what had been several Gothic-style buildings. Slowly, they coasted over the ruins of the Medical Complex. Here and there, dead littered the landscape.

Chekov's teeth were clenched. "Someone must answer for this . . . this . . . " He sought an adequate word, but could not find one.

They hovered over what had been the central square of the medical school campus. No one came out from hiding in response to the racket of their engines.

Finally, Chekov took them up and away.

Look for _Star Trek_ fiction from Pocket Books

CRISIS ON CENTAURUS

BRAD FERGUSON

A STAR TREK®
—NOVEL—

PUBLISHED BY POCKET BOOKS NEW YORK

Another *Original* publication of POCKET BOOKS

POCKET BOOKS, a division of Simon & Schuster, Inc.
1230 Avenue of the Americas, New York, N.Y. 10020

This book is Published by Pocket Books, a Division of
Simon & Schuster, Inc. Under exclusive License from
Paramount Pictures Corporation, The Trademark Owner.

ISBN: 0-671-65753-4

First Pocket Books Science Fiction printing March, 1986

10 9 8 7 6 5 4 3

Printed in the U.S.A.

For Linda,
who read it first during a very special time

Chapter One:
The Spaceport

As BEFIT THE capital of an old, successful colony planet, New Athens had built for itself the biggest (and, local boosters said, the best) spaceport on Centaurus—or anywhere else in the Federation.

The main concourse of New Athens Spaceport hummed and bustled with the gentle roar of twenty thousand travelers, each intent on getting to his (or her, or its) departure gate as quickly as possible. Not much had changed since the nineteenth century on Earth, when the locomotive had introduced humans to mass transportation; all that had been added was four hundred years of so-called progress in passenger handling. Perhaps one day the technology of the transporter would become advanced enough to allow cheap point-to-point transfer on the surface of a planet at no more risk than, say, getting there by shuttlecraft, or even airplane . . . but not yet. Until that welcome day, there would be a need for monster facilities such as New Athens Spaceport.

Most of the travelers hurrying on their way through the concourse were humans—but by no means all were. A sharp-eyed observer could easily pick out several individuals from virtually every member race of the Federation among the thousands of humans.

There was even a pair of Klingon traders heading quickly from one of the local gates to an interstellar flight bound for a neutral treaty port. New Athens was a cosmopolitan city, in the literal sense: Beings from *everywhere* lived in New Athens and did business there.

Souvenir stands lined the concourse. They did a brisk business in the traditional knickknacks bought by vacationers who, when home, knew better than to buy such junk. One small stand had been doing very well for years, selling overpriced replicas of the Statue of Liberty with SOUVENIR OF CENTAURUS and I LOVE NEW ATHENS stickers on their bases, even though the real statue still stood in New York Harbor—a mere 4.3 light years away—and had no sister on Centaurus.

Snack bars inadequately fed the hungry. These places, sometimes called "refreshment centers," depended on high volume, quick turnover, and the nimble wits of their human cashiers, who needed no computers to quickly translate Federation credits, Cygnian gold pieces, Vulcan work units or French francs into Centaurian pounds platinum, or to give the correct change in whatever currency the traveler desired—subject to a service charge, of course.

Snack bars, five-sensory computer games, bootshine parlors, and other facilities for private and more personal forms of amusement—all were open, and all were doing a brisk business.

But the most interesting attraction of the hour was to be found in Passenger Lounge B2 of Pan United Spaceways. About fifteen vending machines lined the walls of the lounge, stocked with everything from Coca-Cola to disposable shirts. A group of onlookers had formed around an American Express Travelers' Cheque Dispenser. The center of attention was a burly Tellarite businessman, who was arguing with the balky machine.

"Machine, I address you directly!" grated the Tellarite. "I am Gar, chief of the Knock tribe and with Gold Card number 02551-09334-97372, with suffix Delta-Zebra-Oscar! Satisfaction is what I demand! *Satisfaction is what I will get!*"

The machine remained silent.

"Give card back, you damn dumb machine!" roared Gar, flailing his arms. The watching humans inched away.

The machine flashed a hologram in Gar's eyes:

PLEASE CONTACT
YOUR LOCAL AMERICAN EXPRESS OFFICE
FOR ASSISTANCE.
USE THE VIDEOPHONE TO YOUR RIGHT.
WE APPRECIATE YOUR PATRONAGE. THANK YOU.

*　　*　　*

WHEN IN NEW ATHENS,
STAY AT THE SHERATON CENTAURUS.
COURTESY FLITTERS ARRIVE AT GATE HG26
EVERY TEN MINUTES.

"What?!?" exploded Gar. *"Commercials?!?* No more will I take; this I swear, by honor of Knock tribe!"

With a battle cry evocative of his porcine evolutionary path—a prejudiced human observer might say the Tellarite bellowed like a stuck pig—Gar smashed a meaty fist into the brittle plastic console of the American Express machine. It shattered, sending pieces flying into the air; the machine began to smoke and emit sparks. The Tellarite tore off what remained of the console's surface and quickly found what he was looking for: his American Express card, held firmly in the jaws of the machine's computer scanner.

With both his thumbs, Gar bent back the jaws and neatly extracted his card. Still facing the now-ruined machine, Gar assumed the Posture of Victory and gave out a mighty Tellarite victory howl, waving his slightly singed card in the air. Those watching Gar were silent for a moment.

Then they began to applaud and cheer.

Gar turned, startled, but recovered quickly. "Gar has won battle with machine," he announced. "You all go away now." But those in the lounge were now in no mood to leave and, in truth, Gar appreciated the presence of an audience. So Gar did not *insist* that anyone leave; he merely kept his desire at request level, continued to wave his American Express card in triumph, and drank in the approval of those around him.

But Gar's sharp, predator's eyes soon spotted two spaceport cops making their way quickly through the throng on the concourse. The Tellarite hurried into the crowds, there to lose himself among scores of other Tellarites, who were themselves lost among many thousands of beings from other races. The others in Lounge B2 had predator's eyes only slightly less keen; they spotted the approaching cops a few seconds later and scattered.

But there was someone else in Lounge B2 watching the progress of the spaceport police.

He was a nondescript, middle-aged human, wrapped in an ill-fitting and stained trenchcoat of standard Centaurian manufacture. There was nothing at all conspicuous about him. He was seated in a chair across the lounge from the ruined American Express machine. He had a small box on his lap. He treated it carefully.

He had been sitting there for seven hours, undisturbed.

At times he had pretended to doze, but sleep was the

farthest thing from his mind. That business with the Tellarite had made it impossible now to feign sleep; that swinish fool had simply made too much noise. The man regretted that; no one ever disturbed a dozing passenger waiting for a flight. It was a good cover. But now the pig-faced Tellarite had created all that commotion, and now everyone in the lounge—except, glaringly, for himself—had left quickly afterward. The man's anonymity had evaporated with the crowd.

Forty-five minutes past the deadline and still no word, the man thought fretfully. *Has the organization been penetrated? Did we have a spy in our midst after all?*

Perhaps they're looking for me even now, he worried.

The security guards arrived at Passenger Lounge B2 and looked around. The older of the two shook his head sadly. "Third vending machine we've lost this month," he grumbled to his partner. "We never find these guys."

"So what do we put on the report, Sarge?"

The sergeant shrugged. "We interview witnesses, try to get a description. Then the spaceport authority can issue an interstellar warrant for a misdemeanor charge, if it wants to."

"They wouldn't be that dumb, would they?"

"Nah. But the lieutenant wants reports. He *loves* reports. So we'll give him a report." The sergeant pointed to the man with the box. "That guy looks like he's been here for a while. Ask him what he saw; I'll look at the machine. Damn, I wish they'd fix these things so they stay fixed. Then people wouldn't bash 'em." The sergeant trudged off; his partner, notebook in hand, walked toward the man with the box.

Oh, no, thought the man. *He's coming over. Dammit—be calm!*

"Excuse me, sir," the younger cop said politely. "I'm Corporal Schmidt, of Spaceport Security."

The man looked up blandly. "How do you do, Corporal?"

"Fine, sir. I'd like to know if you saw or heard anything concerning the wrecking of that machine over there . . .?" The cop pointed over to the smoking, sparking wreck.

The man looked regretful. "I'm sorry, Corporal Schmidt. I was dozing and was awakened by this, uh, bellow. I looked, but there were too many people in the way to see anything. Everybody then headed for the concourse, I think."

"Yeah." The corporal frowned. "I can believe it." He whipped out a notebook. "If you don't mind, I'd like your name, please."

The man shifted the box on his lap. He smiled. "Uh, why, Corporal? I've told you I didn't see anything—"

"Just routine, sir. Your name, please?"

The man paused. "Gregory Lebow."

"Residence?"

"Second Try. That's in New Europe."

The corporal smiled. "Really? My mother's from the southern continent, too. Aquinasville. Ever been there?"

"Uh, no, Corporal. I don't get to travel as much as I'd like to."

"Oh. That's a shame. Well, what's your business in New Athens, Mr. Lebow?"

"Pleasure. I was visiting my sister here."

"Well, I hope you had a good time, sir. Uh, got an address in Second Try?"

The man made up something that sounded likely; he'd never been in Second Try. Corporal Schmidt scribbled down the address.

"It's not likely we'll ever bother you about this

incident, Mr. Lebow," the cop said. "Just a lot of nonsense, if you ask me." He smiled. The man smiled back, conspiratorially; inwardly he relaxed the merest fraction. *It's going to be all right,* he said to himself.

The sergeant came back from his brief inspection of the ruined machine. "Total loss. We'll call this in from the Pan United courtesy desk." He nodded in greeting to the man with the box, and smiled briefly.

But the sergeant's smile soon faded.

Oh, no, thought the man with the box.

The sergeant drew his phaser and held it on the man. "Don't move a millimeter," the sergeant ordered. "Schmidt, call this in. Tell 'em we've got Holtzman."

"Holtzman?" The corporal's mouth hung open.

"Move, dammit!" the sergeant growled.

"Yeah, Sarge, uh, sure. Right away!" The corporal hurried off as the sergeant held the phaser steadily on the man with the box.

"You stay still, now," the sergeant said. "I don't want any trouble outa the likes of you."

The man managed to look scared and astonished at the same time. "But, Sergeant, really—I mean, what is this all about? Who is Holtzman? My name is Gregory Lebow! I'm a retired teacher from Second Try. I've been in your city visiting my sister Emma! I have lots of identification and all the proper papers—" He began to reach into his pocket for them.

"Freeze, Holtzman!" the sergeant ordered. The man did. "Hands on your head." The sergeant paused. "You and your kind, always causin' trouble, as if we didn't have enough to go around already . . ."

"But, Sergeant—"

"That's enough!"

The sergeant's shouted orders had attracted the

attention of a growing group of the curious. Members of the crowd stared at the man with the box.

The people were buzzing with the news:

"Did the cop say that guy was *Holtzman?!?*"

"I'm from off-planet. Who the hell's Holtzman?"

"Jeez—he doesn't look like much, does he?"

"Most-wanted man on Centaurus, pal. Scientist, he is. He's a political weirdo. Strictly warp zero, if ya know what I mean."

"Lookit his little beady eyes."

"Escaped from prison three years ago. I think he was doing time for agitation. Or was it sabotage? Maybe it was some other guy."

"He don't *look* dangerous . . ."

"I wonder what's in the box. Secrets?"

"That looks like one tough cop, all right. *I* wouldn't mess with him."

"I wonder if they got Holtzman's friends, too?"

The cop and his prisoner were able to hear most of what was being said. The sergeant smiled humorlessly. "Those are the people you're trying to 'save,' Holtzman. Whaddaya think?"

"I have no idea what you're talking about, Sergeant. Believe me, when all this is straightened out—"

The sergeant glanced at the box. "What's in the box, Holtzman? More hate literature? Poison for people's minds? Lessee." He gestured with the phaser. "Open it *up,* Holtzman."

That's it, the man told himself. *There is nothing I can do. I am gone.*

"Very well, Sergeant," the man said calmly. "I don't mind opening the box."

But, instead, he poked the box in a certain spot in a very particular way.

Carry on the struggle, my friends was Holtzman's last thought.

A specially designed magnetic field collapsed inside

the box—and a small chunk of antimatter was allowed to touch the cheap cardboard.

New Athens Spaceport and everything else for eight kilometers around vaporized in the barest fraction of a second . . . and a terrible fourth sun rose high into the beautifully blue Centaurian sky.

Chapter Two:
The *Enterprise*

RRRAAASSSP.

James Kirk stirred in his sleep.

RRRAAAASSSSSSPPP!

Kirk's eyes opened, and as they did a sensor-linked relay turned his bunkside lamp on to DIM. *Whuzzat noise?* he thought confusedly, slow to awaken. *Wherezit from?*

RRRAAAAAAZZZZZZZZZ . . . CRACK!!!

At that last, sharp sound, the captain of the U.S.S. *Enterprise* came fully awake. *It's from the vent!* he realized quickly. *The air circulators!* As he threw his bedcovers aside and the lights in his quarters came up full, Kirk felt a chill. *Temperature's down, too. We've got big problems.*

No sooner had Kirk's bare feet hit the deck than he was sent sprawling by a huge and sudden increase in his body weight.

Flat on the floor, Kirk grunted; he felt as if two men of his own size had jumped on him and pinned him to the deck. *Lucky,* he told himself. *My head just missed the bunk support.* The captain tried moving his arms and legs; it was difficult, but nothing seemed to be broken. He estimated his apparent weight at some-

18

thing like 250 kilos, or more than 550 pounds in what Bones McCoy usually called "Grandma's kitchen system." That meant there had been a sudden surge of at least two G's in the usually even-tempered one-G output of the ship's artificial gravity generators. *Heat, air, gravity—the whole environmental section's gone out,* Kirk thought as he gathered his strength to get up from the floor. *I've got to contact the bridge . . . .*

Kirk dragged his arms toward his chest and placed his palms flat on the deck. Carefully he pushed himself up—

—and found himself rising quickly toward the overhead. *Gravity's cut out entirely!* Kirk thought with a shock.

Reflexively, Kirk twisted in mid-air so that his feet, and not the back of his head, struck the ceiling. As his momentum bounced him back toward the floor, Kirk somersaulted and landed on his feet; he allowed himself to collapse on the deck to soak up as much of his velocity as he could. Kirk bounced again, but much more slowly this time; he reached out his right hand and grasped the edge of a small table, jarring it. The table's legs were bolted to the deck, but several objects, put into motion by Kirk's spent momentum, began to rise off the tabletop and bobble around the cabin.

The hell with it, thought Kirk. He steadied himself, carefully judged the distance to his desk, and pushed away from the table with a slow, steady thrust. The captain floated across his quarters. As he slowly approached his desk, he saw the intercom begin to bleep for his attention—just as the soft green light on the status board over Kirk's bunk changed to a harsh yellow and an electronic alarm began to beep insistently.

"Alarm off," Kirk ordered as he flew through the air.

The alarm continued to beep.

Kirk repeated his verbal order to the computer; again it was ignored. *So we have an order-interpretation problem on top of everything else,* Kirk thought, annoyed.

At last Kirk had floated close enough to his desk to grasp it. He pulled himself in, hooked his left foot under the center drawer, and pulled himself down. *The Eagle has landed,* Kirk thought as he pushed himself into the chair. Kirk's bathrobe hung loosely on the back of the chair; the captain shrugged the robe on as best he could—*Sure is getting cold in here,* he thought—and thumbed the intercom on.

The face of Pavel Chekov, the nightwatch duty officer, swam onto the screen, floating in and out of pickup range. Kirk could see a bloody cut just over Chekov's left eye—an eye, Kirk thought, that looked like it had a good chance of becoming a full-blown shiner before long.

"Report, Mr. Chekov," Kirk snapped.

"Ve are on yellow alert, Captain," answered the young Russian ensign. "Zero grawity conditions obtain throughout the ship. Air circulation and temperature control systems are out. Ve have lost some computer functions, mostly in housekeeping. Specifically, the computer vill not respond to werbal commands, nor vill the computer run any of its galley or plumbing subroutines—"

"Yes, Mr. Chekov," Kirk said impatiently. "Security status?"

"Sensors are fully operational and show no wessel, friendly or othervise, vithin range. Ve do have injuries; there are a number of medical cases on the bridge, but none appears to be serious. I have not yet had a report from the medical officer on duty. I am trying to locate Dr. McCoy as vell. Our computer problems are making some intraship communications difficult." Chekov turned away from the pickup and spoke to someone for a moment, then turned back and said, "Captain, Mr. Spock has reported in and is making his vay to the bridge. You also need to know that Mr. Scott is already in Engineering, and Chief MacPherson is the Engineering officer presently on bridge duty. He vas here vhen ve got into trouble."

"Very good, Mr. Chekov," Kirk said. "Maintain yellow alert. Priority one: Get all hands up and moving. Everybody out of bed, *now*. Remind Sickbay to get air circulating somehow around sleeping patients, even if the head nurse has to wave a magazine around the room. And I want a full security sweep of all sections to pick up any unconscious or immobile injured."

Kirk knew that, in zero gravity and with no air movement, exhaled breath tends to accumulate in an invisible, deadly globe around a person's head. An unmoving, sleeping member of the crew could smother in carbon dioxide while surrounded by a sea of fresh, good air. Kirk knew that, even without air circulation, there was just enough air in the ship to sustain life for about three hours; that made fixing the air problem his top priority.

"While you're talking to Sickbay," Kirk continued, "tell them I want a medico designated for bridge duty. You get your eye attended to. I'll be up there as soon as I can."

"Aye, aye, Captain."

"Kirk out." The captain clicked the intercom off. *Now all I have to do,* Kirk said to himself, *is try to get dressed while floating around the cabin.*

The door to Kirk's quarters squeaked open and the captain coasted on through and into the corridor, fetching up against the opposite wall. Kirk glanced off it at an angle and managed to send himself floating down the hall in the direction he wanted. The corridor was beginning to fill with people; Chekov had, indeed, awakened everyone.

Along with his concern for his ship and crew, some part of Kirk's mind came up with a snatch of song he'd heard as a child, back in the American Midwest. *Oh, he floats through the air with the greatest of ease, dum-dum dee dee dum-dum the flying trapeze—now just what was the rest of that?* Kirk wondered as he floated down the corridor toward the turbolift.

The captain rounded a bend by scrabbling across a wall, killing little of his momentum.

"Watch out!!! Hot water!!!"

Kirk looked ahead toward the source of the shout—and saw a translucent glob surrounded by a cloud of steam rolling and pitching toward him. People in the corridor were dodging this way and that, zooming wildly and sometimes crashing with thuds against a wall or a door. The amoeba-like blob looked alive as it floated down the corridor.

Kirk quickly reached out and grabbed a doorframe, stopping his forward motion. He dragged himself down the frame and pushed himself against the deck. There was nothing for Kirk to hook his feet into, so the captain concentrated on making himself as small as he could; he drew his knees toward his chin and rolled himself into a ball.

The glob wobbled on, narrowly missing Kirk. From the deck he felt the heat on his face as he watched the weirdly shimmering thing pass over his head. *I have to get someone to take care of that,* Kirk told himself. He shouted, "Corridor! Mid-air glob of hot water! Watch out!" But that was merely a precaution; the captain could see that the corridor behind him had been cleared.

The captain heard a *thump* nearby. He turned his

head and saw Lieutenant Sulu, his best helmsman, one-handedly holding onto a wall intercom panel. Sulu was wearing nothing but a towel and was holding several others in his free hand. The trailing end of Sulu's towel floated along with everything else; Kirk decided that zero G was no aid to modesty.

Sulu looked worried. "Captain, are you all right?" he asked anxiously.

Kirk nodded. "No harm done." He pushed himself easily off the deck. Keeping his grip on the doorframe, Kirk asked, "What happened, Mr. Sulu?"

"Well, sir," the lieutenant said, "I was taking a shower—"

"A hot shower."

"A *very* hot shower, sir, and all of a sudden—"

"—the gravity went off."

"The gravity went off, sir, and all this water came out of the shower head and splashed around all over the washroom—"

"—and gathered itself into a ball and wandered out into a public corridor."

"Yes, sir, and I've been chasing it around and trying to soak it up with these towels—"

"—and you haven't been having much luck," Kirk finished.

Sulu considered it. "Yes, sir, that's about it—except that the shower wouldn't turn off when I ordered it to, and the emergency shut-off system didn't work, either. The thing just shut off by itself, eventually."

"Thank you, Mr. Sulu. Carry on."

"Uh, sir?" The lieutenant seemed hesitant.

"What is it, Mr. Sulu?"

"Sir, the, er, facilities did about the same thing."

"You mean the toilets?"

"Uh, yes, sir. There's flying water all over the place. But it's *cold,* sir."

Kirk tried not to smile. "I'm sure whoever gets hit

by those particular globs will appreciate that. Get after yours, now."

"Aye, aye, sir. Thank you, sir." Sulu pushed away from the intercom panel and began sailing off after the glob of hot shower water. *I wonder how much water I've got floating around inside my ship*, Kirk thought as he watched the ensign drift away, *and how many other problems have I got, ones I can't even guess the nature of yet? Well, Jim, that's why they gave you the fancy gold shirt . . . .*

Kirk thrust himself away from the doorframe and made for the hatchway of the turbolift. About halfway there he saw its doors part; the turbolift was empty. *Chekov must have sent it for me*, Kirk thought. *He's on the ball, as usual.* Kirk saw no need to alter his course; he simply shouted "Gangway!" Then he somersaulted in mid-air and sailed feet-first into the turbolift, softly landing on the wall.

He grabbed the handrail and told the computer, "Bridge."

Nothing happened. Kirk swore to himself and grasped the handle for manual override. The turbolift doors slid closed, and Kirk was finally on his way.

The bridge looked to Kirk like a human aquarium.

Mr. Spock was at his station—squatting placidly in mid-air, his legs folded under him as if he were in meditation. But Kirk knew from the set of the Vulcan's shoulders and the aura of concentration he projected that the science officer was communing not with the unseen, but with the ship's ill computers. Lieutenant Uhura was sitting at her communications station, held in her seat by a tied length of fabric. *Her nightgown, I think*, thought Kirk. *Why didn't they install seat belts in this ship?* A medico—Nurse Constance Iziharry, Kirk recalled—was tending to Chekov's eye; both the ensign and the nurse seemed to be doing an aerial *pas de deux* about a meter above the navigation console. The nightwatch helmsman—Lt. Peter Siderakis—had slaved the navigator's board to the helm and was running both stations.

Somehow, somewhere, Siderakis had procured a sweater and was wearing it against the chill. Kirk envied him the sweater—a silly, garish thing with I LEFT MY CASH IN SAN FRANCISCO emblazoned on it— but it looked *warm*.

"Course, Mr. Siderakis?" Kirk asked.

"Captain, our course remains three forty-five mark five, warp two. No glitches in our navigation and guidance systems, at least."

"Fine. Steady as she goes, then. Lieutenant Uhura, what's our communications status?"

"I've gotten several audio lines through to belowdecks, Captain," she replied. "Video is impossible at present; I can't get the computer to give me enough signal to push through."

"Good enough, Uhura. Thank you." Kirk continued his quick visual inspection.

To Kirk's left, at the Engineering station, was Chief Alec MacPherson, perhaps the biggest Scotsman Kirk had ever met. If genetic engineers were ever given a contract to design the ultimate, essential Scot, they might come up with something like MacPherson—two meters tall, broadly built, red-haired and red-bearded, with the blood of mighty Celtic kings in him.

MacPherson was a fierce-looking man with the gentle and appreciative soul of a poet—gentle and appreciative, that is, unless he were confronted by incompetence or stupidity.

But he hardly *ever* hit anybody.

MacPherson was a relatively new arrival aboard the *Enterprise*. He had worked with Scott on a scout-class ship, the U.S.S. *Gagarin,* years before. Scott had eventually been assigned aboard the *Enterprise* and had quickly risen to chief engineer; MacPherson had risen to chief engineer on the *Gagarin* about as quickly.

About a month back, the *Gagarin* had been decommissioned and her crew thrown into Starfleet's reassignment pool. MacPherson had sent his friend Montgomery Scott a short subspace message—NEED WORK. GOT ANY? CHEERS, MAC.—and Scott had requested Kirk to get Personnel to assign MacPherson aboard the *Enterprise* as Scott's new number two. "He's th' only mon I really trust t' watch me engines while I sleep, Cap'n," Scotty had said. "He's a good 'un, take me word for it."

Kirk had never before heard Scotty admit that someone else in Starfleet might be qualified enough to tighten a bolt on the *Enterprise* without the chief engineer's personal supervision; impressed, the captain had put the *Enterprise*'s request for MacPherson through Starfleet repple-depple marked with a PERSONNEL PRIORITY ONE code.

Scotty's word had been good. In the past few weeks the Engineering section's efficiency rating had risen substantially. Kirk found Scotty's habit of calling MacPherson "lad" and "laddie" amusing—MacPherson was less than three years younger than Scott—but the two worked superlatively well together. Most of the ship's personnel had taken to calling Scott and MacPherson "the twins." It was as if there were two Montgomery Scotts aboard; each man had a sure knowledge of the skills and engineering approaches the other might take in a given situation. If a problem needed solving, and an engineer could choose from among fourteen equally valid but different ways to solve it, Scott and MacPherson were each likely to avail themselves of the same solution, without consulting each other—and neither man would find the coincidence strange or unusual. "Thot's just good engineerin'," Scotty might say.

And MacPherson clearly liked working for Scott. The *Enterprise* was considered good duty in Starfleet; she was a ship whose captain brought his crew back home safely from exciting missions which had more than a whiff of adventure and danger. Also, going from number-one engineer aboard a scout ship to number two aboard a cruiser was a good career move in the fleet; MacPherson saw working aboard the *Enterprise* as a challenge, and working with Scott again a pleasure.

But he doesn't seem to be having a very good time right now, thought Kirk.

The big Scot was, incredibly, standing upright at his station. Then Kirk noticed that MacPherson had doffed his boots and hooked his toes under the lip of the Engineering station's console runner. MacPherson's left hand kept a grip on the station, while his right hand gripped a personal communicator—into which MacPherson was bellowing.

"Aye!" MacPherson was shouting. "An' next I suppose you'll be tellin' me there's no reason whatsoe'er why th' gravity controllers aren't functionin', so we're all floatin' aroun' here just for th' sake of it! *Aaaaggh!* Put Scotty back on, ye moron!" The big Scotsman snorted in disgust.

MacPherson turned slightly and saw Kirk floating in the entrance to the turbolift. "Cap'n on the bridge," MacPherson said formally, and nodded politely. "Good mornin', sir."

Kirk nodded back. The captain planted a foot against the turbolift wall, sighted himself carefully, and thrust himself toward his command chair. He sailed through the air and stopped himself by reaching out a hand against the back of the chair.

"Good navigatin', Cap'n," said MacPherson approvingly.

"What's our status, Chief?"

"Oh, things are still up in th' air, so t'speak, sir," MacPherson answered. Before Kirk could respond, the chief hurried on, "Mr. Scott has got his second-best man with him down in Engineering, and th' first thing they'll be goin' after is th' air circulation problem."

"Second-best man?"

"Aye, sir," MacPherson said, surprised. "I'm up here, after all."

"Oh. When do we get our gravity back?"

"Soon, sir—very soon. 'Tis a matter o' pinnin' down th' original problem and patchin' it. Th' problem is, th' gravity generators are puttin' out a zero-G' field in default mode because th' poor babies were beginnin' to run wild. It's not thot th' *generators* are out, y'understand, sir; it's thot th' *controllers* are out o' whack . . ."

"Fall to, Chief."

"Aye, aye, sir." MacPherson put the communicator back to his ear and said quietly, "Scotty, are ye there? Ach, good . . . ."

Kirk spun around and faced Spock's sciences station. *Am I crazy,* thought Kirk, *or does Spock look a little, er . . . greener than usual?* The captain got his bearings and launched himself toward Spock's position.

"Mr. Spock?" Kirk said softly when he had arrived and steadied himself. "Are you all right?"

Spock looked at Kirk. "I am quite able to function, Captain." *He does look ill,* thought Kirk. *What's the matter?*

Kirk hesitated. "I don't mean to pry, Spock, but I must know—are you, er, feeling unwell?" *I've got to be careful of his feelings on this*, Kirk thought. *Lord knows Vulcans are closemouthed about such things . . .*

Spock hesitated. "Captain, I assure you that my . . . physical condition . . . is quite manageable."

Kirk looked Spock in the eye. "Spock, forgive me— *are you spacesick?"*

The science officer hesitated, then said, "Yes, Captain. I have rarely experienced weightlessness, and have never liked it. I find that I am affected adversely by a lack of gravity. You would term it 'motion sickness'—"

"Something like that."

"—and I am handling the problem with such discipline as I am able to muster. I am fully able to man my post, with no loss in personal efficiency. That is why I have answered your questions in the manner I have. Of course, I would not mind a return to normal gravity and temperature status as soon as Mr. Scott and Chief MacPherson can effect such."

Kirk smiled wryly. "I wouldn't mind that very much, either. Very well, Mr. Spock. Thank you for your candor."

Spock nodded. "Of course, Captain." The Vulcan turned back to his close consultation with the ship's computers, and Kirk launched himself back to his command chair.

I hadn't thought of space sickness, thought Kirk. He kicked himself mentally. *If standard figures hold, half the crew must be down with it.*

More than a century before Kirk had been born, all types of spacecraft—humble orbital tugs and majestic starships alike—had begun carrying gravity generators as standard equipment. In fact, artificial gravity, along with inertial control and other byproducts vital to modern spaceflight, had come wrapped in the same neat package in which the great Zefrem Cochrane had given the Federation the secret of warp drive. Any pilot working in Federation space—legally, that is—had to pass a zero-G proficiency test to get his license, and zero-G fields were used routinely in medicine, entertainment, professional sports and a host of scientific applications. But nobody *had* to live or work in zero G anymore. Starfleet Academy demanded that its graduating cadets demonstrate proficiency in zero-G maneuvering, just as it demanded that cadets know how to conn a sailboat, fly a glider and master other ancient skills.

So there were few aboard the *Enterprise* who had more than a nodding, long-ago acquaintance with zero-G conditions. Kirk thought of all the accidents that could—and probably would, and probably *had*—happened aboard his ship, and he shuddered inwardly. *That hot-water glob was just the beginning,* he thought. *Never mind all the water and trash that must be floating around and getting into the ship's most vulnerable places.* The captain looked around the bridge; he saw people, trash, a few writing styli, an empty coffee cup and other flotsam meandering in the air.

And it was still cold, and getting colder.

Kirk fretted. *Come on, twins,* he said to himself. He shivered again, but told himself it was merely the chill on the bridge. Kirk again envied Siderakis that sweater; he wondered if hot coffee was possible, despite the problems with the computers' galley subroutines.

"Cap'n?" MacPherson called out. "Would ye please talk t' Mr. Scott on th' communicator band? That'd be frequency three, sir."

"Thank you, Chief." Kirk thumbed a button on the armrest of his command chair. "Yes, Mr. Scott? What can you tell me?"

"Some good news, I hope," the chief engineer replied. "We've rigged emergency fans at all th' main vent outlets, so ye should be gettin' air circulation back in a moment. We've also installed space heaters next t' th' fans, so ship's temperature ought t' be headin' up nearer normal very soon now. Still workin' on our gravity problems, Cap'n, but I think Chief MacPherson kens a temporary solution. Any orders?"

"None. Uh, what are we doing about all the debris and liquid floating around?" Kirk asked. "Won't that stuff get into the works?"

"Aye, I'm glad you mentioned thot," Scotty said. "Not t' bother you wi' it, but I've got short circuits and things blowin' out all over the ship, thanks t' water gettin' inta th' wirin'. Nothing the apprentices canna handle, and I'll be doin' a thorough inspection later—but for now we've rigged submicronic filters in th' main air channels. They'll catch just about anythin', includin' th' water. I just hope th' filters catch everythin' afore the wirin' does. Ah, and there's th' air fans, goin' on now."

"Very good, Scotty," Kirk said. "Anything you need, just ask; I'll stay out of your hair."

"No problem, then, Cap'n, and thank ye."

"Don't mention it. Kirk out." He thumbed the communications channel to DISENGAGE and said over his shoulder, "Lieutenant Uhura, have we heard from Dr. McCoy yet?"

"He's just calling in now, sir; please stand by." Uhura said something into her lip mike, then turned to the captain. "The doctor's on frequency four, sir."

"Bones!" Kirk greeted. "What's going on?"

"Busy down here, Jim," came the gravelly voice of the ship's chief medical officer. "I've got a sick list that's seventy-three names long so far—almost all trauma cases. Most of those are from that wallop we took when the gravity first went haywire, but some

31

people are down here with typical zero-G problems: muscle strains, bumps, bruises, space sickness and so forth. I've even got a crewman who damn near drowned in the water from his own sink. No dead, though, and no one in any real trouble. Glad you got the air moving again, Jim; Nurse Chapel looked pretty silly waving those medical charts around in here."

Kirk smiled. "Anything else?"

"Yeah. If you could release Iziharry from bridge duty, I could use her down here."

"Done. Kirk out." The captain looked up in the air over the navigation console again; Nurse Iziharry was still poking at the flinching Chekov's injured eye. "Nurse?"

Iziharry, all concentration, did not respond.

"*Ahem!* Nurse?" Kirk repeated.

With a start, Iziharry looked down toward Kirk. "Oh! Yes, Captain?" she said.

"Miss Iziharry, if you're finished up here, Dr. McCoy needs you in Sickbay."

"Oh, I'm done. Thank you, Captain." Constance Iziharry turned back to Chekov. "Now, Pavel," she lectured, "stay away from sharp corners and swinging doors for at least a week. You've got the pain medication, but I'm not going to give you anything for the swelling. It'd just make you drowsy, and you don't really need it anyway. Just tie some ice in a rag and hold it against your eye; that's what Grandma would have done. Okay?"

"Hokay, Connie," Chekov replied. "Sorry for the trouble."

"No trouble," Iziharry answered, and smiled. *God, she is gorgeous*, thought Chekov. *Vhy did I never notice before?*

From his chair Kirk watched Chekov and Connie

Iziharry orbiting slowly around each other. The captain hid his smile. *It's an ill wind,* thought Kirk as Iziharry pushed off Chekov and headed for the turbolift; Chekov, automatically sent in the opposite direction, headed toward the ceiling, came up against it with his hands, and pushed himself toward the deck. The ensign landed neatly by the navigation console, grasped it with a hand, and lithely swung himself into his seat. "Thank you, Peter," he said to Siderakis. "I'm ready now." Siderakis smiled, nodded, and unslaved Chekov's board from his own.

"Welcome back to duty, Mr. Chekov," said Kirk.

"Happy to be back, Captain."

Just then, Spock called out, *"Captain! Shut down the warp engines immediately!"*

"Do it, Siderakis!" Kirk yelled. The helmsman's hands blurred across his board; Kirk heard the subtle whirl of the *Enterprise*'s powerful warp drivers die away quickly.

Kirk turned his head to face the science officer. "What's happening, Spock?"

"Another system failure, Captain," Spock answered. "The matter-antimatter balance in our warp engines was suddenly disrupted—by what, I do not yet know—and the computers did *not* order a protective shutdown. Had this not been noticed, we would have undergone an involuntary self-destruct sequence with no warning. Captain, we can no longer trust the computers to do anything for us. I suggest we convert to manual operations until the computers can be overhauled and reprogrammed."

Kirk frowned. "Thank you, Mr. Spock." Spock nodded in acknowledgment, once. The captain addressed Uhura over his shoulder. "Lieutenant, get me Starfleet Command. Message: 'Am diverting to Starbase Nine for emergency repairs to *Enterprise* computer complex. See Appendices A and B for details.' Uhura, stick a list of our problems at the end of this; stick Mr. Spock's recommendation at the end of *that*. Uh, 'Our ETA at Starbase Nine is'—Mr. Chekov?"

Chekov consulted his board. "At best speed on impulse power only, Captain, ve vill arrive not earlier than stardate 7516.7."

" '—7516.7, subject to delay.' Sign it and send it, Lieutenant. Mr. Chekov, lay in a course for Starbase Nine—best speed under impulse power, just as you said."

"Aye, aye, sir."

Just then the lights on the bridge began to flicker and dim.

"Shorted wires throughout th' main pylon," MacPherson called out. "We're losin' current up here. Switchin' t' bridge batteries, Captain." The chief thumbed a button, but the lights continued to dim.

"Switchin's nae good," MacPherson reported to Kirk. "Lemme work on 't for a while." The big Scot pulled himself down and scrambled under his engineering console.

Uhura's communications board emitted a distinctive—and foreboding—audio signal.

"Captain," she said worriedly, "we're getting a priority Alpha-Red message."

Kirk was startled. "Is it genuine, or just another computer foul-up?"

"Genuine, sir. Confirmed. I can't print out the message for you in code, Captain, because the main computers aren't paying any attention to me today—but I *can* give you a printout in the clear."

Kirk considered it, and shrugged. "Nothing we can do about it, regulations or no. An uncoded printout will be fine, Uhura."

"Yes, sir." Uhura did things to her board, and a

34

tongue of paper began unrolling from the right arm of Kirk's command chair. He tore it off and began reading.

MESSAGE BEGINS
MESSAGE FROM STARFLEET COMMAND STOP
BREAK PRIORITY ALPHA-RED STOP
BREAK STARDATE 7513.2 STOP
BREAK EYES ONLY CAPTAIN JAMES TIBERIUS KIRK
      SC 937-0176 CEC COMMANDING USS ENTER-
      PRISE NCC-1701 STOP
BREAK BREAK MESSAGE FOLLOWS
BREAK PERMISSION TO DIVERT TO STARBASE 9
      DENIED REPEAT DENIED STOP STAND BY FOR
      COMMAND ORDERS STOP SECOND ALPHA-RED
      MESSAGE FOLLOWS IMMEDIATELY STOP
      SIGNED BUCHINSKY CINC STARFLEET
BREAK BREAK MESSAGE ENDS

Bull Buchinsky? Starfleet's commander-in-chief? With an Alpha-Red? Now just what the hell does Bull have in mind? Kirk wondered.

Uhura's board made that insistent, foreboding sound again. "Second message coming in now, Captain," she reported. "Printing it out now . . ."

MESSAGE BEGINS
MESSAGE FROM STARFLEET COMMAND STOP
BREAK PRIORITY ALPHA-RED STOP
BREAK STARDATE 7513.3 STOP
BREAK EYES ONLY CAPTAIN JAMES TIBERIUS KIRK
      SC 937-0176 CEC COMMANDING USS ENTER-
      PRISE NCC-1701 STOP
BREAK BREAK MESSAGE FOLLOWS
BREAK CODE HELLFIRE REPEAT HELLFIRE STOP
    SUBJECT IS NEW ATHENS CENTAURUS REPEAT

NEW ATHENS CENTAURUS STOP THIRD AL-
PHA-RED MESSAGE FOLLOWS IMMEDIATELY
STOP SIGNED BUCHINSKY CINC STARFLEET
BREAK BREAK MESSAGE ENDS

There was an expectant, worried silence on the bridge.

"Mr. Chekov," the captain quietly said at last, "belay that course change to Starbase Nine, and stand by for new orders."

Kirk crumpled the printout and let it float away.

Joanna McCoy, he thought miserably. *Oh my dear God.*

Chapter Three:
Long Ago

ENSIGN JAMES T. KIRK, the twenty-two-year-old tactical weapons officer aboard the U.S.S. *Farragut,* had been badly wounded in the ship's final battle against the pirates of Epsilon Canaris III—bloodthirsty types who had taken full advantage of the thin spread of Federation law in that sector to set up a thriving business in hijacking, slavery and drug smuggling.

The *Farragut,* outnumbered six to one, had taken a terrible pounding. Toward the end of the battle a heavy stanchion on the *Farragut*'s bridge had come loose and crashed down directly onto Jim Kirk's leg, crushing the knee and shattering the thigh.

The young Kirk had never known such incredible pain, but he had learned his life's lesson in duty that day. He had stayed at his weapons console, keeping a tenuous hold on consciousness. The citation for Kirk's Decoration for Valor—his first Starfleet award—would read: "Ensign Kirk, despite the severe pain of his wound, accurately returned the combined fire of the enemy, round for round. He did not slacken until Captain Garrovick declared the enemy destroyed and the ship safe. Only then did Ensign Kirk report his physical condition."

Kirk had "reported" his condition to Garrovick by dragging himself toward the captain and passing out at his feet. A long time later Kirk had awakened in the *Farragut*'s Sickbay, his leg splinted and encased in a stasis field. The leg didn't hurt at all; in fact, under stasis, it felt dead.

Captain Garrovick had stopped by shortly after Kirk had awakened. He had shaken Kirk's hand firmly and had said only one thing: "You belong in this service, Jim. I'm glad you're aboard my ship."

Kirk had been proud to receive that praise.

Starbase 7 began its career as a tough plastic dome mounted on the ragged equator of an irregularly shaped free asteroid in interstellar space. More than a century before, Starfleet had begun adding to that dome. Now the asteroid was completely covered with several decks' worth of facilities and was staffed by some six hundred Starfleet personnel and civilians.

About two weeks after the Epsilon Canaris battle, the *Farragut* limped into Starbase 7 for repairs to the ship and medical treatment for ship's personnel. Kirk was at the top of the sick list, and the admitting medico from the starbase hospital came into *Farragut*'s Sickbay to see the ensign.

"Good afternoon, Mister, ah, Kirk," the doctor said. He gave Kirk's ruined leg a quick look. "Your captain wasn't kidding me, Ensign," the medico said. "That's a nasty bump you've got there."

Kirk nodded. "What do you think?" he asked a bit hesitantly. "Am I going to lose it?"

The medico shrugged. "Dunno." He scratched his chin and examined Kirk's leg closely.

"Well, I don't *think* we'll have to saw it off," the doctor finally drawled. The corner of his mouth turned up. "I've got something I'd like to try first. It's a fairly new approach; I'd like you to go into this with your eyes wide open, because I'm not giving any guarantees this week. We can talk about it. Okay?"

Kirk nodded. "Anything you say, Doctor—?"

"McCoy. Pleased to meet you, Ensign." They shook hands.

Leonard McCoy took full charge of Jim Kirk's rehabilitation. First, the skilled young doctor teased Kirk's thighbone into regenerating; under gentle pressure from drugs and electrotherapy, the thighbone reformed itself and redeveloped the superstrong interior lattice that is one of the marvels of the human body.

The knee was even tougher—*There are so many things the cells have to be taught to do!* McCoy thought in wonderment and weariness—but, eventually, Kirk's knee regenerated and then regained its range of motion. Then, finally, muscle and skin reformed, without a scar.

Kirk's leg took four long months to regenerate. The ensign was physically whole now—but more months of physical therapy lay ahead; Kirk had to be taught how to *use* his new leg. He was a twenty-two-year-old man who had never used that leg in walking, running, kicking—or even in supporting his own weight unassisted. Kirk had to learn how to walk all over again.

It was a painful process; Kirk's nerves screamed in agony as his new leg muscles were forced to do the hard work of moving him around. Leonard McCoy worked with Kirk every day through that ugly period of pain and despair. "There's still no better way to practice using the leg than to use the leg," McCoy told Kirk once, early on, as the sweating ensign groaned his way through a three-kilometer treadmill walk. "It hurts, Jim, I *know* it does—but you have to get through that pain."

Kirk gritted his teeth and nodded . . . and got through the pain.

Seven months after Kirk's arrival at Starbase 7, McCoy pronounced his patient completely cured. The doctor personally did the paperwork on his patient's discharge. Jim Kirk went to Dr. McCoy's hospital office for his exit interview.

"I see they've cut your orders for a return to the *Farragut* as tactical weapons officer," McCoy observed.

"That's right," Kirk replied. "I'm glad about that; I wouldn't want another ship. The rendezvous flight leaves from here in two months. I've got some R and R coming to me. I think I'll take it—I could go for a long walk in somebody's woods, or something."

"Hmmm," McCoy said. "Sounds better than drawing light duty in Starbase Seven's clerical department." The doctor scratched his chin. "Y'know," he drawled, "I've been working on your case just about every day for the past seven months. This organization owes me some R and R, too, I think. Why don't you tag along with me?" He grinned. "I'll show you some woods that'll take your breath away."

"Delighted, Doctor."

"Call me Bones," McCoy said. "All my friends do."

Bones McCoy's official residence was in a small, private room in Starbase 7's medical dormitory—but his home was on the planet Centaurus, just about half a light-year from the star base. McCoy rated four free trips home per year via available Starfleet transportation—usually a supply ship—and Kirk, still excused from regular duty for medical reasons, rated a trip if his doctor prescribed one.

His doctor did. McCoy and Kirk flew to Centaurus

aboard the U.S.S. *Cook County,* an old, small, impulse-only cargo craft that took nearly a week to get there. McCoy and Kirk spent the time talking about women, playing cards, blue-skying about their career plans, and talking some more about women.

Kirk had never been to Centaurus before; he knew it only as Alpha Centauri IV, an Earth-type planet orbiting a star fairly similar to Sol. The name of the planet had come from the star group's traditional name. "Sure, you need sunglasses on Centaurus," McCoy told Kirk once when the doctor had been in a hometown mood. "Alpha's half again as bright as Sol and a tenth bigger, too. Plus, there's Beta. But so what? Think of a Caribbean island on a hot, clear day and you've about got it. Jim, I tell you, the planet's *lush.* Earth flora and fauna just love it there. Just wait—my sister and her husband have a nice place in Athena Preserve; that's a government park just outside New Athens. You'll see."

McCoy called the planet home not because he'd been born there—he hadn't been—but because his nine-year-old daughter Joanna lived there with McCoy's older sister and her husband. "A starbase is no place for a kid," McCoy told Kirk. "I want her to get sun and fresh air and meet different kinds of people. I never want her to become a Starfleet brat."

Kirk knew McCoy was divorced, but the doctor never talked about his failed marriage and had never encouraged questions from Kirk about it. Once, during the long trip on the *Cook County,* McCoy volunteered the information that he had first met "what's-her-name" in his native Georgia; Kirk had not felt free to pursue the subject.

But McCoy worshiped Joanna. Kirk took it as a supreme compliment that the doctor had given up two home leaves to stay with Kirk during his recuperation. Now McCoy had invited Kirk to go home with him.

Kirk had not been especially close to anyone in the service—part of that was Kirk's basic reticence, and the rest of it was due to his heavy schedule of work and study as an ensign still under review—but Kirk had warmed to McCoy during his long recovery, and McCoy's generous offer of hospitality had cemented their friendship.

The *Cook County* set down at the military field attached to New Athens Spaceport. Kirk generally disliked meeting children, but he liked McCoy's daughter on sight. Kirk first saw Joanna McCoy at the military arrivals gate; she was waiting there with her aunt and uncle.

"Daddy!" she cried happily upon seeing the doctor. She glanced at Kirk, gave him a polite smile of the kind appropriate for strangers, and then turned her full attention back to her father. McCoy dropped his personal kit, snatched up his daughter and hugged her powerfully. "Hiya, Squirt," McCoy said, his eyes watering.

"You big mushball," Joanna said mock-scornfully, too low for anyone but McCoy to hear. "Don't get sloppy on me." Joanna cheerfully ignored her own tears. She was a small girl—brown-haired, blue-eyed and slightly built, just on the edge of the beauty that would be hers beginning in her teens.

Joanna broke her hug and McCoy put her down. She looked at Kirk and waited politely, with an interested expression. "Oh, I'm sorry," McCoy said. "Jim Kirk, this is my daughter, Joanna; my sister, Donna, and her husband, Fred Withers." Kirk nodded politely to Donna Withers and shook hands with Fred; he had a firm, salt-of-the-earth grip.

Kirk then turned to Joanna and extended a hand. Joanna shook it with a ladylike grip, squeezing once and pumping twice. "I'm very happy to meet you, Joanna," Kirk said. "I've heard a lot about you from your father." Kirk addressed her, standing; he felt this child would not tolerate the easy condescension of his stooping to talk to her.

Joanna beamed and McCoy said to himself, *Jim passes inspection. Thank God. Joanna may yet let him enjoy this vacation.* "Well!" McCoy said happily. "Let's get going!" Kirk, the McCoys and the Witherses began threading their way through the concourse crowds, heading for the nearest slidewalk to the transient parking lot.

Ensign Kirk, once and future tac weapons officer of the U.S.S. *Farragut*, was used to the presence of perhaps twenty or so people at any one time; starships are spacious, for the number of people they carry, and hospitals through the centuries have always been known for their empty, lonely, impersonal hallways and corridors.

But the concourse was throbbing with *thousands* of people of all kinds, shapes and sizes.

Agoraphobia? Kirk wondered nervously. *At my age? Or maybe I mean . . . xenophobia?* Kirk felt his hackles rise with a subtle, irrational fear of the crowd of travelers. *There are just too damn many people!* Kirk complained to himself. *I'm not used to this . . .*

Kirk felt a small hand slip into his own. He looked down. Joanna McCoy was looking back at him, very seriously.

"I hate crowds, don't you?" she whispered.

Kirk grinned. After that, he felt much better. Kirk and Joanna walked hand-in-hand all the way out of the concourse.

The leave turned out to be the finest of Kirk's life. McCoy made good on his promise to show Kirk some woods; the McCoys and Kirk borrowed the Witherses' recreational flitter and soared over vastnesses of virgin wilderness. Centaurus's population was growing rapidly but, as yet, most of the people on the planet lived in or near the cities on the northern continent's east and west coasts. New Europe had cities, too: They were established and growing on the southern continent's east coast, and farming complexes were located close to all developed areas.

But everything else on Centaurus was virtually untouched by humans.

Seeds from Earth, brought by the original settlers, had been scattered by the winds and had wandered all over the northern continent, New America; terrestrial elms and maples grew and prospered among Centaurian flapjacks and blackapples. Earthly fauna, selected and brought to Centaurus by skilled Federation ecologists, scampered through the great northern wilderness along with native treeturtles and woodscats.

Kirk saw waterfalls a thousand meters high hidden in mountain ranges that stood five times taller. He saw endless hectares of vibrantly green growth interspersed with the cool blue of freshwater lakes and the clean, light gray of rock that had boiled out of Centaurus's core in ages past. Once, Kirk glimpsed an Earth deer leap and bound safely away from the attack of a Centaurian werebear; Joanna had seen that, too, and had squealed with glee as the deer escaped.

But it was not until the three friends flew over a valley about a thousand kilometers west of New Athens that Kirk fell in love.

Kirk had never found it within himself to love a piece of land. His eyes had always been on the stars, and he had always been grateful that he lived in a century when he could soar among them. Kirk was, at heart, a wanderer; he'd never been willing to settle down in any one particular place. He was loyal to the ship on which he served, and to the Federation he had vowed to defend. But the Federation was an abstract thing; it wasn't *real*, any more than the United Nations had once been *real*. He deeply respected the history and founding philosophy of his native United States, although the strong patriotism his American ancestors had once felt had faded along with nationalism itself.

But he fell in love with this unknown piece of land at first sight.

"Bones?" Kirk asked, pointing down toward the valley. "What's that down there?"

"Dunno, Jim," McCoy replied, glancing down at his control board. "It's not named on the navigation map. I guess it's unclaimed. Pretty, isn't it?"

"Let's land," Kirk said. McCoy glanced at him— and saw the fascination on his face. With a small smile, McCoy slapped the autolanding controls, and the flitter settled gently to the ground. The three got out.

They had landed on the lip of a small palisade overlooking the valley. A clean, swift river ran from north to south through the virgin heart of the area. The hills were festooned with nature's best bunting: the riot of reds, yellows and golds that comes with autumn, be it on Earth or Centaurus. Kirk could see foliage rustle here and there as animals ran freely through the pass on some unknowable business. All around him the mountains flowed into hills, which gently melted into glades and dells and pastures. It was a vista of natural loveliness.

Kirk had found *his place*.

"Bones?" he asked. "What are the coordinates here?"

"On the autotracker, Jim. Why?"

Kirk paused. "I want to stake a claim."

Ensign Kirk returned to the valley three times in the following weeks. The first two times he'd flown there alone, bringing with him some primitive camping equipment but no comb, razor or Starfleet uniform. Kirk camped for about four days each time, drinking in the scenery and the peace of the place. On his third trip Kirk brought along a particularly attractive Starfleet nurse from New Athens Medical Complex, where Kirk had had his final medical debriefing a few days after arriving on Centaurus. They'd stayed for a week. It had turned out to be a fine week; the nurse enjoyed camping—and campfires.

Several days after that, and with assistance from Fred Withers, Kirk hired a good lawyer and formed a one-man corporation under Centaurian law. Starstruck Inc., a not-for-profit corporation owned entirely by one James Tiberius Kirk, bought two thousand hectares in the valley at a very favorable price. Kirk's deed to that land became one of his most prized possessions; he would, much later, fold it small and keep it tucked in the lid of the case that held his Medal of Honor.

All too soon Kirk's leave ended, and he promised the Witherses and Joanna that he'd make time for frequent visits from then on. He rejoined the *Farragut* and soon got back into the ebb and flow of his job as tac weapons officer.

But that phase of Kirk's career came to an abrupt and tragic end when Captain Garrovick and fully half the *Farragut*'s crew died at Tycho IV after an attack by a living cosmic cloud. Kirk, a member of the Tycho IV landing party, could never understand why he had survived when so many others had died; it was a question that would bother him for many years to come.

But one of the things Kirk had done was to send a brief subspace message to his lawyer in New Athens. It read simply: REGISTER NAME CHANGE OF PLOT TO GARROVICK VALLEY IMMEDIATELY. KIRK. It had been done.

* * *

As Kirk's career advanced, so did his salary. Starfleet pays its top officers an almost embarrassing amount of money in recognition of their superior skills, the hazards they face, and the responsibilities of their duties. Most officers Kirk had met simply allowed the bulk of their pay to pile up in a Federation bank.

But Kirk split his income. A generous portion went to provide a trust for his only living relatives, the family of his brother, Sam. When Sam and his wife, Aurelan, died, Kirk transferred the trust to their young son, Peter. But most of the rest of Kirk's money was banked with his New Athens lawyer, earmarked for land acquisition in and around Garrovick Valley. Kirk gave his lawyer loose instructions for investment and growth; Kirk believed in letting his subordinates exercise full authority within logical limits, and Kirk viewed his lawyer as just that—a civilian subordinate.

Twelve years after Kirk's first trip to Centaurus, Starstruck Inc. owned all of Garrovick Valley and the banks of the Farragut River all the way back to its source, thirty kilometers farther north, and for another thirty kilometers downstream. Kirk also owned all exploitation rights in the valley and the land around the Farragut; this guaranteed that no one could touch his property or the river that flowed through it. The lawyer reported frequent offers from land developers and real estate brokers to buy Garrovick Valley at a handsome price—Centaurus's wilderness was opening up rapidly—but Kirk refused to sell. He frequently congratulated himself on his foresight in securing all rights to protect the valley.

Kirk had had a log cabin built on the site where he and the McCoys had first landed the flitter. Kirk was not a mountain man; the cabin was small but had its own independent utilities. Power came from a small geothermal generator hidden not far from the cabin, and water came from the river. Kirk's cabin had a septic tank, too; he was unwilling to run a waste pipe into the Farragut and sully that clean, clear river. It was also the only log cabin in the Federation with its own subspace communications link to Starfleet Command; it had been installed when Kirk had gotten the *Enterprise*.

Kirk resisted the temptation to name the cabin the "Captain's Log"; he did not name it anything. He preferred, instead, to think of the valley and everything in it as *his place*, just as he had when he had first found it.

Captain Kirk had not been back to his valley since assuming command of the *Enterprise*; starship captains cannot take a couple of months' leave and disappear into the woods. While he and the McCoys had stayed there together several times, they had not done so since Bones McCoy had come aboard the *Enterprise* as chief medical officer. Joanna was free to use the place, too—but now twenty-one, she was terribly busy with her courses as a first-year student at New Athens Medical Complex. Kirk had often wanted to take Spock there—*Spock would like it*, Kirk often thought, *because he's able to see the beauty in such things*—but Kirk had not yet had the chance to do that, either.

But Captain Kirk, content, knew that one day far in the future, he'd have a place to go when space was done with him, and he with space.

Chapter Four:
The Enterprise

CAPTAIN KIRK SAT silently in his command chair on the nearly dark, still-weightless bridge of the crippled *Enterprise,* a third and final Alpha-Red message from Admiral Bull Buchinsky in his hand. After a moment Kirk stirred—and noticed his bridge crew looking apprehensively at him. Even Spock seemed a bit . . . disturbed. Kirk took a breath, and began.

"We've received some very bad news," Kirk said. "There's been an . . . incident . . . a tragedy . . . on Alpha Centauri IV, the planet Centaurus. The spaceport at the capital, New Athens, has been destroyed, and the city itself has been very badly damaged. Starfleet says the blast was caused by the annihilation of matter—a matter-antimatter explosion. We don't know yet if it was an accident or not."

The bridge crew was shocked; Kirk noticed Uhura's eyes begin to fill with tears. Kirk noted that even his self-controlled Vulcan science officer seemed—taken aback? Or did it just seem that way, in the gloom? And Lieutenant Siderakis's face had gone extraordinarily pale; even in the dim light, Kirk could see him shaking.

Then the captain remembered. Siderakis was a Centaurian native who'd thrown a well-attended party belowdecks last year on his planet's Founders Day.

"Lieutenant Uhura," Kirk said softly, "if you can get the computers to cooperate, I need a list of all ship's personnel who are legal residents of Centaurus or who have families living there. I'd like to inform those people first, before I make a general announcement. But, first, call Mr. Sulu up here early to relieve Mr. Siderakis. Then get me Mr. Scott, please."

Uhura nodded. "Aye, aye, Captain." After a pause she said, "Mr. Scott's on frequency four."

Kirk thumbed a button on the armrest of his command chair. "Scotty? Give me a status report."

"Lookin' better all th' time, Cap'n," the engineering officer replied. "I was just about t' call ye. With your permission, I'd like t' activate a one-fiftieth G field. I believe we can hold our gravity now, sir, but thot 'n all other important ship's systems will have t' remain under manual control. I fear we'll need a complete overhaul of th' computer complex. I nae know what th' cause of our problems is yet, but I think we can deal wi' th' effects all right."

"Very well, Mr. Scott," Kirk said. "Gravity on."

"Aye, aye, sir."

Kirk felt a slight somethingness wash over him, as gentle as a feather floating in a summer breeze. The captain noticed himself settling slowly into his chair— and that, around the bridge, objects floating in mid-air began to descend to the floor. The 0.02 G field Scott was generating would prevent any of the thousands of objects floating around the ship from crashing abruptly to the floor. At that slight weight, an object two meters in the air would take about four and a half leisurely seconds to settle gently to the deck—instead of crashing abruptly in three-fifths of a second, as it would under full gravity.

"All right, Scotty," Kirk said after a moment. "Everything seems to be back where it belongs—so let's take it up to a full G."

"Right ye are, Cap'n," Scotty said. "Comin' up."

Kirk felt the added weight pour smoothly into him. He flexed an arm and liked the way he could feel the pull of gravity against his muscle movement.

"One G precisely, Cap'n," came Scott's voice. "Also, ye might have noticed 'tis gettin' warmer; thot little trick we've been workin' on with th' heaters in th' ducts seems t'be effective."

"I have noticed that, Mr. Scott, and thank you. Navigational status?"

"We can go where'er ye want us t' go, Cap'n—but if we're goin' t' be goin' there too fast, the matter-antimatter intermix will require careful watchin'."

"Be prepared to watch the engines closely, then, Mr. Scott; I'll want our best speed in a few minutes."

"Aye, aye, Cap'n."

"Back to you later, Scotty. Kirk out."

A moment later the turbolift doors squeaked open and Sulu walked onto the bridge. Uhura motioned Sulu over to her communications station and, whispering, gave him the story quickly. Sulu's eyes widened in shock. He glanced quickly at Siderakis, who now was staring fiercely at the bridge viewscreen, tears rolling down his cheeks.

Sulu walked over to Siderakis and put a friendly hand on his shoulder. The Centaurian bowed his head and his shoulders began to shake with quiet sobs. Sulu bent close to Siderakis's ear and murmured something; Siderakis visibly got a grip on himself, nodded, rose, and headed for the turbolift. Kirk watched him go.

"Peter," Kirk called after him. "We'll do our best. I promise you."

Siderakis paused and looked at the captain. He

nodded his appreciation but, not trusting himself to speak, walked silently to the turbolift. The doors slid open to receive him and closed quickly behind him.

The bridge lights suddenly came back on.

"Aye, thot's got 'er," rumbled Chief MacPherson from the Engineering station, breaking the silence. "Cap'n, ye have yer lights back, but I had t' use th' audio backup circuits between here an' th' recreation deck. I figured ye might not be needin' those as much as ye'd be needin' th' lights . . . ?"

"You figured correctly, Chief. Many thanks."

"No trouble, Cap'n." MacPherson turned back to his station.

"Captain?" Uhura said. "I have that list you wanted." She rose from her seat and walked down into the command well to hand the computer printout to Kirk. There was the glistening of great pain in her eyes.

"I see you've read the names," Kirk said quietly.

Uhura nodded. Kirk's name was on the list as a Centaurian landowner, and Dr. McCoy's was there as well, as both a declared resident of the planet and as the father and brother of Centaurian citizens. The names of McCoy and Siderakis, as well as three or four others out of the total of twelve, were asterisked because they had close relatives in the New Athens area.

"I'm so sorry for your pain, sir," Uhura said to Kirk. "I hope Dr. McCoy's daughter is safe."

For a moment Uhura's pain came into Kirk's eyes, but with a conscious effort the captain put the hurt aside . . . at least for a while. "Thank you, Lieutenant." He gave her a small smile, and rose.

"Navigator, plot a course for Centaurus. Best speed. Helm, lay in it and proceed at your discretion."

"Aye, aye, Captain," Sulu and Chekov replied together.

"Mr. Sulu, you have the conn," Kirk added. "Mr. Spock is busy. I'll be down in Sickbay."

The turbolift doors closed behind the captain, as everyone watched him go. Only then did Uhura lean forward and cover her face with her hands.

And so did Sulu, but not until after he'd taken Kirk's seat and ordered warp five.

Dr. Leonard McCoy was busily at work, setting his twenty-seventh bone of the morning . . . this one a broken third metatarsal in a cargo handler's right foot. The doctor used a compression cast at three atmospheres pressure—enough to guarantee that the break would be held rigid, and strong enough to allow the cargoman to return to light duty. McCoy was a big believer in work-as-therapy.

The doors slid open and Captain Kirk entered. McCoy caught sight of him. "Hello, Jim," McCoy greeted him. "Thanks for getting the gravity back. The swabbies will be cleaning up around here for a week, though." McCoy finished inflating the cast, gave a few words of warning to the cargoman, and signed a treatment form. Then McCoy turned to Kirk, and saw something in his eyes.

"What's the matter?" McCoy asked apprehensively.

"Bones . . . take a break and talk to me," Kirk said quietly.

"Nurse Chapel," McCoy said over his shoulder, still looking at Kirk, "take the next patient. I'll be gone for a few minutes." The doctor wiped his hands on a towel and, dropping it on the deck, followed Kirk out of Sickbay and into the medical library, just across the corridor. No one else was inside. The library doors shut behind them.

A few minutes later the library doors opened again and the two men emerged. McCoy walked briskly back to work; Kirk watched the Sickbay doors slide shut behind him. *How very much like him,* Kirk thought.

Bones McCoy did his job and said nothing outside the line of duty for quite a while.

Soon after that, Kirk had Uhura summon everyone on her list of Centaurians to a special briefing in the ship's small theater—where plays were staged, lectures delivered and where, in the very happiest times, Kirk performed marriages. At the briefing the captain noticed the presence of Nurse Constance Iziharry, who'd been treating Chekov's injured eye on the bridge. Like the nine others attending, Iziharry had the hurt, almost puzzled look of someone suddenly stricken by grief and uncertainty.

The captain gave his ship's Centaurians the news as kindly as he could manage, but with no gloss or other attempt to soften it. Kirk assured them that the *Enterprise* would do all it could to relieve the suffering of their home planet, and that he was sure they would do their part as well. There were tears but, Kirk noted gratefully, they were gentle tears of mourning and sadness, not of hysteria or hopelessness. They were the kind of tears that would allow a tough job to get done.

Captain's log, stardate 7513.5:
For the time being, at least, things seem to be under control. We are proceeding at warp five for Centaurus. The matter-antimatter intermix for the warp engines seems balanced, even under tricky manual control; most of the ship's computers are still down. Gravity remains constant at a nominal one G; ship's inboard temperature is holding steady at 21.6 standard degrees, thanks to Mr. Scott's

quick work with the duct heaters. Humidity is high because of all the free water we'd had circulating throughout the ship; I am a bit worried about corrosion in components—particularly wiring—never meant to withstand unusually high amounts of moisture.

With the ship reasonably secure and well under way, I now feel free to hold a formal briefing regarding our mission to Centaurus.

At Kirk's summons, those department heads who would be working in the Centaurian rescue effort gathered in Briefing Room B. Spock, in his dual role as first officer and science officer, was there, of course; Alec MacPherson represented Engineering, since Montgomery Scott could not be spared from his watch on the warp engines; Dr. M'Benga, Bones McCoy's chief assistant, represented Medical; Uhura was there for Communications; and a bandaged, black-eyed Pavel Chekov was there for Navigation and Ship's Systems. Their initial shock had been replaced by numbness at the scope of the horror in New Athens. Kirk could see that numbness in their faces—except, of course, for Spock's; the Vulcan was—outwardly, at least—unperturbed. *Such loss of life, such waste, must sicken him,* Kirk thought. *How does he control himself? I've never understood it—and sometimes, like now, I envy him that control. So might Bones, I think. Oh, Joanna . . . .*

With a conscious effort Kirk broke that train of thought. Standing at the head of the briefing table, he looked over the expectant faces of those waiting for him to say something, to give them some guidance. It was clear to Kirk that none of them knew, or cared, that he knew nothing more at this point than they did. They needed *the captain* now, the superman in the gold shirt—not the vulnerable Jim Kirk who was aghast at the tragedy in New Athens and almost sick with worry about what might have happened to Joanna McCoy. They didn't want, or need, the human Jim Kirk who bled for his friend Bones, Joanna's father, who was working like a dog in Sickbay to keep his grief from overwhelming him.

The captain took a breath and began.

"Thank you all for coming," Kirk said. "I wanted to go over with you just what I've been told about the situation on Centaurus, what I propose to do about it, and what help we might expect."

Kirk had brought with him the printout of Bull Buchinsky's long third Alpha-Red message; he took a quick look at it again. "Communications with Centaurus are out. The first indication we had of the disaster at New Athens was a total loss of routine communications with the Starfleet office at the spaceport. At the same time, the Federation Foreign Office lost touch with its consulate in the downtown section of the city itself. A trade group—the Amsterdam and New Athens Precious Metals and Stones Consortium—reported a loss of its private subspace communications lines at the same instant. Other loss-of-signal reports are still coming in.

"At about the same time, Starbase Seven, located a little less than six light-months from Centaurus, noted large tachyonic readings from the direction of the planet, indicating that there had been an explosion caused by annihilation materials—that is, the uncontrolled merging of matter and antimatter. This flood of tachyons was our first indication that something terrible had occurred on Centaurus. If the ship's computers had been up to par, we'd have noticed it ourselves. That burst of infinitely fast particles crossed the universe from one end to the other, instantly.

"Tracing back, and given the reports of communications losses by Starfleet, the Foreign Office and that trade group, it was determined that the radius of total destruction was between six and ten kilometers. Subsequent reports have confirmed this. A computer simulation of what must have followed indicates that the city of New Athens itself, although located at some distance from the spaceport, was largely destroyed by heat and blast effects."

Kirk paused.

"Starfleet estimates the number of dead at more than nine hundred thousand," he said bluntly. There was a sharp intake of breath around the table. Spock closed his eyes.

The captain continued. "The number of injured is probably less . . . if only because most of those affected by the blast were killed outright. Radiation will be a problem. I must also point out that tachyonic interference is blocking all subspace communication with Centaurus. Starbase Seven reported getting a weak, almost incoherent signal from the planetary government office at McIverton—that's a coastal city three thousand kilometers west of New Athens—but the signal faded completely as tachyonic levels rose. Starfleet notes that a lightspeed signal—radio, for instance—will easily penetrate a tachyonic blanket. However, no ship is close enough to Centaurus to have received such a lightspeed signal yet. As we approach, we'll monitor all lightspeed radio frequencies for Centaurian traffic. Lieutenant Uhura, they might be using some pretty old stuff: AM, low-band shortwave, ham operator bands, laser and so forth."

"I'll be looking everywhere for them, Captain," Uhura said.

Kirk gathered his thoughts. "That's all we know about the situation at this moment. Our orders are to provide whatever relief we can to the civilian population and investigate the circumstances of the accident. If arrests are warranted, Starfleet's ordered us to bring any suspects back to Earth for trial before a Federation court. Federation law supersedes planetary authority in cases involving the possession or use of annihilation materials. As for why we've gotten the job—well, while Centaurus is not in our assigned quadrant, of course, the *Constitution* is in drydock for resupply and renewal of her warp engines; we were the next closest ship."

"Captain?" MacPherson broke in. "Beggin' yer pardon, but ye know we've got problems belowdecks. Will Starfleet be sendin' any help our way?"

Kirk nodded. "That's my next point, Chief. Starfleet is sending the *Hood* to Centaurus as soon as she can be released from her current mission; the *Hood* will also be taking over the *Constitution*'s patrol duties once she's gotten a handle on the tragedy in New Athens. Unfortunately, the *Hood* won't be available for at least a week, perhaps two. No other cruisers are available."

MacPherson shrugged. "An' I say, who needs 'em, anyway? Don't wurry, Cap'n; me 'n Scotty'll hold things together for ye."

"Thank you, Chief," Kirk said, amused—despite the circumstances—by the big Scot's show of confidence. "Let me add that private agencies are dispatching aid to Centaurus. The first vessel is due there by stardate 7514.0—a Red Cross rescue ship, the *Sakharov*—"

"Ah!" came Chekov's pleased voice. "Russian!"

"Well," Kirk said, "Eurasian Union, anyway—and manned by doctors and nurses from most Eurasian countries, under Federation auspices. Also on the way are the British Confederacy's *Edith Cavell* and the USA's *Thomas Dooley*. Those two will arrive soon after the *Sakharov*. We'll pull in soon after the *Dooley*. Unfortunately, it seems the Federation has no ships of its own capable of delivering medical aid on a massive scale, such as will be needed on Centaurus—but some of Earth's remaining national governments do, as do nations on other Federation worlds. Earth, of course, is the closest major Federation planet to Centaurus, so Earth ships will get there first."

"It is a matter of nationalistic pride, Captain," Spock observed. "Although all Earth nations are now members of the Federation and are subordinate to it, there still remain points of national honor. One of these points is a nation's ability to deliver humanitarian aid when and where needed. I must say it is a constructive outgrowth of the old nationalism. It will certainly serve the people of New Athens."

"Thank you, Mr. Spock," Kirk said. "That leads me to ask you, Dr. M'Benga, just what kind of aid the *Enterprise* herself can give to Centaurus."

The tall African shifted uncomfortably in his seat. "I'm afraid the *Enterprise* can't do much in the way of patient care," the doctor said regretfully. "We simply aren't equipped to handle more than a few serious cases at any one time. We'll work hard—but there are only a certain number of patient beds aboard. Perhaps our biggest contribution might be to transport the more severely injured to competent health care facilities, perhaps on Earth and the Jovian satellites; we must assume Centaurian health care facilities will be swamped with the injured. But, Captain, we may be talking about treating *hundreds of thousands* of burn and radiation cases. I don't know what we can do about *all* of them." M'Benga suddenly looked miserable.

"How many do you think we can transport?" Kirk asked.

"Perhaps eleven or twelve hundred at a time," M'Benga replied, "if we crowd them into the corridors. I would not hesitate to do that, Captain, if it would save lives—but some patients will certainly require stasis fields to keep their conditions from deteriorating. How can we provide so many field generators—and even if we could, how are we to monitor them without perfect computer control? I fear we would be killing those we are trying to save. If I might, Captain, I'd like to ask a question of Mr. Chekov."

"Please go ahead."

"Thank you," M'Benga said. "Mr. Chekov, at our fastest safe speed, how long would it take for us to go from Centaurus to Sol?"

Chekov thought about it. "A little over four light-years at warp six, if Mr. Scott can hold our speed—"

"He can!" MacPherson said emphatically.

"Then I would say not more than two days, Doctor."

M'Benga sighed; he waved his lithe hands. "Do you see, Captain? It is the mathematics. Figure a day, if not longer, to get a load of patients aboard and make them comfortable. Two days' journey to the Sol system and its fine hospitals, and two days back. Then we do it all over again. If we estimate five hundred thousand people injured severely enough to require hospitalization—and I think that is a conservative estimate—then it will take *six years* to transport everyone to Sol. And *that* assumes we are at work every day. I believe this morning's unfortunate events with the ship's computers proves we cannot rely on being operational day in and day out for six years."

"I'm afraid you're right," Kirk said. "Your conclusions?"

M'Benga sighed. "Captain, we cannot deliver aid to everyone on Centaurus who will need it. No one can. The logistics of the problem are insurmountable. There is not enough transportation in the Federation to bring all the patients to the hospitals quickly enough—and there are not enough hospitals in the

Federation to handle all the patients. As hard as it may be, we and the Red Cross ships must limit aid to those we can help the most. When these patients are well, they can assist us in helping the next group of patients, and so on. I see no other way."

Kirk said, "But some of the ones we skip over will die."

"Yes," M'Benga said. "Some will die without treatment. God help us. Captain, it is all just so *overwhelming!*" M'Benga sagged wearily in his seat. "I will be up many nights because of this—and not because of the work I will do on Centaurus, but because of the work I will *not* do." The doctor fell silent and stared at the overhead.

No one knew quite what to say, except Spock.

"Dr. M'Benga," the Vulcan began, "I speak as one who has had sufficient reason to appreciate your medical skills. I consider it fortunate that a specialist in Vulcan medicine is assigned to the *Enterprise*. That fact has saved my life at least once."

M'Benga stopped gazing at the ceiling and looked at the Vulcan. This was the closest Spock had ever come to thanking him.

"Permit me, on that basis, to ask you a question," Spock continued. "Do you allow yourself to dwell on the patients you have *not* saved during the course of your career?"

M'Benga looked surprised. "No, Commander. I regret losing a patient—but I must keep my mind clear so that I may treat the next. If I did not have such an attitude, I could not function."

Spock nodded. "Precisely. I would expect the same answer from Dr. McCoy, if he were present at this meeting. Without considering the number of victims who are sure to need treatment on New Athens, Doctor, are you certain you could do your duty toward those patients you *could* treat?"

"Certainly, Mr. Spock."

Spock gestured slightly. "I do not see that you have a moral dilemma here, Dr. M'Benga. You cannot possibly treat half a million people. This ship cannot accommodate that many. Yet this ship is bound for Centaurus, and she will do her best once she is there. You must come to realize that a healed, healthy patient is just that—a healthy patient, one who has benefited from your skill. He does not represent a number of patients you could *not* help; he represents only himself. If all of us do not see the situation in this light, then there is no reason for this ship to go to Centaurus at all."

M'Benga looked down at the table. "Mr. Spock," he said, "I thank you for your words. They make a good deal of sense. I will do my best, we *all* will—yet I am still frightened, if you will pardon me, of the magnitude of the job we must do."

Spock nodded. "But if we are dissuaded from our duty by the size of our task, then we are beaten. I do not propose to be beaten—particularly by a group of mass murderers."

Captain Kirk looked at Spock. " 'Mass murderers,' Spock? What makes you say that? We have no word on that."

Spock said, "I have been considering the circumstances of the explosion, Captain. It could not have been accidental. There are no antimatter power plants on Centaurus, and none are under construction. The Centaurians have breeder reactors using a uranium-plutonium cycle. We can also dismiss the possibility of a ship accident at the spaceport. While ships equipped with warp drive store antimatter aboard for fuel and weapons, no warp-capable ship *ever* lands on a planet. Even if a warp-drive ship were to crash into a planetary surface at terminal speed, its antimatter supply would be protected from contact with matter by an unbreachable series of magnetic fields; the antimatter can always be recovered safely. We have had such cases happen. Impulse-only craft, such as shuttlecraft, *do* land—but such craft do not use antimatter for fuel *or* weapons. Further, spaceports do not store antimatter; starbases do, for reasons of safety. There was no antimatter 'fuel depot' at the spaceport. Therefore, I conclude that any antimatter at the spaceport had to have been brought there on purpose, for use in an annihilation device."

"Who, then, Mr. Spock? Who did it?" Uhura asked.

"Unknown, Lieutenant. Annihilation weapons can be created quite easily once one has the antimatter, which, I must point out, is quite difficult and costly to make. No individual or terrorist group is capable of manufacturing antimatter. This effectively limits the possession of antimatter to military organizations under strict Federation security. Also, no theft of antimatter has been reported; I would venture to think no theft is likely to have happened. But the construction of an annihilation device, once antimatter has been obtained, is not difficult. We ourselves built one with comparative ease to destroy the cosmic cloud on Tycho IV—and, of course, we routinely load antimatter for use in our photon torpedoes. But I believe I can partially answer the question of who did *not* bomb New Athens."

Kirk had a thought. "The Klingons didn't."

"Correct, Captain," Spock said. "The Klingons could not have been responsible. Any attack by the Empire against us would fall under the list of actions proscribed by the Organian Peace Treaty. We do not know how the Organians enforce the treaty they imposed on us and the Klingons; we know only that they do. I presume they would not have allowed an attack on New Athens. The Klingons would have been stopped."

"The Romulans, then?" Chekov suggested.

"Unlikely, Ensign," Spock said. "The Romulans are certainly capable of building and delivering an annihilation device to Centaurus—but what would it gain them? There are far more likely targets—the Federation capital at Geneva, for instance, or Starfleet headquarters in San Francisco. New Athens is—was—merely the capital of a successful colony. It had little or no military importance. The Romulans must also realize that any such attack would bring a quick Federation response—one that they would find devastating. The Federation has many more ships and much more firepower than do the Romulans."

"Well, then, Spock? Who did it?" Kirk prompted, echoing Uhura's question.

"There is not enough data yet to place the blame for the attack, Captain," Spock said. "I said only that I know who did *not* bomb New Athens. But I must note that this is the first attack on a civilian city with a weapon of mass destruction since Earth's Eugenics Wars. Through all history, such weapons have been in the hands of military forces alone."

Spock paused. "Now it appears that, despite all safeguards, someone *else* has them."

Chapter Five:
The Computer Room

MR. SPOCK HAD spent a small part of his very busy day getting reacquainted with his personal set of microsuitable tools. He had paid top credit for them some years ago in a specialty shop on Orion; Spock had no idea where the Orionites might have gotten them. But the tools had served the Vulcan in good stead. They weren't Starfleet issue; they were far better. Spock would never admit it—he wouldn't see the point—but some of the more observant people aboard the *Enterprise* had noticed long before that Spock was, at heart, a tinkerer.

It suited the Vulcan to improve the instruments with which he worked every day. The original designers of Spock's science station on the bridge would no longer recognize some of its innards; Spock had streamlined here and double-circuited there, always improving, changing and reworking things for his benefit. For instance, the chattering of the computer—the trinary code in which parts of the computer "spoke" to other parts—was never meant by its designers to be audible. Spock had changed that; he preferred to hear what was going on. The ship's humans were at first amazed, and then amused, by Spock's ability to understand that computer chatter as if it were a language—which it was, in a way. Similarly, Spock had tinkered with his standard-issue tricorder, improving it until it did things never intended, or imagined, by its makers. Spock had also had an idea or two about improving warp engine performance to a point where a starship could achieve a consistent and safe cruising speed of warp fifteen—but those were just ideas; Spock had nothing practical to present to the captain . . . yet.

Tinkering gave Spock a very personal pleasure—something to which he would never admit, and would barely admit to himself—but he justified it by telling himself that any improvement of the ship's instrumentation allowed the ship to do its job better and was, therefore, beneficial to the ship and the service: a logical and desirable outcome. The Vulcan preferred not to notice that the logic of his reasoning was precisely human and the subject of many Starfleet regulations written to encourage personal initiative for the benefit of the service.

With the environmental chaos aboard the *Enterprise,* Spock had not had a chance to study the ship's computers themselves; the science officer had spent most of the day patching manual controls for ship's functions and interrogating the computer software to see if the source of the ship's problems lay there.

It didn't. Spock had quickly found that all software errors could be attributed to a hardware breakdown of some sort. Spock wondered about that: In all his experience, he had never seen a computer hardware breakdown of such magnitude. The Vulcan had never heard of even a minor breakdown involving the quintuply-redundant computers aboard a Starfleet cruiser. If one component should fail, its four backups would handle traffic until someone could make a repair.

In the *Enterprise*'s case, all the main computer

systems—except for navigation and a handful of others—had failed utterly; the backups had not taken over. Spock intended to find out why, and had gone down to the computer room to find out.

The Vulcan was dressed in an immaculately clean coverall; he was gloved and booted, and he wore a face mask, tool belt, air tank and fishbowl helmet. His equipment had been carefully vacuumed. A grounded wire trailed Spock to carry static electricity away from his body. The precautions were not for Spock's benefit, but the computers'. No grime, no dust could be tolerated here. An operating theater was a germy pigsty compared to a Starfleet computer room.

Spock had not been in the room in more than two years—not since he'd had to repair damage done to the primary memory banks by a disgruntled records officer named Finney. Finney'd been in and out of the computer room repeatedly, without having taken sanitary precautions; Spock had even found a food wrapper on the floor. The Vulcan had almost gotten angry.

The *Enterprise* carried two hundred thirty-six computer banks, all tied together into one megasized electronic brain. The banks were closely stacked like a row of thin dominoes and were seated in a protective chamber set flush into a specially constructed bulkhead. Spock thought it not incorrect to liken the structure of the computer banks to a set of printed-on-paper books sitting on a library shelf—except that *this* shelf held the cultural inheritance of many planets and races.

The capacity of the computers aboard the *Enterprise* was at least one hundred times greater than the total computer capacity available on Earth in the year 2200. The computer banks represented more than three hundred years of progress in the design and manufacture of artificial intelligence machines. Its incredible memory held all the knowledge the ship needed to function, an encyclopedia of all historical and scientific facts, a library of all major and many minor literary and artistic works from all Federation worlds—in short, everything anyone ever wanted or would need to know about *anything*.

But now the computers were nearly mute and couldn't tell Spock much at all.

The Vulcan faced the wall of computer banks and consulted his tricorder. His right eyebrow went up in surprise as the instrument's sensors began to wiggle. *Radiation?* the Vulcan thought. *Primary, secondary, tertiary—characteristic of nuclear fission . . . very strange*. Spock saw from his readings that he was in no danger; the radiation level was not harmful to a humanoid. But the radiation level in this protected room *should* have been zero.

Spock noted that while the tricorder indicated the aftereffects of nuclear fission—or something like it—there was no trace of fissionable material anywhere in the room. The science officer quickly set his tricorder to make a full sweep of the computer room, using all sensors at once.

Ah, Spock thought with some satisfaction. *A temperature anomaly . . . in the direction of the computer banks. A very slight warmth*. He looked at the long row of computer banks, set into the wall. Nothing seemed wrong, at least at first glance. By touch Spock located the inertial screwdriver on his tool belt and walked over to the middle of the computer banks. As he approached he looked the banks over carefully. Spock saw nothing.

Spock stood before the thirty-fifth bank and touched it with the 'driver on the correct spot; the bank withdrew itself from the wall, sliding out easily. The wafer-like bank was about as tall as he was, only six centimeters thick, and about a meter and a half wide; four centimeters of bulkhead insulated this bank from the next one in the series. The Vulcan touched his inertial 'driver to each of the small screws holding the cover of the bank onto its chassis. He watched as the 'driver disrupted the field attaching the screws to the chassis, allowing the screws to pop up for removal by hand. Spock pulled out the screws, gathered them together, and carefully placed them in a pouch on his tool belt. He then gripped the face of the bank and pulled it away from the chassis.

Spock's right eyebrow rose in surprise. There was a tiny, clean, perfectly circular hole drilled into the super-tough material of the computer bank grid. As a result the bank was disrupted, shorted out, wiped clean: It was utterly dead.

Spock inspected twenty more banks chosen at random before concluding that more than eighty-eight percent of the ship's computer capacity was irretrievably gone. All the affected banks had that mysterious, tiny hole in them in exactly the same place, just below and to the right of the center—and as small as it might be, a hole such as that was more than enough to shatter the delicate molecular balance of a grid; each bank depended on that critical balance for its rationality. The only banks still working were the fourteen leftmost and the twelve rightmost, where only a few of the ship's routines were stored. The ship still had navigational control because those routines were stored in banks five and six—but the gravity control routines, for instance, were stored in bank fifty-three, and that bank was dead.

The Vulcan quickly satisfied himself that everything that had gone wrong aboard the *Enterprise* could be traced to the destruction of the computer hardware. Spock fretted at not being able to attack the problem immediately—and he was not sure what he could do, anyway—but the captain had to be informed that the brain of his ship was gone and could not be restored.

Chapter Six:
Near Centaurus

Captain's log, stardate 7513.9:

We are finally nearing the Alpha Centauri star system—and apparently just in the nick of time.

I have received Mr. Spock's report on the condition of our computer banks. I am very disturbed by this—yet a full investigation must await the resolution of more immediate problems on Centaurus. My first thought was of sabotage, perhaps in connection with our current mission, so I have quietly ordered Security to be alert in watching for any such attempts.

But it hardly seems that further sabotage—if there was any in the first place—is necessary. The ship's electrical systems have begun to fail again. Chief MacPherson is now using just about every internal communications channel to carry power—as he'd done on the bridge earlier—but the free water that was floating around the ship this morning seems to have gotten into everything, despite Mr. Scott's efforts at filtering. The ship may re-

quire a nearly complete rewiring . . . a job only a starbase can handle.

Mr. Scott continues to keep a close watch on the matter-antimatter intermix for our warp engines—and he reports more and more trouble in keeping things balanced. With almost all computer systems irrational, Mr. Scott has been controlling the intermix manually—and no human can deliver the billionth-of-a-second balancing corrections needed for smooth operation of the engines. Those small imbalances are beginning to add up—and the best we can expect is an engine burnout, perhaps soon. The worst—well . . .

The bridge crackled with anticipation as the main screen began picking up a visual of the triple-sun Alpha Centauri star group—the bright yellow star Alpha Centauri, half again as bright as Sol when seen from Earth; Beta Centauri, a fiery orange star bigger than Alpha but only a quarter as bright; and, very hard to see, Proxima Centauri, a small red dwarf orbiting Alpha and only 1/13,000th as bright as Sol, its closest stellar neighbor. The planet Centaurus—Alpha Centauri IV—orbited Alpha at an average distance of nearly two hundred million kilometers; those on the bridge strained to see it, but at that distance it was impossible, even at full magnification.

The *Enterprise* continued to make a steady warp five, thanks to the steady hand of Mr. Scott's manual intermix control, Sulu's smooth helmsmanship, and the superbly tolerant design of the ship's much-abused warp engines.

But the ride couldn't last much longer.

The three suns grew steadily larger as Kirk and the others on the bridge watched. Spock, again seated at his science station, looked steadily into his viewer for some faint sign of subspace communications with Centaurus. In her headphones Uhura heard only an occasional squawk or gasp that could have been a transmission—or mere star chatter.

"Crossing into Alpha Centauri system now, Captain," Chekov reported.

We made it, Kirk thought gratefully. "Mr. Sulu, reduce speed to warp one and take us in to Centaurus," he ordered. "Mr. Chekov, get us a course for a standard orbit around the planet; I want to slip in without delay or undue ship's movement. Lieutenant Uhura, begin full monitoring of non-subspace frequencies, as we discussed; we're only a few light-hours from Centaurus now."

The orders were acknowledged and Kirk swung his chair to face Spock's station. "Anything, Mr. Spock?" Kirk asked.

"No, Captain," the Vulcan replied, still gazing into his viewer. "I am picking up energetic tachyonic readings from the direction of Centaurus; I presume those are from the site of the explosion. I am also picking up a great quantity of subsidiary nuclear radiation, but I am not sure of its source . . . except to say that it is on or near the planet. Studying the data will give us a better idea of precisely what is going on—but without the computers to help, I feel we will be at Centaurus before I can come up with anything useful—"

"Captain," Uhura interrupted. "I have a very weak transmission coming in from Centaurus in the kilohertz range."

"Put it on audio, Lieutenant," Kirk ordered.

A rush of sound came through the speakers on the bridge. There might have been a human voice, or a hundred, in there.

"Can you filter that, Uhura?" Kirk asked, concentrating on that strange, echoing rush of sound. He left his chair and walked over to the communications station.

"I'm trying, sir," the communications officer said over her shoulder. "We're stretching the sensors to the limit. Part of what you're hearing are four-year-old radio transmissions we're picking up from Earth and the other planets around Sol."

Uhura bent to her task as the others on the bridge remained silent, their ears straining to pick something sensible out of that eerie, vast conglomeration of raw sound. Gradually Uhura whittled the noise down to a group of not more than a dozen transmissions; she played them in the clear one by one.

Kirk listened as the first came up: a play-by-play report of a World Series baseball game between the Tokyo Giants and the Moscow Dynamos from four years before. That had made its way from Earth, of course, and Uhura squelched it. On the second try Uhura got a transmission from Sol's asteroid belt: a program of news and music for the lonely miners there.

But the third try was the charm. A male voice, a bit shaken but authoritative for all that, came up on the speakers. It was very low, almost inaudible, and nearly swamped by static. "I'm sure that's Centaurus, Captain," Uhura reported. "It's very close. I'm getting it on an old shortwave distress frequency; they must be punching the signal through their atmosphere."

"Can you clear it up any, Lieutenant?" Kirk asked.

"I'll try, sir—wait! Emergency call from Mr. Scott!"

Just then the ship shuddered badly; Kirk, the only one standing on the bridge, was thrown onto his hands and knees as Chief MacPherson, still at the Engineering station, gave a cry of betrayal and outrage.

"Cap'n!" the big Scot shouted. "Everythin' is off the board! Engines beginnin' t' run wild—aye, and there's th' shutdown. Scotty's on it, all right." MacPherson sighed with relief.

The bridge lights flickered and then went out; the emergency lights glowed redly. Kirk got to his feet in the gloom. "Put Mr. Scott on audio, Lieutenant."

"Aye, aye, sir." Uhura threw the call from Scotty onto the bridge speakers. "Yes, Mr. Scott?" Kirk said into the air.

"Cap'n, as ye must know, we've lost th' warp engines. Burned out, crystals an' all. I'm sorry, sir, but we did our level best. Th' imbalances just got t' be too much for th' poor babies."

"Is there anything you can do?" Kirk asked.

"There's nae way around not havin' th' dilithium crystals in th' system," Scotty replied. "They're th' one irreplaceable item wc've got. I can get ye t' Centaurus on impulse power, it's safe enough—but I ask ye t' keep in mind we've an impulse-only ship now, not much good for fancy maneuverin', or fightin', for thot matter."

Kirk sighed; he hadn't really expected a different answer. "Very well, Mr. Scott. I thank you for your efforts. Kirk out." The captain turned. "Mr. Sulu, best speed to Centaurus on the course Mr. Chekov's given you. Full impulse power."

"Aye, aye, sir," Sulu replied. He consulted his helmsman's board; the ship still seemed quick and responsive to his touch. "She's handling pretty well, Captain."

"That's all we can ask of her, Sulu," Kirk said. He resumed his command seat. "Uhura, let's have that Centaurian transmission back on audio."

"Aye, aye, Captain." Uhura pushed a button and a thin, tinny voice came from the speakers. The howling and crackling died away gradually as Uhura twiddled dials and guesstimated reinforcement frequencies.

And, all of a sudden, the voice came through clearly.

"This is the Emergency Control Center at McIverton, Centaurus," the voice said. "A notice of non pratique is hereby given. Repeat, a notice of non pratique is hereby given. Federation craft take note: This is your code seven-ten. Repeating for Federation craft: This is your code seven-ten."

"Code seven-ten?" Chekov wondered out loud. "Ve are forbidden to approach?"

"Yes, Mr. Chekov," Spock answered from his station. "The 'non pratique' message is perhaps meant for ships registered in this system; it is an ancient, seagoing expression from Earth. It means that a ship is denied permission to enter a port." The Vulcan paused and bent over his viewer. "Captain?"

Kirk swung his chair to face the science officer. "Yes, Mr. Spock?"

"I was given to understand in your briefing that three Earth-registered medical ships were to arrive here before us?"

"That's right."

"I see no ships—but there is scattered debris in orbit around Centaurus which could be the remnants of such ships."

Kirk looked at Spock, shocked. "Do you know what you're implying?"

"I believe so, sir. I am not aware of any case in which a Federation ship has ever been fired upon by a Federation member—but I suspect we might have such a case here." Spock paused. "Or three of them."

Kirk nodded and swiveled his chair to face frontward. "Red alert, Mr. Sulu," Kirk said determinedly.

The bridge's emergency battle lights came on full, as red-alert sirens throughout the *Enterprise* began to wail. Kirk continued, "I want all available power channeled to the ship's shields. Lieutenant Uhura, try to raise that person in McIverton. I want to talk to him *now*. Chekov, what's our distance to standard orbit around Centaurus?"

"One point six million kilometers and closing quickly, Captain," the navigator replied.

"Hold your course. Sulu, weapons status?"

Sulu consulted his board. "With all available power to the shields, we can't manage more than one-eighth of full power on phasers, Captain. And that won't last long. But photon torpedoes are intact and ready to go. We'll have to aim and fire them manually, however."

Kirk considered it. *That should be enough to knock down incoming fire,* he told himself, *or slow it down enough so the shields can handle it. I'm not interested in attacking anything or anybody—yet.* "Fine," he told the helmsman. "Stand by with photon torpedoes. I hope your aim's as good as it ever was, Mr. Sulu."

"Captain," Uhura said, "I've gotten an audio signal through to a station that says it's the Ministry of Communications for the Centaurian government. The transmission is from the city of McIverton, sir."

Kirk nodded grimly. "That must be them, Lieutenant. Who will I be talking to?"

"A man named Erikkson, sir. He says he's the president pro tem."

"Put him on."

Uhura did. Kirk addressed the air. "This is Captain James T. Kirk of the U.S.S. *Enterprise*. President Erikkson?"

There was a brief *crackkkkle* of static as Kirk's voice, traveling over shortwave radio, made its way at the speed of light to the city of McIverton. Kirk was used to the swift comeback speed of subspace communications; even the short delay involved in waiting for an answer from Centaurus fretted him.

But it finally came. "Captain Kirk, this is Erikkson. No time! There's a code seven-ten in effect. For God's sake, move off before it's too late!"

Kirk was startled at the urgency in the man's voice. "Just what is the problem, Mr. President—"

It was at that moment that Sulu eased the *Enterprise* into a standard orbit around Centaurus—and a titanic explosion engulfed her.

Chapter Seven:
Gregory's Landing

THE SMALL RESORT town of Gregory's Landing was spending the night under the same canopy of stars Old Earth had always known—except, of course, for the different planets that travel the Centaurian sky, and the bright yellow star in Cassiopeia that was Sol. Centaurus's red-dwarf third sun could also be seen dimly in the night sky, but it did nothing to inhibit the welcome darkness. There was a glow on the southern horizon that represented the millions of lights of McIverton; to the west there was nothing but the sleeping, dark sea.

It was all very restful.

But there was no sleep for five men hiding in a small neocolonial house at the foot of Elm Street, in the southern part of town. The men had been sitting in the darkened, shuttered room for many hours, not saying very much to one another. Two of the men had been smoking cigarettes, one after another; the air was stale with haze and the smell of nervous sweat.

Whatever worried thoughts they might have been having were interrupted by slashes of bright, intolerable light through the shutters. One of the men rose quickly and unblocked a window. He looked up, squinting. "Way high, sir," he reported. "Explosion's still spreading."

"Close the shutter, Max—and, next time, ask me first."

Max's eyes widened a bit in fear as he nodded a quick assent. "Yessir," he said quickly. "Sorry, sir."

The man who had ordered the shutter closed—a plump, pink, unruffled, fiftyish man dressed in vest and tie, and the only one of the five who seemed calm and unhurried—nodded and directed his attention to another part of the room. "That was another one," the man said. "Turn on the 3V, Dave. Let's get some news."

Dave licked his lips nervously and nodded assent. He rose from his chair and walked to a small panel inset into the living room wall. He flicked a switch and, after a moment, something bright formed in the opposite corner of the room. The writhing swarm of light quickly resolved itself into a life-size, three-dimensional picture of a woman seated at a desk, a news script in her hands; the corner itself was replaced by the flat image of a backdrop that read NAN'S NEWSNIGHT. The picture flickered badly.

"Still a lot of interference, Mr. Barclay."

"Um."

Dave twiddled several dials, and the image became a bit clearer. He turned up the volume; there was static and buzzing under the woman's voice. "Best I can do, Mr. Barclay."

"Shut up. I want to hear this."

"—and the Ministry of Defense has confirmed this latest disaster. The destruction of the three medical aid ships was visible in daylight throughout the northern hemisphere. The Ministry says each ship was listed as carrying a crew of fifty and a complement of three hundred or more doctors, nurses and other medical personnel, and that they must all be assumed dead. Reports from sources in McIverton say the American, British and Eurasian Union ships were each hit by at least one nuclear warhead in the multimegaton range almost immediately upon taking up orbit around our planet—"

"That was unexpected," mused Barclay to no one in particular.

"—despite warnings over emergency frequencies from ground control not to approach. It's assumed that the ships were not monitoring those frequencies, since they are seldom, if ever, used. Regular subspace communication has been impossible since the antimatter blast in New Athens."

The woman paused, shuffled her papers, and continued. "The government still has not given an official estimate of the number of casualties in the destroyed capital, but unofficial figures now put the toll at perhaps a million dead—"

Three of the men in the room shuddered; Barclay and the fifth man continued to watch the newscast calmly.

"—and somewhat fewer than that injured. Government sources admit they're hard-pressed to get relief to New Athens, and as one Ministry of Health official told New American News Service when word came of the destruction of the three medical aid ships, quote, 'I don't know what we're going to do now.' "

The woman looked down at a monitor on her desktop; she quickly read what was there and continued: "And this word just in: There has been another nuclear explosion at standard-orbit altitude. Reports from witnesses all over the west coast indicate the detonation took place above, or nearly above, the new capital of McIverton—"

Barclay sat up straighter; he waved his hand for

silence as the woman paused and read something on her desktop monitor.

"—and we now have confirmation of the blast from the Ministry of Defense. In a very brief statement, the Ministry says the explosion was touched off by a Federation starship attempting to take up standard orbit. The statement does not identify the starship, but the Ministry says there had been brief two-way communication with the ship immediately before the blast, and that it had been warned not to assume orbit. No word yet on the starship's fate."

"Turn it off," Barclay said; Dave did so.

"All right, gentlemen," Barclay said to the group. "As I expected, the Federation has arrived. If this first ship has been destroyed, it matters little; another ship will be here shortly. It is time to put our contingency plan into effect. Max, you have that newspaper?"

"Right here, Mr. Barclay."

"Hold on to it, Max; you and Dave will need it. You're to approach the subject of our concern in McIverton tomorrow morning, tell him what I have told you to tell him, and stay with him until he meets with us."

"But, sir?" Max asked. "What if he doesn't want to cooperate?"

"Then kill him and leave town at once," Barclay said flatly. "But I expect he *will* go along; he's built that way. And Max—if either you or Dave say one word I've not authorized you to say, your own lives are forfeit. Understand?"

Max and Dave nodded together. "Yessir," Max said.

Barclay nodded back. "The keys to the flitter are on the coffee table. Take them and leave now; you ought to reach McIverton about an hour after first sunrise. I want the subject contacted before breakfast. Go." He pointed toward the door; Max grabbed the keys, and he and Dave left quickly. The door eased shut behind them.

"And now, gentlemen," Barclay said to the remaining two men, "it's time for us to move to the other hideout. I expect those two may be caught, and I don't trust them not to crack."

Chapter Eight:
The Enterprise

ONLY THE SHIELDS had saved the *Enterprise* from destruction.

If Captain Kirk had not put his ship on red alert, thus automatically bringing the shields into play, the titanic explosion would have sent more twisted junk— the former *Enterprise*—to join the tumbling debris already in rapidly decaying orbit around Centaurus.

But the starship's shields, while good, were not invulnerable. A small fraction of the raw power of the blast had leaked through to them, to crash against the tough outer skin of the *Enterprise*. That remaining force was more than enough to override the ship's inertial dampeners and cause further problems.

On the bridge, Kirk painfully got to his feet and looked around. Everyone had been thrown to the deck. "Sulu!" he called. "How's our orbit?"

The helmsman had already struggled back into his seat. He consulted his board. "Steady in standard orbit, Captain. Whatever that was, it didn't slow us down."

"Good. Maintain the shields; full emergency power. Chekov, keep a sharp eye out for incoming fire." Kirk glanced here and there around the bridge, looking for problems. There were a couple of minor circuitry fires and a lot of acrid smoke; the circuits in several boards had overloaded. But even as Kirk watched, the automatics cut in and a fog of anticombustible, heavier-than-air gases writhed along the surfaces of the affected stations. The fires died aborning, but there was no telling how much damage might have been done.

"Captain," Spock called. "Our sensors show we were hit by a nuclear explosion with an estimated yield of three million metric tons of trinitrotoluene—"

"TNT" to you and me, thought Kirk.

"—and I am attempting to coax a damage report from the computers," Spock continued. "The blast occurred approximately fifty meters off the port nacelle. I can report that our shields are forty-three percent depleted from deflecting the explosion; we do not have the energy reserves to survive more than one additional blast of similar size." The science officer paused. "It also appears we have lost most of the emergency repairs made by Mr. Scott and Chief Mac-Pherson."

As if on cue, the lights on the bridge began to flicker, which brought a frustrated snort from MacPherson, again standing tall at his engineering station. The big Scot began to hit buttons and slide switches up and down; the lights began to glow more steadily.

"Try your best to keep the air and gravity going, Chief," Kirk said. "Anything else can wait."

"Aye, sir," responded the Scot. "Anythin' else is gonna *have* t'wait, if ye don't mind me sayin' so. All th' backups appear shot—burned out from overload—and we've been usin' most everythin' else t' carry power around the ship. I'll do me best, though, Cap'n."

Kirk looked at the main viewscreen. Things looked quiet. Stars occupied the upper half of the screen, and below them an arc of the planet shone brightly bluish.

There was nothing else. "Anything approaching us, Mr. Chekov?"

"Negative, Captain," the navigator replied. "I am on maximum scan; sensors are nominal. Nothing out there, sir."

Kirk nodded and, limping slightly, walked to his command chair and resumed his seat. He swiveled it to face Uhura. "Lieutenant," he said, "do we still have a line through to Sickbay, or is that gone, too?"

Uhura shook her head. "No line, Captain. No communications lines left *from* anywhere *to* anywhere. I've already had ship's stores begin to distribute communicators to all department heads and anyone else with a need for one, but it'll take a while; Security has to deliver them by hand, since all the tubes are out. I have about half a dozen up here already, though." Uhura ducked and slid open a panel at her feet; she took out several communicators and tossed one to Kirk, who needed both hands to catch it.

"Thank you, Uhura," Kirk said as the communications officer called out, "Mr. Spock? Your communicator, sir." She pitched it underhanded in the science officer's direction. Without looking, Spock snatched it out of the air and, with his eyes still glued to the data readout in his viewer, placed the communicator on his belt. "Thank you, Lieutenant. I will have need of it."

As Uhura distributed the remaining communicators to Sulu, Chekov, MacPherson, and the Security officer on duty, Kirk flipped his open. It tweeted and Kirk said, "Bridge to Sickbay. Bones, are you there?"

A tired but familiar voice answered. "I'm here, Jim. I've been carrying this communicator ever since Scotty told me not to worry about the intercom lines getting fixed. What is it?"

"I need a casualty report, if you can give me one. How's it look so far?"

"We were lucky," McCoy said flatly. "My environmental readouts—if I can trust 'em at this point—show the outer skin of the ship was hit by a level-nine burst of primary and secondary nuclear radiation. That blast couldn't have been far off—"

"It wasn't."

"—but radiation levels inside the ship are so damn near normal, I'm tempted to say forget about it. Level-nine exterior exposure is within safety limits, anyway. M'Benga and a couple of nurses are making a quick trip through the ship to see what's going on, since we can't call around. I'm getting reports from them of injuries from blast concussion—people falling down and being thrown into things—but nothing serious, nothing we can't handle down here, and nothing you should worry about. I'll get you a sick list as soon as I can. Anything I should know about on the bridge?"

"No, nothing major," Kirk said, then paused. "Uh, I think I twisted my knee."

"The right one?"

"Yeah. But it's feeling better now."

"I'll look at it later. I worked too damn long on that knee to have you go and wreck it. Try to stay off it, and I'll see you later. McCoy out."

Kirk flipped his communicator closed as Uhura called out, "Captain, I'm still getting that lightspeed radio signal from the Ministry of Emergency Communications in McIverton. They sound frantic, sir."

"Put 'em on," Kirk ordered, and Uhura did. "This is Kirk, commanding *Enterprise*. Go ahead, McIverton."

"Kirk! This is Erikkson. Thank God you're all right! We saw the explosion and thought you'd had it—"

"We almost did. Just what the—what is going on, Mr. President?" Kirk demanded. He thought the president sounded frantic.

"Captain, our planetary defense system is out of control and has been ever since we lost New Athens.

86

Every effort we've made to shut it down has failed. The system attacks any ship approaching the planet, and we can do nothing to stop it from doing so. We tried to warn you off, but there wasn't time."

"Yes, you did try," Kirk admitted. "We didn't pick up your signal until it was too late. Go on, please."

"Subspace communications are out because of tachyonic interference," the Centaurian president said. "I'm speaking to you over this old lightspeed radio transceiver the Ministry of Communications dug out of the Colonial Museum. It doesn't have much range, but it's the only thing we've got that can penetrate the interference blanket."

"What about the defense system?" Kirk asked. "What's wrong? Why is it attacking Federation craft?"

"Our defense system is similar to that used by most Federation planets," Erikkson explained. "We use ground-based multimegaton-range nuclear weapons to deter approach by enemy forces. The Defense Center complex is near New Athens. Our General Staff says the antimatter blast must have deranged the computers controlling the system so that anything approaching the planet is assumed to be an enemy."

"Have you tried disarming the system?" Kirk asked.

"Nothing's worked, Captain!" Erikkson replied, with some heat. "The stand-down code has been sent thousands of times, with no effect. We've sent repair crews to the Defense Center site; they've made no progress in reprogramming the system or shutting it down!"

"Please, Mr. President, go easy," Kirk said. "I need to know; I'm not challenging your judgment." *This man's one millimeter away from a breakdown of some kind*, Kirk thought. *I don't think I've ever heard a voice riding so close to the edge.*

Erikkson paused, and then continued in a calmer tone. "Look, Captain, right after New Athens went up, everything in orbit—freighters, passenger liners, flitters, satellites, whatever—was targeted and destroyed. We lost scores of ships. Things were chaotic; most of the government was killed in New Athens, including the old president and vice president. I was minister of state in the old president's Cabinet. I and two other members of the Cabinet were making an inspection tour of our west coast government offices when word came of the explosion at the spaceport. I've been trying to run things from here ever since; I've had to deputize half a replacement Cabinet from clerks and career bureaucrats, just to keep things moving along.

"After it became clear that the defense system was attacking anything and everything in our sky," Erikkson continued, "I put the code seven-ten into effect. Then the three medical ships from Earth came. We saw them and tried to warn them—but they apparently weren't monitoring lightspeed radio frequencies. They never heard us, Kirk. They were blasted—and we couldn't stop it. We had to watch those ships die."

"Well, there's one thing we may be able to do right away," Kirk said. "Lieutenant Uhura, how much interference are we getting on subspace channels?"

"The tachyonic blanket is still smothering all space-to-ground channels, sir," the communications officer replied. "We're so close to Centaurus now that there's heavy interference on all other subspace frequencies, too—but I think I can punch a signal through to Starbase Seven."

"All right, do it," Kirk said. "My compliments to the commander of Starbase Seven, et cetera, and make our report. Uh, tell him I've put Centaurus under quarantine, with the approval of its government;

have him inform all ships to stay away until further notice. The *Enterprise* is beginning relief operations. Append a report on our status. Sign it and have Seven relay it to Starfleet Command.''

"Thank you, Captain,'' Erikkson said wearily. "It's a great load off my mind, a great load. Tell me—do you have any ideas about how to disarm our defense system? The minister of defense is here with me, as is the minister of internal security. We are all very anxious to help. Please, Captain, do you have any ideas?'' The president's voice had taken on a pleading whine.

Kirk swiveled his chair to face the science officer's station and looked inquiringly at Spock. The Vulcan nodded, and Kirk said, "Gentlemen, this is my first officer, Commander Spock. Mr. Spock also serves as science officer. I believe he has something helpful to say. Go ahead, Spock.''

"Yes, by all means, by all means,'' Erikkson replied quickly. "Mr. Spock, first let me introduce the men with me: the minister of defense, Daniel Perez, and the minister of internal security, Nathaniel Burke.'' There were brief grunts from the two men.

"Greetings, gentlemen,'' Spock said politely. "Minister Perez, have you considered the possibility of a direct attack on the site of the Defense Center?''

"Certainly we have,'' Perez answered, "and we dismissed it out of hand. Commander, the central processing complex of the Defense Center computers is contained in a shielded vault four hundred meters below the surface. Nuclear weapons won't touch that vault; we built it to last. The only way I know to breach the vault is to hit the Defense Center site with annihilation weapons in series, and I think you'll understand we don't wish to do that.''

"Of course,'' Spock said. "Quite understandable, Mr. Minister. May I ask what happened when, as the president said, you sent the stand-down code?''

Perez sighed. "No reaction at all. The computers ignored the code. We expect that any approaching enemy will attempt to generate a great number of random codes in order to confuse the system. Our stand-down codes are, thus, randomly generated and subject to many different kinds of verification before they are implemented. My experts tell me that, somewhere along the way, the computers have lost a step in that verification process and so will refuse to recognize *any* code as a stand-down code."

"So the computers will not stand down because no stand-down code is possible," Spock said. "The system will attack, and keep on attacking."

Suddenly Spock paused thoughtfully, his right eyebrow arching; he swiveled his seat to face Kirk. "Captain," he said, "I must point out that, while we have been attacked once, there have been no follow-up strikes. I deduce that either the Defense Center computers erroneously consider us destroyed, or they are no longer capable of pursuing an initial attack. Either way, this indicates severe damage to the computers' logic centers. It also suggests a weak point from which the problem might be addressed. If our own computer complex were intact, I might be able to begin my investigation from here. Under current circumstances, however, I must go to the site of the Defense Center to see what, if anything, can be done."

Kirk considered it, and finally nodded. "Mr. President, will you and your Cabinet ministers please stand by? I think we might have an approach."

"Of course, Captain," Erikkson answered. "Standing by."

Kirk whipped out his communicator and flipped it open. "Kirk to Engineering. Come in, Scotty." There was a brief wait, and then the burr of the chief engineer's voice came tinnily from the communicator's small speaker. "Aye, Cap'n. Scott here."

"Scotty, do we have enough oomph left to beam Mr. Spock and a team of, er, two technologists down to the surface?"

"Cap'n, after our original problems, I'd routed every transporter circuit through any spare pathway I could find, but thot was all undone by th' nuclear blast. Th' pathways have been randomized, and I canna reconstruct 'em. Th' compensators are out, too; I could perhaps disassemble a landing party, but I nae could put it back together."

Spock spoke up. "I'm quite willing to take the risk alone, Captain."

The chief engineer broke in. "Pardon me, Mr. Spock, but it's nae risk; it's guaranteed disaster. Take a look at yer readouts and figure it out; ye know th' equations as well as I do." To this, Spock nodded slowly. He'd already seen the transporter data readouts; the mathematics were unassailable.

"Captain?" Spock said. "I might suggest going down to the surface in a shuttlecraft."

Kirk gestured an emphatic negative. "No. Even if this ship is now safe from attack—and that's not guaranteed—the defense system is still tracking and attacking anything that approaches the atmosphere. From what Erikkson said, that includes shuttle-sized targets."

Spock nodded. "However, Captain, there are three possibilities here. One is that we have been marked 'destroyed,' and are being ignored. Similarly, a shuttle departing from this ship will be ignored, perhaps as detached debris. The defense system will not respond to anything we do. To it, we do not exist."

The Vulcan paused. "The second possibility is more risky. The defense system will see the shuttle depart from this ship, judge the situation as a new enemy attack, and fire on the shuttle. I must point out, though, that we were hit upon our arrival only because the system detected our approach and had enough time to launch a missile on an intercept course for us; a shuttle departure will take it by surprise. It will have to intercept the shuttlecraft in the atmosphere; the *Enterprise* herself would be safe. And the shuttle can fly a zig-zag pattern to avoid the intercepting missile."

"And the third possibility?" Kirk asked.

"That the defense system will see the shuttle leave, decide that the *Enterprise* is not destroyed, and launch a new attack on her as well as on the shuttle."

Kirk shook his head. "And what are the odds against avoiding another attack on this ship, Spock?"

The science officer looked as unconcerned as ever. "Unknown, Captain; I have no data. But it *is* necessary for me to go to the Defense Center site, and going there in a shuttle offers some hope of success."

Kirk was about to disapprove Spock's plan because of the risk to the *Enterprise* when he caught himself and paused.

"All right, Spock," he said at last. "You can go. But I'm going, too."

Chapter Nine:
Above Centaurus

UHURA SURVEYED THE bridge from her seat in the captain's command chair—*her* chair, for now. She carefully told herself that she wasn't really nervous and that her symptoms (slight nausea, rapid respiration, a bit of a headache and an acute case of the clammy palm) were simply the result of a slight rise in her adrenaline level. Perfectly natural, of course.

But she felt good, for all that.

Well, I just don't believe it, she said to herself for the fourth time. *Here I am in the big chair at last.*

Uhura liked the idea of being in that chair. Sometimes it seemed to her that everyone, including the ship's third-class spittoon polisher, had taken the conn for Captain Kirk at one time or another—everyone, that is, except Uhura. The problem was, quite simply, that Uhura didn't have much in the way of rank or seniority, although she was in the line of command, albeit somewhere very near the bottom. The conn usually went to the most senior bridge officer able to take it.

But this time Uhura had won the roll of the dice. Kirk and Spock, along with Sulu, Chekov and several other personnel, were about to head for the surface of

Centaurus. Mr. Scott was considered "bridge personnel" and would be remaining aboard, but he'd been busy outfitting the shuttles for the trip to the surface; now he was even busier, working with Chief MacPherson to re-repair the ship's subsystems, further damaged by the close-aboard nuclear blast. Dr. McCoy was neither a bridge officer nor in the line of command. Kirk could have called an off-watch officer to duty and given him or her the conn, but he had given it to Uhura without hesitation.

"I apologize for the circumstances, Uhura," Kirk had told her. "It's a bad time for a first watch, but this is a job I *know* you can do. I have only one order: If this ship comes under attack, try to intercept the incoming missile—but if you have to, then get my ship the hell out of here! We'll take care of ourselves; you take care of the *Enterprise*. Your seat, Lieutenant." Kirk had smiled and gestured at his command chair, and Uhura had sat in it.

Now what am I going to do? She pondered that for a moment. *Hmm . . . I could try giving an order or something . . . .*

Uhura addressed the relief navigator, a young ensign with the unlikely name of Diana Octavia Siobhan "Dossie" Flores. She was doing double-duty as navigator and helmsman. "Sensor readings, Ensign?"

"All clear, ma'am."

That went well, Uhura thought with satisfaction. She looked down and consulted the digital chronograph on the arm of the command chair. *The captain and Mr. Spock and the others should be leaving about now,* Uhura thought. *If the captain's plan doesn't work . . . no, I don't want to think about it. It will work.*

Uhura looked around the bridge. The science officer's station was not being manned in Spock's absence. A big, ugly metal box with lights and dials on it had been mounted smack in the middle of the communications station's desktop. With Uhura in command, communications had been taken over by her most able backup, Lieutenant Sergei Dominico. Uhura watched Dominico twiddle switches and frequency scanners in his seemingly ceaseless—and entirely useless—efforts to pick up a subspace signal from Centaurus.

Uhura noticed that Chief MacPherson was still one-handedly manipulating the controls on his engineer's panel; his other beefy hand was holding a communicator open on a direct two-way feed to Scotty, who himself was lurking somewhere in the more mysterious parts of the ship.

What should I do now? Uhura thought. *It'll look silly if I ask about the sensors again. What would the captain do? Oh, I know* . . . She looked at the controls under her right hand. *Well? Where is it? I've seen him do it ten thousand times, but I've never seen just how he does it! Think, you! Oh, dear, this could be embarrassing* . . . .

Then Uhura remembered. *Oh, yes. Turn this dial here, to cut out incoming pages and calls—even though all the lines are down and I won't be getting any. Then I hit this button right here and just talk* . . .

Captain's log, stardate 7514.1. This is Lieutenant Nyota Uhura, in temporary command of the—oh, strike that. Uh, this is Lieutenant Nyota Uhura, communications officer, recording:

We are maintaining standard orbit around Centaurus. Mr. Scott and Chief MacPherson continue their repairs of, uh, basic systems aboard the ship. A fresh sensor scan shows nothing threatening us. Er . . . oh, yes. We've had no further word from the Centaurian capital of McIverton—or anywhere else on Centaurus—since the captain's conversation with President Erikkson and the two ministers at stardate 7514.0. As the captain ordered before he left the bridge, we will be keeping a close watch for incoming missile fire from the planet's defense system.

Captain Kirk and Mr. Spock are to leave momentarily for Centaurus in separate shuttlecraft. Mr. Sulu will accompany the captain as pilot. Mr. Spock will be going with Ensign Chekov as pilot, two computer technicians selected by Mr. Spock to work with him on the repair job at the Defense Center, and Nurse Constance Iziharry. Iziharry was selected by Dr. McCoy because of her expertise in radiation work; Mr. Spock expects her medical skills may be needed. Chekov's skill as a pilot certainly will be.

Mr. Scott and his people have completed installation of three—how can I describe them?—shortwave radio transceiver sets, specs for which Mr. Scott dug out of one of his old books. Fortunately, Mr. Scott has some of the captain's taste for printed literature and is not totally dependent on the ship's computers for research material. A transceiver has been installed at my bridge station; others have been bolted into the two shuttlecraft. Unfortunately, no one had time to adapt the centuries-old design of the transceivers to come up with something portable—the sets are very big and heavy—so hand-held communicators won't be available to our landing parties for ground-to-space traffic. The landing parties will only be able to talk to us from the shuttles. They can talk to each other on their regular hand-held communicators, though, as long as the range isn't very great—a few meters, no more. For the record, tachyonic interference from Centaurus has not abated. No normal wavelength can get through that wall of static—

There was a familiar squeak behind Uhura, and then came a gravelly voice: "Well, Uhura! Glad to see you've finally made the big time."

Uhura put the log on standby and swung the command chair to face the open turbolift doors. In the 'lift stood Dr. McCoy and Lt. Siderakis. Uhura smiled widely. "Welcome to both of you," she said warmly as the two men walked onto the bridge. "Peter, are you feeling better?"

Siderakis nodded. "Reporting for duty, ma'am, if that's all right."

"I guarantee him, Uhura," McCoy affirmed. "In fact, I guarantee the both of us. I think we're both sick of skulking around—me in Sickbay and Peter in his quarters—so we've decided to come out for some fresh, recirculated air."

"Fine, Doctor," Uhura said. "Lieutenant, I think Ensign Flores is more than ready to give up the helm."

Dossie Flores grinned. "I'll say! Welcome back, Peter."

"Hello, Dossie. Thanks," Siderakis said quietly, sliding into his seat. "What's the situation?"

"Holding steady in standard orbit. Defensive posture: Shields up full, emergency overload capability activated. Keep an eye out for incoming fire. Our position is almost directly above McIverton, a city on the west coast of the northern continent—"

"I know where McIverton is," Siderakis said brusquely. His tone reminded Flores that he was a native of Centaurus; it also made McCoy, standing behind Siderakis, look at him with ill-disguised concern.

"Oh," Flores said after an awkward silence. "Sorry, Peter. Well, anyway, that's our position. Uh, I'm unslaving your board from mine in three . . . two . . . one . . . mark."

"Got it, Dossie. And I'm sorry; I shouldn't have been abrupt."

Flores smiled. "Forget about it, Pete." They both set about doing their jobs. Behind them, McCoy relaxed.

Uhura turned to the doctor and spoke to him quietly amid the murmur of the small sounds on the bridge. "How are you, Doctor?"

McCoy gave a small, wan smile; he looked tired. "As well as can be expected. Talking with Pete helped him a lot; I know it helped *me*. We've both got people in New Athens."

"I know, Doctor," Uhura said. Her eyes were warm and sympathetic.

McCoy sighed. "The worst thing is not knowing about Joanna, Uhura. I wish I'd managed to see Jim and Spock before they went to the hangar deck."

"Don't worry, Doctor. They understand, and I've been up here all the while with the captain. He wants to know about . . . things . . . as badly as you do. He'll check himself, or Spock will. I'm sure of it."

McCoy nodded slowly. "I have to get in touch with my sister and her husband, too," he said. "They're probably as worried as I am. When Joanna started med school about a year ago, they retired down south and sold the house. A good thing they did; they used to live about six kilometers from the spaceport, in a park there. It was a pretty place. Jim stayed there once or twice." He looked at the main screen: Yes, it was a pretty planet down there, a brilliant blue. "You can't see New Athens from here, I guess."

"No, sir. It's slightly below the horizon. We're in standard orbit, of course; New Athens will be out of sight as long as we remain above McIverton."

"I guess I prefer it that way," McCoy said.

The shuttlecraft *Columbus* and *Galileo* stood on the *Enterprise*'s cavernous hangar deck loaded, fueled, and ready to lift. The seven who would crew them gathered for a final briefing by Captain Kirk. All hands were wearing pressure suits, as ordered. *Ve look like actors in wery bad old-time space-fiction motion picture,* Chekov thought. He was irritable; his injured eye was still hurting a little.

Kirk was speaking to the others over a communicator built into his suit's helmet. At this close range—less than two meters in this small group—there was no noticeable interference from the Centaurian tachyonic blanket. "A few last words before we depart, ladies and gentlemen. Messrs. Sulu and Chekov know their departure pattern. We will strap in and *remain* strapped in until I and Mr. Spock give the word to unstrap; maneuvers are likely to be abrupt, and shuttles don't have inertial dampeners. These craft can't take much punishment, and I want no decompression injuries in case of a near-miss by the defense system down there. The suits will keep air coming to you even if your shuttlecraft is hulled. Mr. Spock, since you'll be in New Athens, your group will have to wear the suits on the surface as well. You'll be in the fallout footprint from the spaceport blast."

"Yes, Captain," Spock said. Chekov groaned inwardly, and then checked himself as he realized that spending a few uncomfortable hours in a pressure suit was preferable to spending several evil weeks recovering from radiation sickness . . . or dying of it more quickly.

"All right," Kirk said. "To continue: I expect we'll

have no trouble from the defense system once we're twenty thousand meters or so from the surface. The system's computers have not been attacking Centaurian air traffic, almost all of which operates below that altitude. So we'll get down to that level fast and adopt a standard aircraft flying pattern." Kirk paused and changed the subject. "We'll coordinate via communicator until the subspace interference from below swamps us; then we'll switch to radio. Spock and I will act as communications officers. I believe that's it; any questions?"

There were none. "Very well. Good luck and happy landings. Mr. Sulu? Let's get aboard." Kirk gestured, and the group split up. The captain and Sulu headed for *Galileo;* Spock and his party were already climbing aboard the nearer *Columbus,* even as the landing deck's sirens rang out with the compelling signal to board ship.

Seated and strapped in—the newly installed seat belts courtesy of Montgomery Scott—Sulu and Kirk ran a final check of *Galileo*'s instruments. All indicators were green; the little ship was warmed up, ready and eager to fly; Scotty had done his usual thorough job in the pre-check. "Everything all right on your end, Sulu?" Kirk said into his suit communicator.

"Ready to go, Captain. All lights green; cabin pressure normal. Manual launch in one minute . . . mark."

"Fine." Kirk changed frequencies. *"Galileo* to *Columbus.* Mr. Spock, communications check; how do you read?"

"I read you five-by-five, Captain. Fifty seconds and counting. Mr. Chekov reports our board is green and all systems are nominal. We are ready."

"Read you five-by-five. We're go for a launch. *Gali-*

leo out." Kirk clicked over to a third setting. "*Galileo* to bridge. Lieutenant Uhura, do you read?"

"Perfectly, Captain. Godspeed, sir."

"Thank you, Uhura. Take care of my ship. Kirk out." Kirk clicked to the farthest-right setting. "*Galileo* to hangar deck duty officer. Begin launch sequence; it's time we left."

"Aye, aye, Captain. Air pumps working; full vacuum on deck in thirty seconds. Safe trip, sir."

"Thank you. Out."

Kirk clicked back to talk with Sulu. "You read about things like this in the archives, back in pre-transporter days."

"Yes," Sulu mused. "In those days the chief helmsman always piloted the captain's shuttle to the surface for first contact. They used up a lot of helmsmen that way."

"Not to mention captains."

Sulu grinned widely enough for Kirk to see it through the helmsman's heavily laminated faceplate. "I think the last such significant first contact was with Vulcan. Everything went well until Captain Harrison tried to shake hands with the head of the Vulcan Council. The Vulcans thought Harrison was attacking him."

"And old Harrison wasn't very good at splitting his fingers in the Salute," Kirk said. He laughed. "We should all be glad Harrison didn't try to kiss the Chief Councillor's wife."

A tinny voice overrode Kirk and Sulu's communicator frequency. "Vacuum on deck complete; doors opening. Departure sequence starts."

"It's show time, Mr. Sulu. Raise ship."

"Aye, aye, Captain."

The whine of *Galileo*'s impulse engines rose as the small, boxy craft lifted a meter off the hangar deck and hovered. Kirk switched his copilot's monitor to give a view to starboard. He saw that *Columbus* had also lifted and was ready for departure; she was hovering five meters to *Galileo*'s starboard side.

Kirk looked out the forward ports and saw the huge doors of the hangar deck begin to iris open. He could see a wealth of stars in cold black velvet above the blue arc of Centaurus below. *It's live,* Kirk thought. *I usually get to see this in a viewscreen, but it's never quite as good as the real, naked-eye thing. This is magnificent! I made starfaring my career for a lot of reasons; this was a big one. Just to go and see, that's all. That's all I ever really wanted. My brother and I never went more than fifty klicks from home until we were teenagers. Then I joined Starfleet, like Dad, and I never looked back; Sam, rest his soul, chose colonial life and never looked back either. The Kirks have always been wanderers; I think Mom knew that and understood it, just as she understood it when Dad volunteered for duty on Hellspawn . . . and died there.*

"Five seconds to departure, Captain."

The hangar deck doors had disappeared, folded into the hull of the *Enterprise.* The hangar deck was in hard vacuum, and nothing but naked space lay beyond. Kirk felt a stirring of the old exuberant excitement. *Let's hurry up and get the hell going!*

Kirk switched over to the third frequency. "Hangar deck duty officer, this is *Galileo.* Requesting permission to depart."

"Permission granted, Captain; go well. Duty officer out."

Kirk clicked his transmit/receive switch twice—a communications officer's shorthand for "thank you"—and clicked over to Sulu. "We're clear, pilot. Take her out."

"Aye, aye, Captain."

Kirk switched over. *"Columbus,* we are leaving. Stay close, Mr. Chekov."

"Aye, Captain. Ve guarantee ve vill not bump you on the vay down."

Together, slowly, the two shuttlecraft each rose a little higher and moved toward the hangar port.

"Rear view, please, helmsman," Uhura said.

"Aye, aye, ma'am," Siderakis responded as he pushed a button. The familiar forward scene on the bridge's main screen swam for a moment and then steadied into a similar sternward view—the stars resting timelessly above the planet—except that now two small squarish craft were moving closely together into sight. Each presented its keel to the other, and they were not more than three meters apart. "That's *Galileo* to port, ma'am," Siderakis said. "Good departure pattern."

"Sulu and Chekov are a couple of our best," Uhura said. "Angle the view down, please, helmsman; I want to keep visual track of them for as long as we can." The view changed again; now they were looking downward toward the departing shuttles and fully against the glare of Centaurus; Uhura was forced to squint. "Tickle that down, please, Peter," she said, and the stark brightness of the scene faded to a tolerable level. "Dossie, what do the sensors say?"

"Nothing yet, Lieutenant," the navigator responded. "Everything's clear. I've plotted the five most likely paths of attack between the shuttles and the ground, and there's nothing there yet, either." McCoy, still standing next to the command chair, slipped a hand secretively behind his back and crossed his fingers; Sergei Dominico, sitting at the communications station, saw McCoy do it but pretended not to notice.

* * *

Kirk noticed some interference in *Galileo*'s sensor readouts—some reception modes depended on the frequencies most affected by the tachyonic fallout blanket surrounding Centaurus—but satisfied himself that enough signal was getting through on other wavelengths to allow a safe approach. He could no longer see *Columbus* on his monitor, because *Galileo*'s outboard camera system did not allow a view directly "down"—that is, in the direction of the keel. "Sky is still clear, Sulu," Kirk told his pilot.

"Hope it stays that way, Captain," Sulu said. "Uh, we're maintaining a distance of two point seven meters from *Columbus*. Speeds are matched, courses are parallel. Chekov is hanging on out there like he was bolted on. We're right on track."

"Very good." Kirk switched the vidmonitor for a departure angle. It had been quite a while—a year, anyway—since Kirk had eyeballed his ship close-up from the outside; he rarely went on shuttle rides. He saw the stern of the *Enterprise*, lit brilliantly by the two suns that mattered to Centaurus. From here the starship's long and graceful warp nacelles, starkly white and almost glowing, appeared splayed against the ultimate blackness of space.

Somewhere in the middle of the stern, Kirk could see an even brighter gleam of light, which shrank to nothing even as he watched. That would be the hangar deck, as its giant doors closed again, sealing that most vulnerable part of the ship from the hostile vacuum. The *Enterprise* herself was rapidly growing smaller and smaller as the shuttles accelerated. Kirk felt a bit lost without his ship around him.

"Distance from *Enterprise* nearly one hundred kilometers, Captain," Sulu said. "We'll begin descent in tandem with *Columbus* according to flight plan—now."

Sulu smoothly sent *Galileo* into a shallow, precise

descent while keeping an eye on his proximity readouts with *Columbus*. Kirk saw them, too, and noted that Chekov and Sulu were maintaining no more than three meters' distance between them. *This is one masterpiece of piloting, gentlemen,* Kirk thought. *If we pull this off, I'll be more than happy to process the commendations* . . . .

As *Galileo*'s angle of approach changed, Kirk saw the star-speckled blackness of space supplanted by the glowing blueness of Centaurus; they were headed directly for the surface now, at a speed well within the shuttles' re-entry tolerances. That thought reminded Kirk of another *Galileo,* the predecessor shuttle to the one he was now in. The first *Galileo* had been lost in a burnup over Taurus during a mission commanded by Spock; those aboard had been saved at the last moment by what had been some of Scotty's quickest and most deft transporter work ever.

One thing I don't like about pressure suits, Kirk said to himself, *is that your breath is too loud in your ears. It's like living in a giant nostril.*

His thoughts were interrupted by an indicator light on his copilot's panel. "Sulu, I have a launch indication from the surface," Kirk said calmly. "Data reading in now."

"Damn!" Sulu said. "The defense system's still watching us, after all."

"So now we know." Kirk clicked over to the ship-to-ship communicator frequency; there was now a roar of heavy static, caused by the rising tachyonic interference from below. "Spock, did you get that?"

"Affirmative, Captain. It seems to be a single missile launch from a silo located not far from the Defense Center site itself. Since we are headed generally down toward New Athens, I infer the computer is attempting a quick, direct response to our supposed 'attack,' but it is trying nothing more than a simple interception. I would have expected more . . . finesse . . . from an undamaged computer system of this advanced type."

"I understand, Spock; I hope you continue to be as correct as you have been. Chekov, stand by for Operation Razzle-Dazzle."

"Standing by, Captain."

Kirk clicked over to the fourth communicator frequency, but found he could not raise the *Enterprise;* the tachyonic interference was now overwhelming. He switched on the cobbled-together shortwave transceiver. "Kirk, aboard *Galileo,* to *Enterprise.* Come in, *Enterprise.*"

"Uhura here, Captain. We've seen the launch and are tracking. Phasers ready." Uhura's voice was clear and sharp; Scotty and his people had done a superlative job on short notice.

"Very good, Lieutenant. Kirk out." He looked again at his status board and saw that the incoming missile was quickly gaining speed as it rose into the Centaurian sky. Kirk carefully consulted his board; he could see no evidence of a second launch. *Good,* he thought. *The defense system thinks both shuttles are a single spacecraft, because we're flying so close together—and Spock is* still *right; the defense system's apparently lost its capacity for follow-up attacks. Just as it never hit the ship again, it's not ready to fire on us a second time if this first missile doesn't do the job. There's no backup missile in place, hanging back to 'see' what happens. Advantage, us.*

Kirk clicked back to the first frequency setting. "Altitude now fifty kilometers above the surface, Sulu," he reported. "Missile altitude ten point seven kilometers. Steady track."

"Good enough," Sulu said. "Interception time?"

"Assuming the track remains steady, fifty-eight seconds."

"It'll stay steady—I hope," Sulu said.

"I'm pretty much depending on that myself," Kirk returned. "Fifty seconds."

Kirk heard a signal in his ear and switched the radio to the intership frequency setting. "Captain, this is Spock. Mr. Chekov informs me he is ready to commence Operation Razzle-Dazzle whenever he should get the word."

"Very well, Mr. Spock. Good luck."

There was a pause. "All luck to you and Mr. Sulu, Captain. Spock out."

Kirk consulted his board's chronometer. "Twenty seconds to interception, Sulu." *Galileo*, like *Columbus*, was flying with her nose pitched down toward the planet below; peering out the forward window, Kirk could see a very small, but very bright, point of light against the swirling white clouds of the planet. *Is that the son of a bitch?* he wondered, looking at the tiny pinpoint of fire. "Fifteen seconds, Sulu."

Sulu grunted acknowledgment. "Captain, please tell *Columbus* to stand by; I'm not going to give much notice. This is seat-of-the-pants stuff."

"Right." Kirk radioed the other shuttle. "*Columbus*, stand by to commence Operation Razzle-Dazzle on my signal. Acknowledge, please."

"Acknowledged," Spock said amid loud static.

"Ten seconds," Kirk told Sulu. He could see the helmsman nod quickly. Kirk counted down to himself: *Nine . . . eight . . . seven . . . six . . .*

"Now!" Sulu shouted, and bore down hard on the shuttle's joystick as Kirk shouted "Now, Chekov!" into the radio. The shuttle strained with the abrupt change of velocity; Kirk and Sulu found themselves struggling to retain their seats, even belted in.

Kirk watched Sulu's board; *Columbus* was pulling away in much the same maneuver at rapid speed, plunging outward and downward. He noted with great satisfaction that both shuttles were now—just barely—out of the circle of destruction of any expectable nuclear explosion taking place at the interception point.

Three . . . two . . . one . . . zero.

Nothing happened. Kirk consulted his board quickly. The missile was *still* heading up and was now well above its expected detonation point. *What the hell is going on—my God, it's changing course! But not toward us . . .*

The shortwave unit buzzed for attention; Kirk activated it. "Captain, this is Spock. The missile is now on a direct interception course for the ship. I assume this is a 'smart' missile, and it selected an alternative target upon our 'disappearance' from its sensors. We have apparently provoked the defense system into rediscovering the ship's presence. Estimated interception time is sixty-eight seconds."

Uhura watched the abstract display on the main viewscreen. The two shuttles were small orange dots against the green map of the planet below; the missile was a pulsing red triangle heading directly for the white sphere that represented the *Enterprise*. A digital chronometer in the lower right corner of the screen was counting down the number of seconds to estimated interception time: 0067 . . . 0066 . . . 0065 . . . 0064 . . .

"Phasers locked on target," Dossie Flores reported. "We're ready to go, Lieutenant."

"Let's let it get a little closer," Uhura said. "Helm, are you ready?"

Siderakis nodded. "If Dossie misses, I'll pull us out of here so fast we'll leave a hole in the sky. Impulse engines are at forty-two percent capacity."

Dominico, at the communications station, said, "Captain Kirk is standing by on the shortwave."

"Does he want to talk to me?" Uhura asked.

"He says both *Galileo* and *Columbus* have reached safe altitude, and each is proceeding to its destination. No further missile launches detected. Other than telling you that, he said not to bother you. He'll stand by."

"Thank him, then, and tell him we're fine." *I'm glad he's there,* Uhura thought as she watched the chronometer pass 0050. *Maybe he knows I need him there.*

At 0045 Uhura said, "All right, Dossie. Prepare to fire; this is one that *doesn't* get through!"

"Yes, ma'am!"

0042 . . . 0041 . . . 0040.

"Fire phasers!" Uhura ordered, and Dossie Flores crunched a button. The display showed a line of intense blue leaping between the *Enterprise* and the red triangle that represented the missile . . .

. . . and the triangle blinked three times and disappeared.

"Target destroyed, Lieutenant," Flores said. "Not bad for a minor leaguer, eh?" She gripped her hands above her head in a gesture of victory.

Uhura grinned. "Good work, everybody. Sergei, message to *Galileo:* 'Target destroyed. We are maintaining orbital position and speed. All is well. Uhura out.' "

And Uhura settled back in *her* command chair with a satisfied sigh.

Chapter Ten:
New Athens

THE SMALL SHUTTLECRAFT *Columbus* sliced through the thin air high over the east coast of Centaurus's northern continent, New America.

"Our altitude is twenty thousand meters and holding, Mr. Spock," Chekov reported. "Braking seqvence ended; speed is now seven hundred thirty kilometers per hour. Ve are subsonic."

Spock looked out the trisected forward ports. It was beautiful up here in this clear, clean sky. *Columbus* was flying well above the cloud cover, and so their little craft was surrounded by pleasant shadings of purest blue. Spock had not "cut sky" in quite a while; he found himself admitting—not without some embarrassment—that he liked it.

The first officer consulted his status board and saw that *Galileo* was making good speed westward. At this altitude the planet's damaged defense system would dismiss both shuttlecraft as friendly air traffic. Spock did not see the logic of that—there *was* no logic to it, because an invader was, in theory, as fully capable of mounting an air-to-ground attack as a space-to-ground assault—but the datum helped Spock build a mental picture of what the internal state of the defense system's computers must be. It bothered him that, even after hours of concentrated thought, he had still not found a sure, exploitable flaw in the system's logic. That was why he'd felt it necessary to come down to the surface . . . just as Captain Kirk had found it necessary to go to McIverton for a face-to-face meeting with the leaders of the Centaurian government. *He will deal with the broken human element, as I will deal with the mechanical,* thought Spock. *He cannot rely on this planet's new leaders to do right; neither can I rely on this planet's defense mechanism to work correctly. We must each confront our task directly. The spaceport explosion has left us both with massive damage to repair; we must repair it—but perhaps both of us will face insurmountable problems in our attempts to do so. And I have one other task . . .*

"Mr. Spock?" Chekov said, interrupting the first officer's thoughts. "Ve vill be over the site of New Athens Spaceport in three minutes. Any instructions, sir?"

Spock nodded. "Yes, Ensign. Take us down below the clouds. I desire to make a visual inspection." *Three minutes at this speed puts us at a distance of thirty-six point five kilometers from ground zero,* Spock calculated. *We ought to be able to see the fringes of the blast area by now; our course has us approaching from the southwest, bound for the site of the Defense Center.*

Chekov pushed his joystick forward, and *Columbus* began a quick descent. She pierced the top of the cloud cover at eight thousand meters and plunged on through. The window revealed nothing but the gentle white interior of the cloud . . . and then, very suddenly, the cloud turned a deathly gray.

"Significant radiation readings, Mr. Spock," Chekov said.

"I see them, Ensign." Spock swiveled his chair to

face aft and addressed the three others aboard. There was a gentle hiss of static under his words. "We are now entering the radiation-affected area of the blast. You will notice the greater tachyonic interference on our communicator frequency, but as we will be within very close range of one another at all times, it should not be a significant problem. With radiation in mind, I caution you once again to maintain the integrity of your pressure suits. The readings are rather higher than I might have expected, but they are still well within suit safety limits. It seems likely that weather patterns—high winds from the north, perhaps—have prevented an equal distribution of fallout in this general area. This gives some hope that the region to the north of us might be more free of contamination."

"Mr. Spock?" came a voice. It was Rawlings, one of the computer techs Spock had selected for the repair job; the thin technician appeared engulfed by his bulky pressure suit. "Is there any chance the Defense Center area will be clean enough to operate in without the suits?"

"I think not," Spock answered. "The site of the complex is quite near the spaceport and not sufficiently north of it to matter."

Next time I vill bring vith me a giant radiation-proof Baggie and live in it, after poking two holes in it for my eyes, thought Chekov. *It could not be less comfortable, and at least I could have vith me a sandvich. And I could put some ice on my eye.*

The cloud began to break into a wispy pattern of gray and deeper gray. Chekov spoke up. "Mr. Spock? Ve are beginning to see the ground. Range to spaceport is now twenty-three point four kilometers northeast of our present position."

"Thank you, Ensign." Spock gazed intently out the window as Rawlings, Nurse Iziharry and the other computer tech, a man named Hudson, watched the same scene on their video screens. *Columbus* continued downward.

And then, suddenly, they were in the open air.

"My God," Chekov breathed for all of them.

Columbus was two thousand meters above the ground. There was no green anywhere at all; there was no movement. There was nothing but black and gray, the charcoal colors of death. Everything below had been burned, blasted, and burned again; heavy black smoke still rose here and there. There had been buildings and houses and roads and cars and people below, once; all were now gone, cremated and covered. The area below *Columbus* was well outside the eight-kilometer circle of total destruction from the spaceport explosion, but secondary heat and blast effects had been more than enough to wipe out everything that had been here. If there had, somehow, been survivors, they'd fled long before now—and Spock, for one, could not imagine how anyone might have escaped. *Perhaps by flitter, the aerial craft most often used on this planet,* he considered. *But how would one fly such a flimsy thing in the maelstrom that must have existed here? I believe they must have been forced to walk out . . . through a sea of radiation and death. No, there can be no one left.*

Spock's face suddenly contorted with overwhelming emotional pain. He recovered almost immediately and realized his helmet had hidden his weakness from the others; no one had seen. Yet even in his personal shame he knew that there was no discipline, Vulcan or otherwise, which would allow a being to view this hell without cost.

"Tventy kilometers from the spaceport," Chekov said in a dazed voice. "No one down there, no one at all."

Spock opened his eyes—the pause had helped—and consulted his map of the area. The *Enterprise*'s map storage banks had been lost in the ship's mysterious computer breakdown. What Spock had in hand now was a paper map of the area; he'd borrowed it from Lieutenant Siderakis, who was from New Athens. The relief helmsman had been reluctant to give it up, and Spock had understood that; the map had become a precious souvenir of a lost home town. But Siderakis had quickly come to see for himself the necessity of Spock's having the map for this mission, and had surrendered to the logic of the situation without argument. Spock had appreciated that, and planned to do his best to return the map undamaged.

The Vulcan took a quick look at the shuttle's coordinate plotter and mentally translated the figures onto the face of the map. Spock put a finger in the lower right quadrant of the map and showed it to Chekov. "Here we are, Ensign."

The young Russian took a quick look. "This used to be a protected park area?" he asked. He looked down at the flattened, charred landscape.

"Yes. It was called Athena Preserve. I believe Dr. McCoy maintained a residence here at one time."

"It's not there now," Chekov pointed out unnecessarily. Nothing was there.

Spock consulted the map again. "We appear to be two kilometers from the southernmost boundary of the spaceport." He looked at his board. "Radiation readings high, but still within safety limits. Outside temperature twenty-three standard degrees, and there are brisk winds from the north; I cannot determine a true wind velocity while we are in flight. Mr. Chekov, I suggest we cruise slowly over the spaceport to see what we might see."

"Yes, sir. But I don't think there'll be much to see; ve're now passing ower the lip of a crater."

And that was all there was below them for the next three kilometers—the glassy floor of a hole in the world, burned and chewed out in one unimaginable, terrible instant. The crater looked to be several hundred meters deep at its lowest point, but it was hard to tell; water had collected in it already. One day this might be a small, strangely circular—and dangerously radioactive—inland sea.

Columbus flew on slowly.

They passed the northeastern rim of the crater. Spock was more watchful now; the Defense Center was nearby. Captain Kirk had been told that repair crews had been sent to fix the defense computers, but Spock saw no compelling reason to accept this. There was no direct evidence that the crews had ever arrived: The computers were still not fixed. It was too bad. Spock would have liked to rely on the crews' landed flitters as a clear landmark for the location of the entrance to the defense installation.

Spock did not want his party to spend very much time on the surface, even in pressure suits. The Vulcan wanted to find the entrance to the underground complex quickly; being below the surface would afford a great deal of protection against radiation, and that would gain them more time to solve the problem of the Defense Center.

But there were no landmarks left . . . not a lake, not a bridge, not a road. Dead reckoning would have to do—that, and a little guesswork. Spock looked again at the coordinates on his board and translated them to his map. The Defense Center site was not more than three hundred meters from their present position. "Mr. Chekov, please hover. We're very near the site, and I must get our bearings."

"Aye, aye, sir."

As *Columbus* stood by, Spock thought. There was nothing but rubble below and no evidence of any repair flitters—but wasn't there a little *less* rubble over that way, about two hundred and fifty meters to port?

And wouldn't something like a defense site be relatively "unbuilt," with most of its facilities underground? Or was the clearing simply an accidental cancellation of blast patterns in one very small area?

There was only one way to find out. "There, Mr. Chekov," Spock said, pointing. "Overfly that area very slowly, please." Chekov nodded and complied; *Columbus* dropped closer to the ground, now moving about a meter per second, at a height no more than two meters above the scattered debris. Rawlings, Hudson and Iziharry left their seats and moved forward to stand behind Chekov and Spock. Connie Iziharry laid a trembling, pressure-gloved hand on Chekov's left shoulder; he never felt it. The five of them, together, watched the devastation flow slowly around them as they floated above it.

A few minutes later Hudson cried out, pointing. "There, at ten o'clock!"

Then they all saw a twisted, blackened sign welcoming visitors to Planetary Defense Command Headquarters. There was the remnant of a heavily protected entrance, and Chekov landed *Columbus* precisely in front of it.

The massive doors which should have shut the Defense Center off from the outside world upon detection of the spaceport explosion hadn't worked. They were still open, both sides of them scorched with terrible heat. The *Columbus* party walked on through, with Spock in the lead. The Vulcan's DayBrite lantern picked out heaps of rubble here and there—and, every so often, a corpse in military garb. The center had remained open to heat and radiation, and there had been no warning at all. The dead military personnel were the first casualties the five from the *Enterprise* had seen on Centaurus.

"There can't be anyone alive down here, can there?" Connie Iziharry asked.

"Perhaps lower down," Spock said doubtfully. "There may have been other protected areas . . . but, as we saw, the primary doors were open."

"Is it possible someone opened them after the explosion?" Rawlings wondered.

"I think not," Spock said. "Both sides of the doors were affected by great heat, and we saw rubble from the outside down the entryway. It could only have been thrown that far by the blast."

"Oh. Of course."

Hudson spoke up. "If that's so, then I wonder what condition we'll find the equipment here in. I thought we might be able to use some of the stuff they had here already."

Spock considered it. "Some might well be usable. Such electronics as we will find here are sometimes delicate, but I assume they were produced according to military specifications. I would also assume the central command center was protected somehow, although I cannot be sure those protective measures were effective."

"I vonder how many personnel vere stationed here," Chekov said.

"I don't know precisely, Ensign," Spock answered. "However, I once visited a similar defense installation on Big Top. That one had some forty officers and five hundred enlisted personnel."

Iziharry waved her medical tricorder. "There's really too much tachyonic interference to get a decent reading here, Mr. Spock. But I can tell you there's no one alive within fifty meters of this spot, except us."

"I do not expect survivors, Nurse Iziharry."

There was silence after that. The five of them trudged on and down into the Defense Center, Spock's lonely light leading the way.

Chapter Eleven:
McIverton

KIRK AND SULU relaxed as *Galileo* streaked westward at supersonic speed across New America. It was a beautiful day. Sulu flew the little ship just a few hundred meters above the clouds. Kirk drank in the warm, pleasant light of the suns, filtered to gentle warmness by *Galileo*'s hyperpolarized viewports.

It had felt awfully good to take the pressure suits off. They lay limply on the aft deck behind the passenger seats, looking like a couple of rubbery people with all the air let out.

Sulu stretched in his pilot's seat and relaxed. "I remember a day in Hawaii like this," he said.

"Hmm," Kirk grunted pleasurably. "Sometimes I miss this sort of thing a lot." He closed his eyes and enjoyed the warmth. It was blissfully quiet in the cabin, since they were supersonic, and Kirk hadn't had much sleep lately . . . mmmmm . . .

"Captain!" Sulu said. Kirk came instantly awake. "Sensors show unknown craft approaching us. Six bogies, tight formation. Bearing two five two, coming up from below. Fast!"

Damn! Kirk thought. "All right, Mr. Sulu. Let's meet 'em. I'll try to raise 'em on the radio." *Too bad shuttles aren't armed. Add that to the wish list, Jim.*

"Attention, unknown craft. Attention," Kirk said into the microphone. "This is Captain James T. Kirk of the Federation starship *Enterprise,* aboard shuttle-craft *Galileo.* Come in, please."

There was a pause and a burst of static, and then a crackling voice. *"Galileo,* this is Colonel Duncan Smith, commander of the Thirty-sixth Air Wing, Centaurus Defense Command. Welcome to Centaurus, sir; glad to see you made it. We will provide escort to McIverton. Over to you."

"Thank you, Colonel," Kirk replied. "Glad to be here. We'll follow you in. Kirk out."

"Roger on that, Captain. Smith out."

He thumbed the radio to inactive status and spoke to Sulu. "Interesting. They seemed to be waiting for us."

Sulu frowned. "That's not necessarily bad. Don't Federation governments usually provide an escort of honor for a starship captain arriving by shuttle?"

"Yes—but I specifically told Erikkson I didn't want one; this isn't a ceremonial call. He's shoving an escort down our throats anyway. I don't like that much, Mr. Sulu; it makes me think we're being herded."

"That may be the idea, Captain."

"That's what I'm afraid of."

A moment later, a squadron of six combat jets took up a precise formation around, over and under *Galileo,* providing a standard escort of honor. Kirk could not help noticing that the shuttlecraft was effectively boxed in. He also couldn't help noticing the sleek air-to-air missiles slung under the wings of each jet, a pair to port and another to starboard. Of course, it was normal enough for a warplane to carry such weapons . . . but the sight of them disturbed Kirk nevertheless. He felt vulnerable, and he didn't like that at all.

The shuttle and the jets continued flying in formation above the clouds, across the rest of New America, all the way west to McIverton. Kirk no longer enjoyed the trip.

About an hour after rendezvous, the seven craft dipped below the clouds just south of the new capital and banked to starboard, beginning their approach to Government Field. The shortwave radio crackled. "Here's where we leave you, *Galileo*. Your bearing to the field is niner-two degrees; pick up the tower on four five three kilohertz. Been a pleasure, Captain Kirk. Smith out."

"Thank you, Colonel. *Galileo* out." The six jets peeled away from the shuttle as Kirk twiddled a frequency dial on the shortwave console; there had been no time for Scotty to construct a digital readout, so Kirk searched back and forth within a narrow range for 453 kHz. Finally he heard something, and upped the gain.

It was a woman's voice, brisk and businesslike. "*Galileo*, this is Government Field Tower. Welcome to McIverton, Captain Kirk. You are cleared to land on the president's flitterpad; we will feed you a directional cue over this frequency. Please let us know when you have visual contact; the pad is marked with a red target. Please acknowledge."

Kirk pushed the talkback. *Now I know exactly how Uhura feels*, he thought. "Tower, this is *Galileo*. We are, er, thirteen kilometers south of you, bearing niner-two. Altitude eighteen hundred meters and descending. Send us the cue at your pleasure. Kirk out."

A not unpleasant tone came from the shortwave speaker. As long as Kirk and Sulu could hear it, it meant that *Galileo* was on a correct heading for the flitterpad; if they lost the tone, Government Field Tower would issue a course correction, which Sulu would follow. But Sulu was very good.

"There's the field," Sulu said.

And it was. Government Field looked like nothing more than the usual civilian airfield one came across on any sufficiently advanced Federation planet—except that this one had an unusual amount of traffic parked in its holding areas. Whatever government was left after the destruction of New Athens had coalesced here, on the other coast, and there had, of course, not yet been time to expand the field's facilities. Kirk did not envy the air traffic controllers their jobs. The arrival of *Galileo* must be causing them some headaches; even with a heavy volume of air traffic in the area, the shuttle had been cleared for landing immediately.

But the landing priority given *Galileo*—the normal sort of priority given any Federation craft bearing a visitor of Kirk's rank or higher—did not reassure the captain. Kirk still sensed an essential *wrongness* about what was going on in McIverton. He had no justification for that feeling, as yet. But it was there . . . and such feelings had served him in good stead more than once.

"Coming in for a landing, Captain," Sulu reported.

Galileo was nearing the presidential flitterpad, a concrete square about ten meters on a side. There was a target in its center—six concentric red circles forming a bull's-eye. Kirk could see three large black vehicles parked just beyond the safety line. *Flitters?* wondered Kirk. *They don't look much like—oh! Limousines; I've seen pictures. Well, I'll be. We're getting the full treatment.* Kirk had rarely ever seen an automobile. Advanced Federation planets still used them on diplomatic occasions, in the same kind of forced anachronism that once had Earth royalty still riding to their coronations and weddings in horse-drawn carriages more than a century after the introduction of the automobile.

Kirk had been in a car just once, on Iotia, a planet whose inhabitants had drawn their entire social and ethical structure from a book on twentieth-century gangster rule in Chicago. He had even tried to pilot the thing—with mixed results, but he'd enjoyed the experience. Despite his present misgivings, Kirk was looking forward to a ride in a car.

The pad was under them, now. "Grounding," Sulu said. The whine of the shuttle's impulse engines began to die away as the *Enterprise* helmsman gradually bled power from them, allowing the boxy craft to drift downward easily. Kirk watched as buildings and other structures began to rise into view in his window.

A light went green on the pilot's status board. "Landing legs down and locked," Sulu reported; a few seconds later there was a negligible bump. "Landed, Captain," Sulu said. "Hope you had a pleasant flight. Please exit from the side door, and remember to take your valuables."

Kirk smiled back. "Nice job, Lieutenant. Thank you." The captain looked out the window; Sulu had oriented the nose of *Galileo* to face the three parked limousines. There was a small group of men waiting there. "Look—a reception committee. And me without my dress uniform."

"Perhaps we could wear the pressure suits instead," Sulu said jokingly.

"Not on your life. Let's crack the hatch and meet the people, Mr. Sulu."

It was early in the local morning, but already the light of the two major Centaurian suns was dazzling. It danced on the white concrete runways and flitterpads, darting painfully into Kirk's eyes. *Knew I forgot something,* fumed Kirk. *Sunglasses! I should have remembered.* Squinting, he and Sulu walked down *Galileo*'s landing ramp and over to the welcoming party. A tall, balding man of about forty had his hand out; Kirk shook it firmly.

"Greetings, Captain Kirk, and welcome to Centaurus. I'm Thaddeus Hayes, chief of protocol. Pleased to make your acquaintance, sir."

"Thank you," Kirk said. "Allow me to introduce Lieutenant Sulu, my pilot and confidential aide." Sulu allowed no surprise at his sudden status as aide to appear on his face; he had learned long ago to simply go along with anything Captain Kirk might say. Sulu shook Hayes's proffered hand and wondered what a confidential aide was supposed to do. *Probably remain very quiet when the captain's talking,* Sulu decided.

Hayes turned and indicated two much younger men. "These two gentlemen are my chief deputies: Roland Samuels and Winston Churchill McKnight." More hands were shaken. "I think that completes the introductions, Captain—oh, I forgot. You'll probably want these." Hayes stuck out a hand, and McKnight gave him two leatherette objects. "Sunglasses," Hayes explained. "I trust they'll fit you both . . . and if you wear yours, we'll be able to put ours on, too." Hayes smiled apologetically. "Please forgive my bluntness, but it *is* terribly bright today."

Kirk grinned. "No problem, Mr. Hayes." He slipped the glasses out of the leatherette holder and put them on; the hyperpolarized lenses did much to cut the glare. "Much better. We appreciate your thoughtfulness."

Hayes and the other two men slipped their sunglasses on. "You'll find sunglasses are pretty necessary items here, Captain," the protocol chief said.

"Yes. I must have a dozen pairs of these things kicking around somewhere. Not much use for them Out There, though."

"I'd imagine not, Captain. Well, shall we go? The president is waiting for us."

"Certainly."

"This way, then."

Kirk and Sulu walked toward the second of the three limousines, gently directed by Samuels; a silent chauffeur saluted deferentially and opened the door. Hayes climbed in after them, and only then did McKnight and Samuels head for the third limousine. Then they were off, with the howl of several sirens and the flashing of many red strobe lights clearing the way.

The windowglass of the limousine was itself hyperpolarized; Kirk, Sulu and Hayes took off their glasses. It was Sulu's first trip to Centaurus, and Kirk himself had never been in McIverton.

They were approaching the city from the southeast. McIverton was the only city of any size on the west coast of New America; further expansion would have to wait a few generations. There were villages, though, mostly settled by highly individualistic types who thought McIverton, a town of two hundred thousand, was too big. They were passing through one such now: a conglomeration of houses of all architectural designs, from traditional suburban to NeoFuller. But all the houses had lawns, shrubs and cultivated plant growth. A few people could be seen taking their ease in those gardens, protected by sunbrellas; no one dared sunbathe during this planet's long summer without taking special precautions.

"This road's in good repair," Kirk remarked to Hayes. "Smooth ride."

"Thank you, Captain," Hayes said with pride, as if he'd had something to do with the maintenance of the highway himself. "We don't have much automobile traffic anymore, but quite a few people keep motorcycles and mopeds for recreational and commuting purposes. Lord knows this planet has plenty of oil to crack for gasoline; no one ever exploited it before we got here, and we've been careful not to remake Earth's mistakes. Oil is a nice little export business for us, considering Earth's so nearby."

Kirk knew that "nice little export business" accounted for billions of credits in the Centaurian treasury annually; Earth's hunger for petroleum had never abated, despite that day in the middle of the twenty-first century when the last drop of terrestrial oil had been pumped.

Fortunately for Earth, though, by the middle of the twenty-first century Earth was not the only possible source of petroleum. There were, for instance, the virgin oil fields of Centaurus.

Although Earth now used the precious fluid only for the production of plastics and pharmaceuticals, Earth produced a *lot* of plastics and pharmaceuticals. Liquid hydrogen, small nuclear fission and fusion power plants, microwaved solar power and a range of less efficient but environmentally friendly alternatives met Earth's energy needs.

But Centaurus's spacefaring supertankers were grounded for the duration—until Spock and his crew could solve the Defense Center problem. *Add economic dislocation to the list of problems we have to solve,* thought Kirk wearily.

The limousine surmounted a hill, and the highway began to dip. McIverton lay ahead of them.

Hayes pointed. "I was born here," he said. "McIverton's a port, but we don't do much ocean shipping. Everything goes by cargo flitter. But we have a lot of recreational boating. The east coast has a little shipping, but the east is much more heavily settled. New Europe, the southern continent, has a few settlements that are out of easy flitter range of New America, so we'll sometimes run a ship or two down that way. Easier to use airplanes, though. They might be old-fashioned, but they get the job done."

"What about the third continent, across the Western Ocean?" Sulu asked. "Any settlements there?"

"Not yet, Lieutenant," Hayes answered. "We don't plan to open up New Asia until the next century, at least. Some people go there for vacations in the wild, but there are no facilities except for a handful of scientific stations. Mostly they handle zoological studies and other things you can't do very well from orbit." Hayes paused. "Of course, with all the satellites out, we might have to continue some space-based surveys from the ground. We'll have to see."

"You mentioned zoology," Sulu said. "I once specialized in biology. I know Centaurus has a goodly stock of Earth flora and fauna. What I was wondering was, how does it all cope with the nightless days you get here at maximum solar separation?"

Hayes nodded. "That was tricky, all right. We've got three stars in this system, of course, but only two of them count for anything. Proxima Centauri is a red dwarf that orbits Alpha about a sixth of a light-year out. It's dim, cool and not worth worrying about." Sulu nodded; that was elementary cosmography.

Hayes continued. "Most of Centaurus is semitropical; Alpha Centauri is pretty bright. Beta's smaller and dimmer but adds a little warmth, too. Centaurus orbits Alpha, while Alpha and Beta orbit each other, like a big bolo in space." Both Kirk and Sulu grinned at that; it was quite an image. "Alpha and Beta were as close as they ever get to each other about nine years ago; we called it the Great New Year and celebrated like crazy."

Hayes grinned sheepishly. "I could tell you stories . . . but never mind; it's only once every eighty years." Kirk could not help grinning; he'd been there for it. The chief of protocol continued. "The stellar separation on Great New Year is about a billion and a half kilometers, and it gets a little warmer here. Thirty-one years from now, when the suns are at their widest separation—more than five billion kilometers—it'll be cooler."

"But what about nightfall?" Sulu wondered. "I can see the twin suns are together in the sky now, but there must be several months during your year that the suns are on opposite sides of the sky. And it must get worse as the suns draw away from each other; one will eventually rise half a day after the other, which effectively wipes out your nighttime. Or did I miss something?"

Hayes nodded. "Then we use Big Blotto."

" 'Big Blotto'?"

"Our handy-dandy sun eradicator."

"Oh," Sulu said, catching on. "You blank out one of the suns. Beta, I guess?"

"That's right. Big Blotto is an automated station in a Luna-type orbit about half a million kilometers from Centaurus. It makes one complete turn around the planet per standard month. The station sets up a giant hyperpolarized field, and Beta's effectively gone from the sky, blotted out. Of course, it's really still there, but its heat and light never reach Centaurus because the planet sits in the 'shadow' of the hyperpolarized field. Then we get an artificial night on the side of Centaurus not facing Alpha; we get a mild planetary winter out of the deal, too, not to mention all the solar power the field absorbs. Big Blotto costs a bunch to run, let me tell you . . . but we all think it's worth it."

Sulu looked quizzical. "But doesn't all this have some effect on native Centaurian life-forms? I mean to say, they evolved under vastly different conditions . . ."

Hayes nodded. "There are problems. We think some forms—minor ones—are already extinct. But others are still thriving. Besides which, we *need* a day-night cycle for the Earth forms we brought here; they have priority. Without night, our animals would die and we'd have few if any edible crops—and a colony that winds up importing all its foodstuffs isn't much of a colony at all."

Sulu nodded agreement. "I've been on worlds that depended on food imports. Sooner or later, there's always some disaster."

"Right," Hayes affirmed. "Can you imagine, for instance, if we were dependent on imports to feed ourselves? We haven't had a ship land on the planet in nearly a week. We'd be running short even now; we'd be starving in another few days. There'd be chaos." Hayes sighed. "As bad as things are, they could be worse. We can at least take care of ourselves."

There was a short silence, which Kirk broke. "I take it, Mr. Hayes, you haven't been chief of protocol for very long . . . ?"

Hayes looked at him with a small smile. "Does it show that badly?"

Kirk smiled back. "Not at all. I bring it up only because you're the first unpretentious chief of protocol I've ever met."

Hayes laughed. "I'll take that as a compliment, Captain. Thank you. No, I haven't been doing this for long. President Erikkson pulled me out of the Ministry of Labor Relations for this job; I used to mediate labor disputes from an office right here in McIverton. The old protocol chief was in New Athens when the balloon went up, unfortunately. Most of us are new at our jobs, as a matter of fact."

"What about the gentlemen we've already talked to? Ministers Perez and Burke?" Kirk asked.

"They're from the old president's Cabinet; President Erikkson asked them to stay on, and they did. The three of them were on a west coast tour together when New Athens was destroyed. They were the only high government officials not in the capital when it was destroyed, as far as I know."

"Do you know the new president well?"

"I've barely met him, Captain. He was minister of state; he wasn't somebody I'd run into very often in the Ministry of Labor Relations. I don't know the other two gentlemen, either, although Minister Burke interviewed me for the job as chief of protocol."

"Mr. Burke is the internal security minister, isn't he?" Kirk asked.

"That's right."

"You had to pass a security check?"

Hayes nodded slowly. "Yes, I did."

"Why?"

Hayes was silent for a moment. "Forgive me, Captain—but I'd rather you talk with the president or Minister Burke before I answer any question in that area."

"Oh. All right." Feeling a touch awkward, Kirk looked out the window. "We seem to be in the city already."

"Yes, we are," Hayes said with all the enthusiasm one can bring to a gratefully changed subject. "This is Gregory Avenue; John Houston Gregory was the first man to land on Centaurus. The actual site is a few kilometers north of town; there's a village there now, called Gregory's Landing. We're using the government offices in Planetary Plaza, not far from here, as a temporary Government House. It's not nearly big enough, but there's nothing we can do except sit on each other's laps. At that, we had to evict umpteen government agencies to do it—including, I might add, the Ministry of Labor Relations." Hayes chuckled. "At least I got to keep my old office."

The motorcade made a left turn onto a wide boulevard—Kirk saw a sign that said FOUNDERS WAY—and it began to slow. "We're arriving," Hayes said just as the limousines entered an interior driveway leading to an underground garage. There were armed guards on both sides of a narrow pedway parallel to the ramp. Kirk and Sulu's car continued downward, stopping sidewise to a large elevator.

"Sorry for the back-door route, gentlemen," Hayes apologized, "but we have security problems at the present time." There were more guards here; one of them opened the passenger door and saluted smartly. On leaving the limousine Kirk smelled a peculiar odor, at once smoky and oily, not unlike one of Scotty's cruder lubricants; he could not place it because he had never before in his life sniffed the distinctive smell of a gasoline-powered internal combustion engine in a confined space. It wasn't pleasant.

"The elevator, gentlemen?" Hayes beckoned. He gestured toward it, and the three of them entered.

Chapter Twelve:
The Defense Center

Spock and the others had gained easy entry to the heart of the Defense Center, the control room. The blastproof door, like all other such doors they'd come across, had been wide open. Spock felt sure that there had been some fundamental breakdown here, that the untried protective systems in the center had failed when they were needed the most.

They had found no one alive. Spock had held some faint hope that, if anyone had been left, they would have gathered here, in the control room, the most protected area in the whole Defense Center—but no one had. There hadn't been enough time.

There were bodies sprawled here and there. It was apparent that death had come swiftly and nearly painlessly from an overwhelming wave of radiation. Heat and blast hadn't reached down this far; there hadn't been much, if any, overt physical damage, and ground shock from the spaceport disaster hadn't touched the control room. Spock imagined the whole place had been built on springs; such a technique was standard practice and was used to combat abrupt ground movement from blast concussion. The control room was dark and without power, but intact.

Now they were in the central pit of the cavernous control room, surrounded by disabled consoles, read-out screens, and dead men and women slumped at their stations. Spock aimed his DayBrite up into the catwalks and galleries surrounding the pit. The light faded into the darkness high above.

Nothing. No one.

"Gives me the creeps," Rawlings said. "No place should be this dead." He set his equipment down; Hudson did the same. Connie Iziharry bent to inspect the body nearest her; Chekov, feeling useless here, stood nearby. "This one's a general," Iziharry announced. "Perhaps he was the commander." She conducted a quick, efficient search. "No papers on him, Mr. Spock."

"Can you determine the exact cause of death, Miss Iziharry?" Spock asked.

She considered it. "Not without a lab to work in, but I can make a good guess. Radiation. See—there's not a mark on him. He wasn't burned or blasted. By elimination, that leaves radiation. I'd need to do some tests to be sure, though."

"Thank you." Iziharry's independent diagnosis agreed with Spock's own, so he treated the question as tentatively settled and turned his full attention to other matters. He aimed his tricorder around the room. He got a fairly constant radiation reading at level twelve— certainly enough to kill an unprotected human, or Vulcan, in moments.

"No one could live more than a minute or two without protective gear," Spock announced. "The readings in this area are nearly as bad as those we found above. We will not be able to take off our pressure suits." The science officer paused. "Our first priority is to re-establish power in this room. Mr. Rawlings, if you'll be so kind as to give me that portapack, I believe we can couple it to the circuits servicing the standby generator over there." He pointed to a large gray cube in a corner of the room. Thick wiring led to and from it.

Spock brought the portapack—a small, heavy and efficient short-term power producer—over to the generator. Sure enough, there was a specialized socket for backup. The portapack lead wouldn't fit into it, but it was the work of a moment for Spock to clip the portapack plug off and fashion a new one from spare parts. He threw a switch on the portapack, and the room lights came on to the glad cries of the four humans.

The center's consoles came alive; data began reading onto screens all over the room. Rawlings and Hudson seated themselves at stations marked NUMBER TWO and AUXILIARY COMMAND; Spock came over and sat at one marked WATCH COMMANDER. The computer consoles were old-fashioned typewriter keyboards, the kind humans had been using for hundreds of years; Spock was thoroughly familiar with such, having built several in his younger days, before he'd been directed toward more practical pursuits.

The Vulcan began to type and caused several errors. *Oh, of course,* he realized. *How stupid of me.* His gloved fingers were too big to fit the keys. "Miss Iziharry," he asked, "will you give me a medical probe of some sort? A tongue depressor, perhaps?"

She did, and Spock used it to hit the keys one by one. A bit of reasoned mathematical analysis quickly gave Spock the passwords he needed to get into the center's computers and talk to them; it was actually quite simple, much more so than Spock had anticipated. Spock then activated the keyboards on Rawlings's and Hudson's stations, so that they might be free to pursue the problem in their own ways. *I will not dismiss human intuition on this occasion,* Spock thought. *It is not logical to give intuition free rein, unbound by logic—but it is more illogical to deny intuition its chance to deal with this problem. Humans designed this system; perhaps humans will be able to sense its makers' intent more easily than I.* Spock typed, and the computers replied.

> *Stand down.*
> NEGATIVE FUNCTION.
> *Priority command. Stand down.*
> NEGATIVE FUNCTION.
> *Deactivate defenses.*
> NEGATIVE FUNCTION.
> *Peacetime condition. Stand down. Go to inactive status. Priority command.*
> NEGATIVE FUNCTION.

Spock thought for a moment. Through the baffles in his pressure suit helmet, he could hear the tapping of keys to his left and right: Rawlings and Hudson, trying their own approaches. Rawlings would groan occasionally; Hudson seemed silently intent. Spock began typing again.

> *Define mission. Short form.*
> DEFEND PLANETARY NEIGHBORHOOD FROM APPROACH BY INVADING FORCES. NEIGHBORHOOD DEFINED AS ARBITRARY LINE DRAWN AT STANDARD ORBIT ALTITUDE TO AIR TRAFFIC CEILING.
> *Stop. Define defense policy. Short form.*
> DETECT INVADER. TARGET INVADER. COMMAND AND CONTROL GROUND-TO-SPACE MISSILES TO DETER INVASION. MAXIMUM EFFORT INDICATED.
> *Define maximum effort.*
> DESTRUCTION OF INVADING FORCES.
> *Define possibility of missing target on first launch.*

ZERO. DESTRUCTION ASSURED.
State policy regarding friendly forces during invasion.
NO DATA.
List catalog of friendly forces.
NO DATA.
List current status.
WAR. INVASION IN PROGRESS.
Give nature of enemy.
NO DATA.
Give catalog of enemy forces.
ENEMY FORCES ARE DEFINED AS SPACECRAFT MEASURING ABOVE FIVE POINT SIX THREE CENTIMETERS FROM BOW TO STERN AND/OR EQUIPPED WITH WARP AND/OR IMPULSE DRIVE APPEARING IN NEIGHBORHOOD OF CENTAURUS AS PREVIOUSLY DEFINED.
List targets destroyed in current invasion. Short form.
LIST INCLUDES 39 CAPITAL SHIPS, 621 LANDING CRAFT, 157 CLOSE-ORBIT SATELLITES LAUNCHED BY ENEMY. MINOR OBJECTS NOT INCLUDED.
Stand by.
WAITING.

"I know what is wrong now," Spock announced. "Some of my preliminary suppositions were correct. Mr. Rawlings, Mr. Hudson, how far have you gotten?"

Rawlings sighed heavily. "Nowhere, Mr. Spock. I can't even get the computers to admit there's any such thing as a friendly ship."

"Same here," Hudson said. "The computers assume everything and everybody is an enemy, and they go after it. They also won't react to stand-down codes. I've even tried to tell them Centaurus lost the war and surrendered. Nothing works."

Spock's eyebrow went up; a fake surrender was something he hadn't thought of, yet there would have to be provision for something like that so enemy forces could land on and occupy the planet in relative safety. Otherwise, an enemy might exact bloody reprisals against the conquered civilian populace.

"What happens when you enter the surrender codes, Mr. Hudson?"

"I get a 'no data' readback, sir."

"Interesting." Spock thought for a moment. "My own investigations show the following: The system is active and alert in many ways, most notably in its detection of so-called 'enemy' ships. It will conduct an initial attack, but refuses to believe that such an initial attack will not result in the destruction of the ship. As we already know, gentlemen—and Miss Iziharry—a properly shielded ship can withstand at least one, and perhaps two, large nuclear detonations close aboard.

"The computers define an enemy craft as *any* craft of a length greater than about six centimeters." Spock heard Rawlings and Hudson grunt; they'd missed that. "That is, of course, an absurd definition; one of our communicators is larger than that. Further, the computers believe that Centaurus is at war. They will not recognize any order to stop attacking, which is in fact the easiest order to give, since no one desires to carry out or continue an attack by mistake.

"These and other factors tell me that the problem with the computers lies in their logic centers. The computers have forgotten large blocks of data—such as listing of friendly ships, configurations of possible enemy ships, and so forth—and have joined unrelated blocks of data together to form new, and dangerous, standing orders."

"Excuse me, Mr. Spock," Chekov broke in. "Vhy do ve not simply destroy the control room?"

"I would, if it would do any good, Ensign," Spock

replied. "However, the errant logic centers are not located here, but in a vault several kilometers below us. They are deeply seated in rock and are unreachable by human agency, not even for repair; they are serviced by robots on permanent station. We could not even beam down there, were the transporters aboard the *Enterprise* working; the vault is too deep. Several annihilation devices, exploded in series just over the vault, might do the trick—but that, of course, is not desirable."

"So vhat do ve do?" asked Chekov.

"I have to think about that, Ensign."

They all waited while he did.

Chapter Thirteen:
Gregory's Landing

IT WAS MUCH later that same day, and Reuben Barclay was not at all nervous. Barclay and his two companions had made it safely to the new hideout in the prefirstdawn hours; no one had seen, and no one had followed them.

Several hours ago, Max had called on the shielded line to say that their quarry had been contacted and had agreed to Barclay's terms, all as Barclay had planned; it had not been necessary to kill him, or even to threaten to do so. It was going well. Max and Dave would stay in town to keep an eye on things; they did not know where Barclay and his friends were now, anyway. The address of this second refuge was a secret, and would remain so until early the next day—when, if all continued to go well, Max and Dave would be informed of the new address and would rejoin Barclay and the other two men.

(The address was doubly secret because the late owner of the property had been in New Athens on the day of the explosion. But he'd been a good League member, and had given his sector chief a spare set of keys for use if and when the need arose.)

Well, with any luck at all, they would be out of this

hole by tomorrow. And there had already been plenty of luck: A later news report had identified the nuked starship as the U.S.S. *Enterprise,* commanded by one James Kirk—and had added that the ship had survived the blast and that the captain would confer with the new president and his top advisers on the current situation.

As one of the authors of the "current situation," Barclay could not help but smirk. He'd use Kirk, just as he'd used all of them. It was good, very good, that it was Kirk who'd come. A quick background check of the captain had turned up an interesting fact about him: He knew the man Max and Dave had contacted this morning. He knew him very well indeed.

That was an edge. Barclay was used to riding the edge—and he never, ever lost his balance. It was one of the many qualities of leadership and human purity for which Barclay would, one day, be recognized on worlds not yet numbered.

All that would start once Barclay and his two friends left this dismal planet. That fool Holtzman had nearly destroyed the League—but, then again, Holtzman had removed all pretenders to League leadership in one stroke. He'd also done incredible, incalculable damage to the current order. That in itself was invaluable. Barclay could plan a return to Centaurus a few years from now—and be acclaimed as leader. It was as if it had all been . . . planned. Well, perhaps it had been. Barclay did not automatically dismiss the existence of Providence, as long as it served him.

On that glorious day when Barclay would finally become leader, and his leadership was extended to other worlds, perhaps he could install Holtzman as a martyr to the cause. The League could use a martyr or two. (Never mind that Holtzman was a total fool who didn't know when to cut his losses and who mixed misguided loyalty with his pragmatism. Barclay was pragmatic enough for ten men, and he'd be writing the history tapes. He knew Holtzman was an idiot who would dynamite a high-rise building to kill a sandbug in one of the closets, but he could use Holtzman anyway. All he had to do was lie about him. Extensively.)

Barclay looked again at his watch. Nearly the midhour; it wouldn't be long now. The rendezvous would be the next morning. That was when it would all begin.

Chapter Fourteen:
McIverton

KIRK, SULU, AND Hayes walked into the presidential conference room atop the newly designated Government House. The three men already in the room rose as Kirk and Sulu entered. *Erikkson—he must be the one at the head of the table,* Kirk thought.

He was. Erikkson was a small, balding man of about sixty. He looked tired. His suit was wrinkled, and he hadn't shaved for perhaps two days. He also looked nervous—but, for all that, he drew himself up, walked around the conference table, and extended his hand to Captain Kirk. "Henry Erikkson, Captain. And this must be Lieutenant Sulu. I'm very pleased to meet you both. Allow me to introduce the other two gentlemen: Minister of Defense Daniel Perez, and Minister of Internal Security Nathaniel Burke." All shook hands with Kirk and Sulu.

Perez was a short, swarthy type; he looked like a grubby veteran of the kind of hand-to-hand infighting that still haunted the political precincts of the Federation. Perez looked subdued, though, as if recent events had deflated him somewhat. But Burke looked to be a military type: square-jawed, short-haired, and shaved blue. His suit wasn't a bit wrinkled. He was every inch an internal-security type; he looked utterly capable.

So why don't I like him? wondered Kirk. He didn't have an answer for that yet.

"Thank you for bringing them, Thaddeus," Erikkson said to Hayes. It was a dismissal; the chief of protocol nodded, smiled and left.

They had quickly seated themselves around the table, the president at the head, Kirk and Sulu to his right. Perez and Burke sat opposite the men from the *Enterprise*. Coffee and sandwiches had arrived, but they remained untouched. There had been silence after an initial few minutes of meaningless small talk. Perez and Burke continued to look uncomfortable. President Erikkson fidgeted with a paper clip, bending and unbending it; finally it snapped apart.

Enough, thought Kirk. "Mr. President?"

Erikkson roused himself. "Yes, Captain?"

"Forgive me, Mr. President, but I think we need to talk about this situation. There's a lot I don't know yet." The two ministers looked relieved. *Hmm,* Kirk said to himself. *These two gents know there's something wrong with Erikkson, just as much as I do.*

"Anything I can do, I will do," Erikkson affirmed. "Ask any question. Go right ahead." The president made a "gimme" gesture with his hands.

"Very well, sir," Kirk said. "It's been clear to me since before our arrival in orbit here that the explosion in New Athens was no accident. An accident with antimatter simply wasn't possible." Kirk felt he was on solid ground here; he agreed with Spock's initial analysis and had seen nothing on Centaurus to change his mind. "I need to know whatever you know about the incident. From the beginning, sir."

Burke shifted in his chair; Kirk caught the movement. *You can't keep a state secret in a situation like this, Burke,* thought Kirk. *School's out. I'll have my answers—or I'll have your carefully combed scalp, one way or the other.*

Erikkson looked uncomfortable. He glanced sideways at Burke, but Burke was busy looking at a spot on the opposite wall. The president cleared his throat.

"Captain, I'll be blunt. The destruction of New Athens was due to nothing more than error upon error upon error, all committed by the government." Perez was beginning to look ill; Erikkson noticed his discomfort. "Dan," he said, "there's no time to gloss things over, and I'm not one to indulge in recriminations. We were stupid, period, and it's cost a million lives. Captain, please understand me. I find it difficult to live with this. No one outside this room knows the whole story. Please try to understand what I'm going to tell you."

Kirk nodded. "Go on, sir."

Erikkson took a deep breath, and began. "About ten years ago, some people on this planet who should have known better formed a political fringe movement called the League for a Pure Humanity. Their numbers were never very great, but they exerted influence by means of demonstrations, clever literature and the occasional paid political 3V broadcast."

"I've heard of them, Mr. President. Word gets around."

"Their leader was a university physics professor named Holtzman, Isidore Holtzman. He was rather famous as a political personality from the fringe. Holtzman enjoyed a measure of importance well beyond the numbers of his group or the votes they could draw in any given election. If a newscast needed a dramatic quote on anything from agricultural policy to the weather, they'd get such a quote from Holtzman. Most people dismissed him as a lunatic."

"Was he one?" Kirk asked.

"He was never diagnosed," Erikkson said, "and this government was not one to force a rationality test on a man simply because of his political philosophy. We simply tolerated his tirades. As I say, he did not have much of a following."

"If I may, sir," Sulu said, "what were his group's views?"

Erikkson sighed. "The League favored a new political agenda for Centaurus, under which we would pull out of the Federation and expel all non-human citizens and residents from the planet. There was evidence that the League wished to limit citizenship here still further to humans of certain, ah, racial types. I apologize, Mr. Sulu."

Sulu frowned. "From that, sir, I take it Mr. Holtzman did not like persons of Oriental stock?"

"Or Negroid stock, or anyone else who wasn't Caucasian—but he was willing to 'tolerate' those non-whites who would help advance his political fortunes. But as it was, few if any non-whites joined his movement. Certainly no non-humans did." Erikkson shook his head in disgust. "Fortunately, not many humans remain racist today; it's hard to hate your fellow human in an era of interstellar travel, when scores of non-human races are known."

"Some manage it anyway," Kirk said grimly. "Go on, please."

Erikkson continued. "Holtzman contented himself with agitation on the fringe for a decade. I don't believe the League was ever successful in electing even one representative to the World Congress, despite a great deal of politicking on its part. People simply didn't buy Holtzman's message."

"But something changed," Kirk said. "What was it, sir?"

"A month ago, Holtzman asked for and received a

personal appointment with the old president," Erikkson said. "He demanded a political role for his group. He said that the president had a month to deliver that role—cabinet appointments to begin with, appointments to Congress a little later on. Holtzman said they'd waited long enough. If the president did not comply, the League would destroy New Athens."

Erikkson sighed. "The president, of course, summoned security forces and attempted to place Holtzman under arrest for threatening the peace. But Holtzman said that if he were arrested, New Athens would be destroyed before nightfall. The president chose to believe the threat. Holtzman was allowed to leave, unmolested. He was followed, of course, but they lost him; he covered his tracks very well."

"Why did the president believe the threat?" Kirk asked.

"Whatever his faults, Captain, Holtzman was a talented nuclear physicist. The president chose to assume that Holtzman was capable of carrying out his threat. I think it would have been unwise to assume anything else." Erikkson paused. "But the president—all of us—assumed one thing, anyway: that the weapon of Holtzman's blackmail would be a nuclear bomb. It was not."

"Holtzman got his hands on an annihilation device," Kirk said. "How?"

"We don't know," Erikkson said. His voice grew shaky. "Perhaps, Nat, it would be better if you continued things at this point."

Burke nodded. "Captain, in the following month we conducted security sweeps in the New Athens area. We detected every gram of misplaced U^{235} and plutonium there was to find. We had sensors at every point of entry into the region, ready to howl should somebody try to smuggle in a nuke. We didn't give a thought to antimatter, Captain; it was simply not a substance we thought could get into civilian hands. We weren't geared to detect it; instead, we wasted our time securing every nuclear facility on this planet. Meanwhile, the deadline approached."

"So New Athens died," Kirk said quietly.

Erikkson nodded sadly and, shakily, took up the narrative. "The explosion occurred about an hour after Holtzman's deadline. Nothing's been heard from the League since then—certainly nothing's come from Holtzman. Perhaps he died in New Athens. Maybe the entire leadership of the League did; it was centered there, although there were members everywhere. Or perhaps Holtzman and the rest of the group left New Athens before the deadline."

"I hope they all died horribly," Burke said. His fists were on the tabletop, clenched; his knuckles were white. "My wife and kids were in New Athens."

"And so were mine," Erikkson breathed. He bowed his head; tears fell silently to the desk. Kirk looked at Perez, but the defense minister's face told the captain that Mrs. Perez and their children had been there, too. *So much blood,* thought Kirk. *Joanna, and these people's loved ones, and all the hundreds of thousands of others—and for what? What am I going to tell Bones when I get back?*

After a few moments Erikkson looked up. "Forgive us, Captain. The last few days have been a strain on us. We're not ourselves. I apologize."

"You have nothing to apologize for, Mr. President," Kirk replied. "Nothing at all. No one in this room does." He paused. "You did your best. The former president could not surrender his authority to a madman; you took whatever measures you could to prevent a terrorist attack. This Holtzman hit you with an unexpected weapon. You cannot blame yourselves."

Perez grunted softly. "Sometimes I think that, perhaps, we could have played for time somehow . . . or we could have evacuated the city . . . saved our families . . ."

Burke was quick to respond. "I can't afford to think that, Danny. Sooner or later, Holtzman would have hit us. Hell, he told the president he'd blow up the town at the first sign of an evacuation—or at the first sign of an evacuation of Cabinet families."

The internal security minister looked at Kirk. "Captain, thank you for what you said just now. The guilt of this thing is something the three of us must live with for the rest of our lives. We'll never know if we did enough to prevent it. It cost us everything we loved."

Kirk nodded; he knew something of what Burke meant.

Sulu broke in. "Forgive me again, Mr. President, but has there been any attempt to draw up a list of survivors yet? We have a number of people on the *Enterprise* who have relatives in the New Athens area." Kirk looked at Sulu gratefully; the captain would never have asked for himself . . . but Sulu knew that, and so had asked for him.

Erikkson nodded. "We have some names. We understand there are a good number of survivors in the northern part of the city. It might be easier if you'd give me a list of whoever it is you want to know about, and we can run a check of those names against the ones we already have. We could also give those names to the Red Cross and the news organizations."

Sulu nodded. "Thank you, sir; that'll do just fine. I can come up with a list for you fairly quickly. I know most of the crew members involved."

"Fine. Give it to Minister Burke, and he'll run it past his people, too." Burke nodded. There was a short silence, and for the first time since Kirk and Sulu arrived, Erikkson smiled. "You know what?" he said. "I feel like a cup of coffee after all. Will you gentlemen join me?"

For the next hour Kirk and the Centaurians talked easily. Sulu had compiled a list of every person aboard the *Enterprise* he could think of who had a relative on Centaurus. It was no astounding feat of memory: Most of the relatives concerned had the same surnames as the crew members involved, and Sulu knew most everyone aboard well enough to come up with a nearly complete list. Not every great-aunt and second cousin was on it, true—but mothers and fathers and spouses and siblings, yes. And at the top of the list was MCCOY, JOANNA.

Sulu finished and gave the list to Burke, who pocketed it. "I'll put Priority One on this right now, Captain," he said. "Mr. President, with your permission . . . ?"

"Of course, Nat," Erikkson said. "Later, then."

Burke turned to leave, then paused. "You know, Captain, I hope you help us get these guys, if there are any left to get. Terrorist murder carries the death penalty on Centaurus—and I want to pull the phaser relay myself. For Anne and the kids. You understand?"

"I think I do," Kirk said.

"I think you do, too," Burke said. "Good afternoon, everyone." He left. *I understand you, Burke,* Kirk thought, *but I can't help you. I'm under orders to deliver them for trial on Earth . . . and I have enough of a struggle reconciling those orders with the vengeance I want to take for Joanna. And if we catch anybody and if they stand trial on Earth, the most they'll draw is a life sentence in a rehabilitation col-*

ony. And if I tell you that now, Burke, you'll never help me get them. And I want them. Bad.

The phone rang. Erikkson looked at it, puzzled. "That's the special military command network line," he told Kirk. To Perez he said, "Dan, I didn't realize we had the audio-only lines reconnected yet."

The defense minister shrugged. "We don't. The command communications system was wiped out when New Athens bought it. Nobody's been able to patch it yet."

"Don't you think you ought to answer it, Mr. President?" Kirk prompted.

"Umm, yes." He did. "Hello, Erikkson here . . . . *Who* is this? From *where?* . . . Yes? . . . I see. Yes, he is. . . . Certainly. Hold on, please." The president covered the receiver with his hand. "Captain, this is your Mr. Spock. He's calling from the Defense Center."

"Who the hell is Mr. Spock?" Perez wanted to know.

Erikkson looked annoyed. "Come on, Dan, you talked to him on the radio just a few hours ago, when he was aboard the *Enterprise.*"

"Oh, that guy. Yeah."

Kirk reached for the handset. "Thank you, Mr. President. . . . Mr. Spock?"

"Ah, Captain. I thought I might find you there. It seemed logical that you would be with the president, so I simply repaired the Defense Center's hotline to McIverton and called him. I was not sure that the idea would work, however."

"It worked just fine, Spock. You've once again managed to amaze me. What's going on?"

"Captain, I need a command decision. I did not feel the situation would wait for tonight's check-in, when our shuttle-to-shuttle shortwave receivers are more likely to work."

"What's the problem?"

"I believe I have an approach to remedying the dilemma of the defense system computers. My solution is radical, but it will allow ships to once again approach this planet. However, I need your approval and that of the president as well."

Kirk paused. "The defense minister is here, too. Will this decision involve him?" Perez's ears picked up at the mention of his title.

"Yes, Captain, it will."

"Hold on." Kirk turned to Erikkson. "Mr. President, is it possible for you to put this call on a speaker? Mr. Spock tells me he has something to say to all of us regarding the defense system."

"I think there's a button here somewhere," Erikkson said. He pushed it, and there was a howl of feedback. "I think you have to disconnect the handset," Perez said helpfully. The president did so, and the howling ceased.

"Gentlemen, are you still there?" came Spock's voice from a speaker in the ceiling.

"We're here, Spock," Kirk answered. "Go ahead."

"Very well, Mr. President, Mr. Minister, Captain . . . it would take several hours for me to justify it to you in terms of diagrams and logical approaches, but I believe there is but one way to stop the attacks by the defense system on ships approaching this planet. I feel I need your approval before I begin."

"What do you want to do, Mr. Spock?" Erikkson asked. "I think we'll all take your word for it that, whatever it is, it's necessary."

Spock paused. "Very well."

The Vulcan briefly described what he wanted to do. First Perez, and then Erikkson, objected loudly—and, Spock felt, without much logic. But Captain Kirk defended Spock, and after more than an hour and a half of argument and appeals to reason, Erikkson and Perez acquiesced. They, at last, saw the necessity for what Spock was planning. It was radical, and it had never been tried before. It was the stuff of nightmares—but Erikkson gave the order.

Chapter Fifteen:
The Defense Center

SPOCK STUDIED THE output indicator of the portapack connected to the command center's standby generator. *Thirty-eight point six percent left,* he thought. *It will have to do.*

"Mr. Chekov?" the Vulcan called. "I will require your assistance. Come here, please."

"Yes, Mr. Spock?"

"I understand you have some facility with the portapack?"

"Vell, yes, sir. Ve used to use them in remote areas on the collective farm, back vhen I vas a ciwilian."

"Very well. Please watch this one and keep it working. Its continued functioning will be critical."

"I can believe that, Mr. Spock. I vill vatch it most closely."

"Miss Iziharry, please assist Mr. Chekov . . . thank you. Now, gentlemen," Spock said, addressing Rawlings and Hudson, "you will have to follow my lead in every particular. Much depends on your skill today. At the least sign of something going wrong, call out sharply and I will abort. I cannot emphasize this too strongly. The safety of many people on this planet rests on it."

The two computer technicians nodded their understanding.

Spock checked the time. "All right. By now, the captain should have notified Lieutenant Uhura of our intentions; the *Enterprise* should be ready. Fortunately, the captain is in a much better position to communicate with the ship than we are. We approach zero hour. Beginning the count, Mr. Rawlings—*now*."

Rawlings hit the ENTER button, and a series of codes—all previously typed in laboriously by Spock—disappeared off his NUMBER TWO console screen. New numbers and codes began to appear on the screen at the WATCH COMMANDER station. Rawlings swallowed nervously. What they were about to do had, indeed, never been done before, not even on Earth . . . thank the stars.

"Countdown to missile launch, sixty seconds," Rawlings reported. "All nominal."

Hudson merely said, "Confirmed. Fifty-five seconds."

Chekov watched with Connie Iziharry. Spock stood behind the chair at the WATCH COMMANDER station, his gloved hands clasped calmly behind him. *Is this vhat it vould have been like, if Earth had committed suicide vith these veapons long ago?* the Russian wondered. *So calm, so surgical? Or vould there have been tears, or shouts of anger, or cries of joy, or anything?*

Chekov could not see it, but Spock was swallowing nervously. It was something that Spock did sometimes; the Vulcan was never aware of it and so did nothing to control it. The only one who had ever noticed it was Kirk, and he had never said anything to Spock about it.

"Thirty seconds, Mr. Spock," Rawlings reported. "Everything's go."

"Power reading, Mr. Chekov?" Spock called out.

"Thirty-four point zero, falling slowly."

"Mr. Hudson, recheck the launch communications lines for clarity of signal, please."

"All's well, Mr. Spock. Response one hundred percent. All birds check out, all systems go. We're ready, sir."

"Fifteen seconds, sir," Rawlings said. "Telemetry checks out."

"Power reading now thirty-two point nine," Chekov said.

"Ten seconds, Mr. Spock."

Spock of Vulcan, thoughtful being of peace and culture, was about to order the launch of a full-scale nuclear strike.

Rawlings was watching the clock. "Five . . . four . . . three . . . two . . . one . . . mark!"

"Fire all missiles," Spock said quietly.

Rawlings and Hudson input one last series of prepared commands.

"Ignition across the board, Mr. Spock!" Hudson called out seconds later. "Missiles heading up!"

Chekov noticed a severe drain on the portapack. *Twenty-six point four and falling more rapidly now,* he told himself. *I do not think this is the time to bother Mr. Spock, oh, no.*

"There they go," said Uhura on the bridge of the *Enterprise.*

The main viewscreen showed an entire hemisphere of Centaurus. All over the globe, tiny pinpoints of light appeared . . . and began to move.

"I get seven eighty-four in this hemisphere, five sixty-eight in the other, Lieutenant," Pete Siderakis called from the helmsman's station. "Jeez, look at all that tax money going up in smoke." It was a cemetery watchman's joke, the kind told nervously in the dead of night when one is filled with fear and surrounded by unknowns. No one laughed.

Thirteen hundred and fifty-two missiles, total, Uhura thought. *It checks: Spock got them all off. God, did they really need all those missiles?*

The pinpoints of light kept climbing. Dossie Flores, still at the navigator's station, kept an eye on her readouts. "All missiles still heading up, and none coming this way. Phasers standing by, ma'am."

Uhura smiled. "Okay, Deadeye." The new nickname for Flores had stuck immediately, bestowed by an appreciative crew after her quick and flawless interception of the incoming missile a few hours before.

"Missiles approaching atmospheric limit, Lieutenant. All on track."

Now comes the tricky part, thought Uhura. *Will they keep on going . . . or will they re-enter?*

As he'd told Kirk and the others in McIverton, Spock had seen but one solution to the problem of the defense system. Since it was intent on attacking everything in sight and could not be dissuaded from doing so, Spock probed to find something the computers *could* be persuaded to do.

They could be persuaded to attack the planet's star, Alpha Centauri. It was a target in space; all Spock had had to do was redefine the outer limit of the Centaurian "neighborhood," and tell the computers that one of the local suns had become a military threat. It was insane . . . but so were the computers. They only knew what Spock told them, and Spock had told them nonsense. The computers, being computers, believed every word.

If everything worked, the missiles would head directly for the sun—and, after several weeks in flight, would coast into its photosphere and be destroyed. They would in all probability never get the chance to detonate—but even if they did, their combined megatonnage would be the barest fraction of Alpha's output in any given microsecond. Alpha Centauri would chew on the terror of an entire world, grind it up, and swallow it whole.

Or so Spock hoped.

"Sixty percent of the missiles have reached escape velocity, Lieutenant," Siderakis reported. "We can forget those. Still nothing headed this way."

"Good. Deadeye, keep an eye on the rest of them."

"Aye, aye, ma'am."

Chekov was hunched over the portapack. He was beginning to worry. The supply was down to less than eighteen percent of capacity; the defense system was making heavy power demands for telemetry and course guidance requirements. Without that data, those missiles which had not yet achieved escape velocity would fall back to Centaurus. *Damn!* thought Chekov. *Vhy does the system not use its own independent supply? It vas doing vell enough vithout a portapack vhen it vas shooting at us!* Then the ensign realized that the demands on the system at that time were much, much less than they were now. The system's own backups must have been exhausted early in the mass launch . . . which also accounted for the accelerated drain of the portapack supply.

"Mr. Spock?" Chekov called out. "Power supply down to fifteen percent and falling more quickly."

Spock turned. "Do what you can, Ensign."

Chekov looked up at Connie and shrugged; she laid a gauntleted hand on his shoulder. *Do your best, Pavel,* she seemed to be saying. Chekov thought back to the days on the collective, when the days grew longer and the exhaustion of a portapack threatened to ruin an entire day's work. There was a trick. It always ruined the portapack, but the canny Russian farmers knew the government would be good for another one.

"Connie," Chekov asked, "could you dig into your medikit and perhaps find for me a conductive metal object about so long?" He held his hands apart about twenty centimeters. Iziharry paused in thought, and then selected a stainless steel surgical probe. "Will this do, Pavel?"

"Fine, fine! Stand back, now, and I vill show you one of the original Russian inwentions."

Chekov looked at the power reserve dial. *Six point one!* he thought frantically. Carefully, he laid the probe across a positive and a negative contact atop the portapack. There was a bright spark, at which Spock spun around. "Ensign? What's happening?"

"Emergency recharge, Mr. Spock." It had worked! In shorting the portapack terminals, Chekov had forced it to yield up everything it had, including the seed current it kept for recharging. The pack could never be recharged now—but it was delivering more than nineteen percent of capacity. Impulsively Chekov rose and hugged Connie; even through a pressure suit or two, she felt very good.

And she hugged back.

Chekov touched helmets with her to transmit sound; he did not want what he had to say broadcast over the intersuit communicators. "Connie? Forgive me for saying it . . . but I wery much vish ve vere alone now."

She looked up at him. "Pavel . . . oh, God, so do I. Soon."

Chekov grinned broadly. "Think I love you, Connie. Do you mind this thing?"

"Not if you don't, you crazy Russian." She squeezed him harder.

"Mama said vatch out for girls like you. I did, and

finally found vone." He grinned even more widely. "Back to vatching output meter now."

Siderakis stretched. "Lieutenant Uhura, boss, I have the distinct pleasure of telling you that all missiles have reached escape velocity, and all are on course for Alpha Centauri, to arrive there eventually. You can tell Deadeye over there to relax now."

Uhura laughed. "Mr. Spock does it again."

"His legend grows by th' hour," agreed MacPherson from his engineering station. "I ken Spock's approach ta things. He's direct. Th' missiles bother ya, then get rid o' th' bloody things. No foolin' around wi' thot one. I don' know anyone thot coulda done better. 'Cept perhaps Deadeye over there, o' course. But wee Deadeye's a legend in her own right."

" 'Wee,' is it?" fumed Flores. "Keep to 'Deadeye,' you hunk; I kinda like it."

"Ah, lass, but 'Wee Deadeye' it'll be. You'll see."

Rawlings and Hudson leaned back in their chairs. "All missiles away, out of the atmosphere, heading at better than escape velocity toward Alpha Centauri," Rawlings said. He sighed. "Man, I never want to do *that* again. It's like every old apocalypse movie I ever saw." Hudson, for his part, had nothing to say.

"Thank you both for your efforts," Spock said. "Mr. Chekov, you can shut down the portapack and strap it for carrying."

"Oh, that von't be necessary, Mr. Spock," the ensign replied. "I had to wreck the portapack to increase the yield. It is finished, sir. Junk."

"Then I suppose you might leave it behind here, Ensign, if you're in the mood to do so."

"Yes, sir."

Spock allowed them all to relax for a few minutes while he picked up the command phone and called the president's conference room in McIverton to report to Kirk, Erikkson and Perez. It was a short conversation, during which Erikkson shakily congratulated the Vulcan on a job well done.

Then Kirk got on the line. "Mr. Spock, well done."

"Thank you, Captain," Spock said politely. "We are now about to commence the second part of our mission here."

"Very good. I understand there are survivors in the northern part of the city, where the effects of the spaceport blast were less severe. You might try there first."

"An excellent idea, Captain. I will, of course, report to you at the earliest opportunity."

"Thank you again, Spock. Kirk out."

Chapter Sixteen:
McIverton

IT WAS ABOUT a half hour after second sunset, and nightlife in McIverton—such as it was—was in full swing. There was a thin crowd of couples in the streets, and a bright glow from restaurants and advertising signs washed against the sky. What ground traffic there was—mostly motorcycles and a few automobiles—found it slow going on the streets, and horns were appropriately honked.

Kirk watched the scene from his hotel window, all of three stories up; he had never in his life seen a traffic jam. He was fascinated by the chaos. *Noisy out there,* he thought.

Kirk and Sulu had been assigned separate but adjoining rooms in McIverton's one luxury hotel, the Hilton Inn West. It wasn't all that luxurious, either, but it *was* comfortable. There was a nice, big bed, which Kirk had already tried out for ten minutes or so of deep meditation—the kind accompanied by loud snores. The covers were still slightly mussed.

Kirk had checked in with Uhura earlier, over Erikkson's shortwave transceiver. He'd felt vaguely apprehensive about not spending the night aboard the *Enterprise,* but Uhura had assured him that all was well, and that Spock and his party had decided to camp for the night in a wooded area some distance outside the New Athens radiation zone. She'd finished her report by telling Kirk to get some sleep. "Yes, Captain," he'd said, and cleared. Actually, he liked the idea of staying in McIverton overnight; it was a long flight back up to the *Enterprise,* the break in his routine was welcome, and he had the time, for once.

Everything that could be done had been done. Uhura had sent a subspace signal to Starbase 7, with the welcome news that the code 710 had been lifted and that Centaurus was once again approachable. Seven would relay that word throughout the Federation. Kirk knew that ships from all over the UFP would be coming now, loaded to the overheads with the people and supplies needed to help the victims of the New Athens bombing.

Kirk rubbed the back of his neck as he wandered into the bathroom. He felt a bit ill from the cumulative effects of tiredness and sustained effort. He opened the medicine chest, hoping to find something appropriate for the weary traveler. All he found were complimentary razor blades (Kirk used a depilatory every week, so the blades were useless to him and, besides, there was no razor to put them in), a small roll of dental floss, a couple of bars of wrapped soap, a tube of shampoo, and a toothbrush (but no toothpaste). Kirk sighed, and settled for a splash or two of cold water on his face. *Perhaps there's a drugstore or something in the lobby—oh, hell! I don't have any money on me. Well, I didn't know I'd be here so long. Maybe Sulu brought some cash.*

Kirk left his room and went next door to Sulu's. He knocked; no answer. *Damn,* he thought. He went back to his own room and spotted the telephone. Kirk's experience of hotels was so close to zero as not to matter, but he knew you could ask any old question of the person at the front desk, and you might even get an answer. He'd seen it in dramas.

PUNCH "90" FOR FRONT DESK, a sign said. He did, and the phone's small screen lit with the face of a young blonde woman. *Cute,* Kirk told himself. "Front desk. May I help you?"

"Hello, Miss. This is Captain Kirk in room, uh, three forty-one, I think." The woman smiled. "I was wondering if it would be possible to get something for a headache . . . ?" Kirk felt ridiculous. It was much easier talking to Bones McCoy about such things.

"Of course, Captain," the young woman said brightly. "I'll have room service send something up right away."

Kirk mentally kicked himself. *Room service! Damn, I'd forgotten about that. Starfleet doesn't have room service; how the hell am I supposed to know? Jim, you'd make a lousy civilian.*

The woman paused. "Anything else you need, Captain, just ask for Madeleine. That's me." She smiled again.

Kirk smiled back. *Well, why not?* he thought. "Have you had dinner yet, Madeleine?" he said in a certain tone. *It's been a bad and busy time, Madeleine, and all I'm looking for is some pleasant company.*

Madeleine smiled even more. "I'll have room service send that up, too. For one. Good night, Captain." Kirk looked at the blanked screen. *I must be losing my touch,* he thought. Then he shrugged it off.

There were a few magazines on a reading rack in the bathroom, and Kirk thumbed through them: dog-eared copies of *National Cosmographic, Newsweek, McIverton Today!,* and *Analog.* The latest of them was eight months old. He sat on the bed and read the *Analog* until there was a knock at the door. "Room service," came a voice.

"Coming." Kirk tossed the magazine onto the bed and walked to the door. He opened it. There was a small, balding man standing there, tray in hand.

Kirk recognized him. "I *will* be dipped," he said flatly.

"Hello, Jim," said Sam Cogley. "It's been a while. May I come in?"

Samuel T. Cogley was one of the great ones: A lawyer with both dramatic style and an instinctual sense of the law. He had argued cases before virtually every major Federation court, and won most of them.

He was also the first human lawyer ever to plead a case before a Klingonese court. A Federation citizen had been accused of smuggling, and there was no way anyone could get a verdict of "not guilty" from a Klingon jury—but Cogley had tried, and *had* managed to get the man's sentence reduced to expulsion from the Empire. The Klingons had even let the smuggler keep his hands.

Kirk had been court-martialed once, less than a year after he'd taken the *Enterprise* out of drydock to begin her five-year mission. He'd been charged with negligence in the death of a records officer, Benjamin Finney. Samuel Cogley had been Kirk's lawyer and, with Spock's help, had broken the case. Cogley and Spock had proved that Finney, still alive and well (although more than a bit around the bend), had faked his own death to destroy Kirk's career.

Cogley had gone on to defend Finney at his own court-martial and had gotten him off on an insanity plea. That had gotten Finney a small pension and a not-so-long stay at a very good Starfleet mental rehabilitation facility. The cured Finney and his daughter, Jamie, now ran a thriving import-export business on Rigel II. Kirk had gotten a Christmas card from Jamie just the year before. Her father had been carefully taught not to remember Kirk at all.

Cogley put the tray on a table and reached into his coat pocket. He withdrew a flask. "Saurian brandy, Captain," he announced. "Got any glasses?"

"In the head, I guess," Kirk said. He ducked into the bathroom to get them. "Sam, just what the hell are you doing here?" he asked over his shoulder.

"Something that I think might concern you a great deal, Jim," Cogley answered. Kirk came back with the glasses, and Cogley poured. The blue liquor gurgled. Kirk picked his up, saluted Cogley with the glass, found some aspirin in a paper cup on the tray, swallowed the pills, and chased them with the brandy.

"I wasn't born yesterday, Sam," Kirk finally said. "It's about the New Athens thing."

"Yes," Cogley nodded. "I've heard from someone about it. They want me to talk to you."

"Are you representing them?"

"Yes."

Kirk shrugged. "So talk."

"Let's sit down," Cogley said. They did, in flimsy chairs around the table. Cogley's chair creaked alarmingly. "I see they spared no expense."

"It's worth what I'm paying for it, Sam."

"Which is?"

"Zero." Kirk grinned.

Cogley smiled. "Good to see you again, Jim. It's been a while since I defended Ben Finney; your testimony helped. Still, it took the devil's own time to convince the court that Finney had cracked as a result of his service, and that they owed him a few credits every month."

"I wouldn't have begrudged him that."

"*They* wanted to. First they brought that ridiculous case against you, and then they wanted to cover their tracks with Finney. But I managed to convince a few people that the publicity would be worse if they cashiered Finney and dumped him on a rock somewhere, without scat-all for him or Jamie."

"Have you seen them lately?"

"No," Cogley said, shaking his head. "I'm too footloose to keep close to my ex-clients. I trust they'll get in touch if they need me again."

Kirk nodded. "But now you've gotten in touch with *me*. So what's up, Sam? You said you've heard from 'someone.' Who?"

Cogley refilled his glass and did the same for Kirk. "I was in McIverton to give a seminar on civil rights law. I got into New Athens Spaceport and arrived in McIverton by flitter. No sooner had I landed here than the word came that New Athens had been destroyed.

"A day or two later, the local newspaper noticed I was here and ran a few quotes from me about how I felt about still being alive. I felt just fine, thanks. Very early the next morning, there was a knock on my hotel room door. Two guys, big; they looked like muscle-for-hire. They weren't forthcoming with many details; I was simply told that three leaders of the League for a Pure Humanity were in hiding near McIverton and wanted to give themselves up to the authorities."

Kirk sat a little straighter. "Any admissions of guilt?"

"Can't answer that, Jim; they're my clients. But I *can* tell you that my two visitors weren't much interested in surrendering to Centaurian authorities."

"Yeah. And I know why. The death penalty."

"Precisely. Then you'll realize that it's in my clients' best interests to surrender to you, for removal to Geneva for trial on whatever charges, if any, are brought against them. I imagine you have orders to that effect . . . ?"

"Yes," Kirk said. "How'd you know?"

"It's standard procedure in split-jurisdiction cases like this. Federation charges have to be dealt with first, anyway. The Federation court can always surrender jurisdiction to the local authority, but I'd fight that in this case because of the risk to my clients' lives."

Kirk was silent for a moment. "Sam," he finally said, "forgive me—but I don't give a rat's rear end for the lives of your clients."

Cogley looked Kirk in the eye. "I forgive you, Jim—and they're innocent until proven guilty. That hasn't been done yet." He paused. "Will your feelings prevent you from carrying out your orders, Captain?"

Kirk shook his head. "No. They never do, Sam."

Cogley and Kirk talked long into the night. Kirk's dinner congealed into a cold, inedible mess.

Sulu arrived back at his room about half an hour before firstdawn; he was beginning to feel a bit queasy, having sampled some of the baser pleasures of what had turned out to be a *very* friendly town. He thumbed the lock on the door; it swung open. *Oh, my aching head*, thought Sulu as he stumbled into the bathroom.

There was a scrawled note left on the sink:

Welcome back. We're leaving an hour after firstdawn. Mix the contents of the packet with a glass of cold water and drink it. Then sleep. You'll feel much better. Hope it was worth it. Kirk.

There was a small packet in one of the glasses. Sulu looked at the contents list; the stuff inside seemed to be a cure for everything but the black plague. *It has lots of thiamine in it,* Sulu thought hazily. *I need thiamine. Boy, do I need thiamine.*

The stuff fizzed agreeably and tasted good going down. Sulu left the bathroom and barely made it to the bed before collapsing.

Chapter Seventeen:
New Athens

A CONTINENT AWAY, Chekov, Rawlings and Hudson were putting things in order at their campsite as Spock and Connie Iziharry processed the party's radiological tabs. It had been a warm, dry night, with gentle, safe winds from the north.

It was a beautiful morning, with the suns bright in a cobalt-blue sky. The forest screened out most of the glare, so sunglasses weren't needed. That was fortunate. None of the humans had brought sunglasses, and Spock had not thought to do so because he himself would not need them and did not consider that others might. The humans would have to depend on the hyperpolarized faceplates in their suits' helmets, if things became intolerable.

The dirty-dish detail had been delegated to Chekov and Rawlings. Chekov (washing) was whistling; Rawlings (drying) was humming an adequate tempo in three-quarter time. Their slightly syncopated rendition of *Tales from the Vienna Woods* was doing an excellent job of scaring the birds away. Hudson was making sure that the campfire was dead; he took the job very seriously. They had all seen enough burned-out land the day before.

* * *

After leaving the Defense Center, Spock's party had boarded *Columbus* and flown over many square kilometers of blasted territory to the south and west. There had been nothing but death and devastation; there had not even been a recognizable ruin within ten kilometers of the spaceport site. Everything had been smashed flat and burned.

Those aboard *Columbus* had hoped that they might find some evidence of life as they approached less damaged areas. They flew over towns and villages that were more or less intact, but no one had been there; survivors had apparently fled in the face of mounting radiation. One airfield sixty kilometers south of the spaceport seemed undamaged, yet its holding areas were clogged with stalled flitters; no people could be seen. A southbound roadway near the airfield was strewn with ground vehicles of every sort, all of them motionless. Some of them had skewed off the roadway into ditches or collided with others. Hovering close to the ground, those on *Columbus* could see bodies in some of the vehicles. No one was found alive.

There had been one exception to the general devastation. *Columbus* found its first and only survivors of the day some eighty kilometers southeast of the spaceport, in Greenvale, a small and undamaged town protectively nestled in a narrow valley. Initially, no one could be seen on the streets. Chekov had overflown the town, and then some of the residents, alerted by the sound of the shuttle's engines, had emerged from their homes and waved. Chekov particularly remembered a heavyset woman in overalls who had energetically whipped a checkered tablecloth over her head.

Radiation readings were normal. The deadly fallout had missed this valley; the pressure suits would not be needed here. Spock told Chekov to land. By then, all five of them desperately needed to see and talk to some living, breathing people.

No one in Greenvale seemed to be in trouble, although everyone was hungry for news; they hadn't had electricity since the blast, and all their 3V and newspapers were from New Athens anyway. Spock and the others told them what they'd seen and done that day, but assured the townspeople the skies were now safe and that help was coming.

Columbus took off from Greenvale soon afterward. Nothing else remarkable was found, and as first sunset approached, Spock decided to stay on the planet overnight. The others were amenable to that; it had been a long and terrible day. They flew to a safe area in some pretty woods well west of the danger zone.

They landed in a clearing next to a small stream. Spock got a moderately high Geiger reading from *Columbus*'s shell, so Hudson got a long hose and a minipump from the shuttle's small cargo bay and washed *Columbus* down to get rid of whatever radioactive particles were on her hull. Then they built a fire to hold back the night, ate a little dinner, and slept fitfully. Their dreams were not pleasant.

Everything was now packed into *Columbus* for takeoff, and the campsite had been policed. Spock and Iziharry had finished processing the radiological tabs, and fresh ones had been issued.

"We will fly north today," Spock announced. "As you know, we have reason to suspect conditions to the north of the spaceport are less severe than we have found south of it. We will continue to observe and record, and offer aid where it is needed. Any questions?"

There weren't, and they climbed aboard. The impulse engines howled once more, and *Columbus* leaped into the sky.

Chekov flew directly over the spaceport crater again, left it behind and passed over the site of the Defense Center. He could see the slight impressions left by *Columbus*'s landing pads the day before.

Spock consulted his map, the one he'd borrowed from Peter Siderakis. The rubble below them was beginning to resolve itself into ruins; this had been a heavily built-up area. *It is right near here, somewhere,* Spock said to himself. *If I triangulate carefully, assuming that this map is in scale, perhaps I might locate it. We should be very near it now . . .*

"Mr. Chekov, please take us down close to the ground," Spock said. As Chekov pitched the joystick forward and eased back on the power, he asked, "Vhat are ve looking for, Mr. Spock?"

"Some indication of the location of the New Athens Medical Complex," the Vulcan answered. "Dr. McCoy's daughter was a medical student there. I would like to be able to tell the doctor something of her fate."

"Of course, Mr. Spock," Chekov replied. "Ve vill all look wery hard."

Once again, Iziharry, Rawlings and Hudson gathered behind the pilot and co-pilot seats, in order to peer out the forward windows. At last, another kilometer or so onward, Iziharry noticed the stumps of what had been several Gothic-style buildings to port. "I think that's it, Mr. Spock," she said. "I visited here once. I remember thinking the medical buildings here looked like some of the cathedrals on Earth. Nothing else on this whole world was ever built of stone."

Spock nodded. "Closer, please, Mr. Chekov. The location indicated by Miss Iziharry agrees with my map."

Slowly, *Columbus* coasted over the ruins of the Medical Complex and its school of medicine.

"I remember something from the New Testament," Rawlings mused. "Something about 'no stone being left on top of another,' or somesuch."

"The destruction of Old Jerusalem, I believe," Spock said. "Yes."

"This is terrible," Hudson said to no one in particular. Iziharry's eyes had filled. Here and there, dead littered the landscape. Some of them were medical students in their traditional white smocks.

Chekov's teeth were clenched. "Somevone must answer for this . . . this . . . " He sought an adequate word, but could not find one.

Columbus hovered over what had been the central square of the medical school campus for fully ten minutes. No one came out from hiding. Finally Chekov took *Columbus* up and away, still heading north.

"New Athens, Mr. Spock," Chekov announced.

Before them sprawled a massive city, a proper capital for any planet. But this one appeared lifeless although damage, while heavy, did not match the devastation a few kilometers south. There was a haze in the air from thousands of small, still-burning fires. They looked down into the streets on the southern end of town and saw no one.

Columbus pressed on. Toward the center of town, damage was even less pronounced; the streets had been sheltered by the buildings between them and the spaceport blast. *I believe most of this city can be reclaimed,* Spock thought. *I did not hope that anything could be salvaged, but with a great deal of work, at least part of New Athens can be repaired and inhabited again.*

They also started to spot some people on the streets.

There was even a little ground traffic. Attracted by the noise of *Columbus*'s engines, the citizens of New Athens looked up and waved. Although they could not be heard, some were obviously cheering the appearance of the Federation shuttle.

"Do you mind, Mr. Spock?" Chekov asked.

"Not at all, Ensign. I believe some demonstration is called for."

Chekov smiled and, grasping the joystick firmly, flew a figure-eight over the heads of the people below—the traditional salute of a wingless aircraft. Chekov saw the people below them grow even more enthusiastic; there were hundreds of them now, and some were standing on the roofs of abandoned automobiles and jumping up and down.

Rawlings said it best: "They look ragged and dirty as hell, but I'll be damned if they look beaten. These people are amazing."

Chekov, in his soul, agreed. He repeated the figure-eight and then resumed his northerly course.

"I'm glad we found them," Connie Iziharry said. "I needed to see some happy people."

"So did we all, Miss Iziharry," Spock said. He was remarkably unembarrassed by what he was feeling, although he took care not to show it overmuch.

The map indicated a large public park about five kilometers north of the center of the city. Chekov took *Columbus* there on a hunch, after conferring with Spock; the Vulcan agreed that it looked like a likely place to find an emergency aid camp of some sort. In fact, it was the only large cleared area in the city.

Founders Park was packed with people. There was more waving and cheering from those below. Spock's preliminary estimate indicated a closely packed crowd of perhaps two hundred thousand; the park had obviously attracted most of the city's survivors. He could see tents, trailers, shelters and shacks dotting the parkscape. There were small cookfires sending thin wisps of smoke into the air.

The law was here, too. Those aboard *Columbus* could see police flitters on the ground here and there; two or three were cruising over the park. They appeared to be from the city's own bureau of security. As yet, Spock had seen no evidence of any planetary government involvement in alleviating the disaster; the Vulcan was still wondering about the repair crew that had supposedly been dispatched to the Defense Center. The disaster had been days ago, yet people were greeting *Columbus* as if she were the first evidence they had seen of any rescue effort. Spock was beginning to believe that it might be true.

Chekov set about looking for a place to land. One wasn't difficult to find; somebody had painted a large red cross on the roof of a building—perhaps a boathouse—near a large pond. There was a cleared area behind the building; Chekov set *Columbus* down there.

"Exterior radiation readings slightly above normal background, Mr. Spock," Iziharry reported. "We don't need the suits, but we ought to keep the tabs."

"Very well, Miss Iziharry," the science officer answered. He opened the hatch, and they disembarked.

Spock looked around. A few people were approaching them. In the forefront was a tall, white-haired man in a bloodied white smock; a medical tricorder was slung over his shoulder and bounced against his hip as he walked. He was smiling widely, his hand extended. Then he noticed Spock was a Vulcan; he dropped the smile and raised his hand, his fingers split in the Salute. "I am Dr. Saul Weinstein," he said.

"I am Spock, first officer and science officer of the U.S.S. *Enterprise*," the Vulcan said, returning the

Salute. "These are Ensign Chekov, Nurse Iziharry, and technicians Rawlings and Hudson." The humans nodded their greetings.

"Live long and prosper, Spock," Weinstein said formally. Then he grinned again. "How the hell are the rest of you, anyway?"

Weinstein took the five from the *Columbus* on a quick tour of the immediate area. The boathouse was serving as a makeshift hospital; what equipment and supplies there were had been looted—with complete police approval and assistance—from a medical warehouse a few blocks east of the park. "We save most of the patients here," Weinstein told Spock a little boastfully. "It's been tough, though, and supplies are running short. Medikits ran out after the first two days; I've even been *stitching* wounds. But that works just as well now as it did in great-grandpa's time. People still heal themselves, with a little help. We might wind up learning something from all this."

The boathouse-hospital contained makeshift operating room facilities, and a small recovery room had been established in the boathouse cafeteria. There was no intensive care unit; there was nothing to equip one with, nor personnel to staff it.

Tents just outside the makeshift hospital served as patient wards. Nurses—and some civilians pressed into nursing duty—kept a constant watch on patients. "We don't have any monitoring equipment," Weinstein said. "We have to take temperature and pulses, watch input/output, and so forth. It's like medical science has retreated three hundred years." He paused. "But you know what? I actually think the patients are getting better faster. The personal touch seems to count for something."

"Perhaps the subject is worthy of study," said Spock. "But, Doctor, such medical care is labor-intensive—that is, the techniques require the work of a great many people to replace the machines you do not have. From where do you draw your staff?"

"We lucked out," Weinstein said. "There's a big medical equipment plant on the northern edge of town. A lot of their stuff's useless to us here—a lot of it's electronic, and we don't have the power to run it— but the plant's staffed by personnel who know what *sanitary* means. That gave us a pool of hundreds of people to draw from for nursing and other purposes. I had enough people to set up auxiliary medical tents here and there around the park, so people wouldn't have to go too far for help."

"It is quite fortunate, Doctor, that the plant was so close to hand," Spock observed.

"More than that, Mr. Spock," Weinstein said. "I was *in* the plant at the time of the explosion. We were taking a tour of the facilities. I'm a professor of diagnostic medicine at the Complex med school, south of town—although I gather the school's not there any longer. I was with a group of my students on a field trip—"

Suddenly Spock *knew* with a sure and entirely illogical instinct that she was nearby. "Miss McCoy!" he called, startling Weinstein and the four from the *Columbus*. "Joanna McCoy! Are you here?"

Not too far away a head turned, searching.

"Oh, yes, that's Joanna," Weinstein said. "Tireless young woman; she's been working like a dog. How do you know her?"

Spock had never met Joanna McCoy, but he'd taken the precaution of seeing a picture of her before he'd left the *Enterprise*. She clearly looked like McCoy's daughter—her smile marked her as such without hope of appeal—but she was a softer McCoy, pretty without glamour. "Thank God she doesn't look like me,"

Spock had heard Bones McCoy say once, but she did.

Now she looked tired. Her smock was streaked with dirt and blood; she badly needed some rest, a shower, and two or three meals. Her nails were broken. She was wearing one earring; the other was missing. Her skirt was ripped. She looked as if she wished she could brush her teeth.

She looks magnificent, thought Spock in a detached way.

Joanna McCoy had been wrapping an elderly woman's leg wound with sterilized rags. An open medikit lay on the ground. As Spock approached, Joanna finished the job, spoke quietly to the woman, and directed two young men nearby—the woman's sons, perhaps—to pick her up gently and take her to the boathouse for observation. Then she rose, stood straight, and looked for whoever it was that had been calling her.

She spotted the Vulcan right away; her eyes quickly found the ship's insigne on Spock's blue shirt, and the similar insignia on the shirts of the four with the Vulcan. She smiled widely. "The *Enterprise!*" she exclaimed. She read the commander's stripes on Spock's sleeves and said, "You must be Mr. Spock. My father's written me about you. I'm Joanna McCoy."

Joanna was polite; she offered the Salute, which Spock returned. "Live long and prosper, Miss McCoy." Spock performed the introductions to Chekov and the others.

"Is my father with you?" She looked past Spock for him.

"No. He chose to remain aboard the ship, for now. He had pressing duties there. I also believe he is undergoing emotional distress concerning your fate."

"Oh, poor Daddy," Joanna fretted. She frowned

just like her father, and Spock was again struck by the resemblance. "He always *was* a worrier. Look, I'll give you a note to take back with you, if that's all right."

"I am prepared to take you up to the *Enterprise*, if you desire to go," Spock said. "I believe your father would be glad to see you."

"I know he would, Mr. Spock. I'd love to go. But I can't leave here now; there's just too much for me to do. Do you understand?"

"Perfectly, Miss McCoy, and I think your father will understand as well." Spock paused. "You do him great honor."

Spock soon had a note, scrawled hastily by Joanna to her father. Now Saul Weinstein gave him a list of desperately needed medical supplies. "If you don't have something, I'll try and make do with something else," Weinstein said. "But I need *something*."

Spock scanned the list quickly. "I believe we have everything you require, Doctor, although not in the quantity needed to service a great number of people."

"So I'll make do," Weinstein shrugged. "Something is better than nothing, *nu?* I'll be grateful for anything you and your people can do for us, Mr. Spock."

Spock bowed his head slightly in polite appreciation.

Connie Iziharry spoke up. "Mr. Spock?"

"Yes, Nurse?"

"Requesting permission to remain behind on detached duty," she stated formally. "I think I can do some good here." Weinstein's eyes lit with greed at the thought of a Starfleet nurse in his makeshift hospital. Chekov's eyes told another story.

Spock nodded his permission. "Dr. Weinstein, I believe the *Enterprise* has just made its first contribution to your efforts here. As for the rest of us, we'll be going. I expect we'll be back with your supplies before very long."

"Till then, Mr. Spock," Weinstein said, and saluted in the Vulcan manner.

As Spock, Rawlings and Hudson headed for *Columbus,* Chekov hung behind. "Connie," he said, fumbling for words, "be safe. Be vell."

"I will, Pavel." She stood quietly, close to him. Her eyes were very large, dark and deep. *So beautiful,* Chekov thought as he kissed her . . . and then he spun away and was gone from her, double-timing it to the open hatch of the shuttle.

Soon they were home again; Chekov cut power to the engines, and *Columbus* settled to the deck.

"Landed, Mr. Spock," Chekov reported. "Landing deck pressurized; engine shut down. Open the hatch at your pleasure, sir."

"Thank you, Ensign." Spock paused. "Gentlemen, you have comported yourselves on this mission in the finest traditions of the fleet. I will be pleased to note same on your service records. I appreciate your efforts." The Vulcan left the shuttle, followed by the other three.

"Landing deck officer!" Spock called out. An orange-garbed woman came trotting over. "Yes, sir?"

"I trust the transporters are still non-functional?"

"That's correct, sir."

"This list, then." Spock handed it to her. "Please have Stores load the items on it, in the quantities specified, onto *Columbus.* I want to leave as soon as possible. After we leave, refill the list; we'll be shuttling supplies to the surface until further notice."

"Aye, aye, sir. Overhaul and fueling routine for the shuttle, Mr. Spock?"

"Refueling and a routine engine check will do. Have

it done as the cargo is being loaded aboard. I do not have very much time."

"Very well, sir." The LDO ran off, Weinstein's list in her hand. Spock headed for the turbolift, followed by Chekov, Rawlings and Hudson. "Mr. Rawlings, Mr. Hudson, you're returned to normal duty. Report to Mr. Scott. Mr. Chekov, secure some refreshment; we'll be leaving again shortly."

The turbolift doors squeaked closed as Spock grasped the manual override handle.

Spock found Bones McCoy in Sickbay, treating a Security lieutenant, the victim of a loosened ceiling panel which had fallen on his head. "You're my last patient of the day," McCoy told the redshirt. "Keep that bandage on for four hours, and you'll be fine."

"Thanks, Doctor." The Security man noticed Spock standing there; McCoy followed his gaze. The doctor's face went cold. The Security man left.

McCoy spoke quickly, but without emotion. He was pale. "Go ahead, Mr. Spock. It's about Joanna. It's all right. Tell me." He closed his eyes.

"Safe and well, Doctor," Spock said. "She sent you a note." He held it out.

McCoy opened his eyes after a moment. "She's all right?" There was a look of disbelief on his face . . . but he was regaining his color.

"Perfectly well, Doctor. She was unhurt in the explosion. She was in another part of the city." Spock rapidly gave McCoy the details. "She trusted you would understand her desire to remain at the emergency medical care facility."

McCoy blinked. "Yes, yes . . . of course." The doctor unfolded the note from Joanna and began reading. His eyes misted, and he blinked more rapidly. Spock watched him struggle for control. *I know that feeling well, Doctor,* the Vulcan thought. *Draw strength from me, if you need it.*

After a moment McCoy looked up; his eyes were dry, and there was a hint of the doctor's accustomed wry expression. "She's all right, all right," McCoy said. "She called me an 'old poop' in the note and told me to get my butt down there."

"I can oblige you, Doctor. Mr. Chekov and I are leaving for the facility again shortly."

"Let me pack a few things, tell M'Benga he's on duty, and I'll be right with you—just as soon as I check in with our lady captain."

McCoy was silent as *Columbus* departed the *Enterprise.* He was silent as Chekov smoothly piloted the shuttle safely through the upper atmosphere of the planet, through a sky now free of the threat of ground-to-space missiles. He remained silent as *Columbus* swiftly fell toward Founders Park and the cleared area behind the boathouse.

Chekov landed without a bump and cracked the hatch from his board. "Thank you both," McCoy said quietly. He grabbed his personal kit. "See you later." Spock and Chekov watched him go.

McCoy swung his kit over his shoulder and began looking around. *She knew I was coming,* he said to himself as he marched through the crowd, stepping over people and narrowly avoiding collisions with others. He moved more and more quickly. *She'd stay close to the landing area, I know she would. She never liked our being apart. She was always right there at the Starfleet arrival gate whenever I'd come home to see her. She's here somewhere.*

And then there was a cry, as there had so often been before. *"Daddy! Over here!"*

She was standing there, tall and proud and alive . . . and waving to him. She was the most beautiful thing

McCoy had ever seen. His vision blurred with the sight.

He pushed his way quickly through the crowds separating them. They met together in a mass of people.

McCoy dropped his personal kit and hugged his daughter fiercely. "Hiya, Squirt," he said softly.

"You big mushball," Joanna said mock-scornfully, too low for anyone but McCoy to hear. "Don't get s-s-sloppy on me . . . Oh, Daddy, I'm so glad to see you . . ." She sniffled.

And then it was finally too much for Bones McCoy, all the worry and the waiting and the conviction that she was dead, and in all that time he had not broken. But now that she was safe and well and in his arms, he hugged his daughter fiercely, sobbing unashamedly with the relief and joy that filled his heart and soul, and he did not care who saw him cry.

Chapter Eighteen:
McIverton

"SULU! SULU! WAKE up, dammit!"

Kirk had been trying to rouse the unconscious lieutenant for several minutes. Sam Cogley had left to bring his flitter around to the front of the Hilton Inn West; he was probably already waiting downstairs.

The captain turned Sulu over. He peeled back one of the helmsman's eyelids; the pupil of his eye was dilated. *He's been drugged!* thought Kirk. *What the hell was he doing last night, anyway?*

Kirk went into Sulu's bathroom to get a glass of cold water and saw the note, the dropped glass, and the empty packet. Instantly Kirk realized what had happened—and that made matters all the more pressing. *It's that bastard Burke,* Kirk thought savagely. *I'll settle his score later.*

Obviously the plan Kirk and Cogley had come up with—Kirk and Sulu to claim urgent business aboard the *Enterprise,* pick up *Galileo,* leave McIverton, head for Gregory's Landing, and pick up the five Leaguers—would not work. Burke (or his men) had done this to Sulu, and they'd be watching.

Kirk heard the phone ring in his room next door.

182

That's probably Sam, Kirk said to himself. *Please, Sam, use the brains God gave a goose and call Sulu!*

Sulu's phone rang. Kirk sighed with relief and thumbed the ANSWER button; Cogley's face swam into view.

"No time, Sam," Kirk said quickly. "Roof pad. Now!" Kirk cleared the circuit. *Now to get Sulu the hell out of here. I hope to God there is a flitterpad on the roof.*

Kirk opened the door. No one was in sight in the hallway. *If I were a cop, where would I hide?* Five meters down the hallway, on the opposite side, was a door marked LAUNDRY. *That's where.*

Kirk dropped to all fours and crept down the hall. He arrived at the laundry chute door, came to a crouch, backed up a bit, and then quickly twisted the knob and yanked the door open. He didn't wait to see who or what was inside; he simply lashed up and out at where he thought a man's jaw would most likely be.

He connected the first time and made his second punch count. The man inside the laundry chute room slumped to the floor. Kirk caught him before his head hit the tiles. After another look up and down the hall, Kirk dragged the man into Sulu's room and quietly closed the door.

Kirk searched him. *Two phasers—good. I can use the clothes, too. There's probably another one or two watching the elevators, maybe more on the roof.* The captain stripped the man efficiently, down to his shorts; he took off his own Starfleet uniform and put on the man's suit. It didn't fit very well. He went through the man's wallet. *Internal Security agent, of course; badge and photo card. Pair of sunglasses. Good, because I can't find the ones Hayes gave me yesterday. Thirteen pounds platinum in the wallet, no Federation money; several charge cards, identification card for the Knights of Columbus, organ donor card, phaser permit signed by Burke himself.* Kirk had been hoping the agent was carrying something *really* good, such as a brace of stun bombs or a couple of gas grenades. *Well, I'll have to make do.*

Kirk dressed the agent in his uniform; it fit him as badly as his suit fit Kirk. He left the agent where he was, face down on the floor. *I wonder how many guys they've got out there?* Kirk wondered.

He opened the door and pitching his voice low, shouted, "Got 'em. Bring the cuffs!" Then he stood behind the open door and waited, phaser drawn and set for stun.

He didn't have to wait long. Two more agents came to the open door, saw Sulu unconscious on the bed and (presumably) the captain out cold on the floor, and stepped into the room. Kirk fired; the agents dropped. He crouched and peeked around the doorsill, phaser ready; no one was in the hallway.

Kirk rolled both agents; one of them (the chief of detail? Kirk hoped so) had a communicator. *His boss is near here. Otherwise the thing wouldn't work, what with all the tachyonic interference.*

What he didn't know was Burke's whereabouts. *I can't believe he's not around here somewhere. Hmmm. If I were Burke, where would I be?* Kirk decided he'd be on the roof, phaser in hand, ready to cut off a last-ditch escape attempt.

And that was precisely where Kirk hoped Cogley was headed. All right—then he'd have to rescue Cogley, too.

Sulu was still out. Kirk hurriedly stripped one of the two agents and pulled his clothes on over Sulu's; dressing a limp body was a tough, clumsy job. After a little thought, Kirk de-pants'd the other agent as well; it might slow him up a bit when he came around.

The captain now had four phasers, one communicator set for the agents' command frequency (as well as the temporarily useless communicators he and Sulu carried), three pairs of sunglasses, three wallets full of false identification (false for Kirk, that is), and a little money—about sixty-five credits' worth, almost all of it in local pounds platinum. *They ought to pay these guys more,* Kirk said to himself.

If Cogley were not a factor, Kirk would simply throw Sulu over his shoulder, go to the lobby, pretend Sulu was dead drunk and call a cab. But Sam was on the roof, presumably in trouble; Kirk couldn't abandon him. Sulu was still doing a good job of pretending to be dead drunk, so Kirk amended his plan a bit, ran it through in his mind several times, and pronounced it good enough. Hell, he'd been through worse than this with a lot less in the way of resources.

Oh. One more thing. Kirk looked in the carboy next to the 3V set; the hotel had thoughtfully provided Sulu a complimentary fifth of not-very-good Scotch. It would be good enough for Kirk's purposes. He twisted the cap (making sure the tax seal was unbroken; he didn't want a piece of Sulu's problem), took a mouthful and swished it around. *Errrkkkkk,* he thought. *Awful!* He spit it out in the bathroom sink, rinsed it, came back out, and sprinkled some of the Scotch on Sulu. Then he did the same to himself. *Sniffff. All right . . .*

Kirk took Sulu in an over-the-shoulders carry and, grunting a little, opened the door. The hallway was still clear; Kirk lurched to the elevators with his burden.

Kirk met a nice elderly couple in the elevator. He grinned sloppily at them, sniffed, and minded his own business. *I'm not an obnoxious kind of drunk,* he told himself. *They leave me alone, I leave them alone.*

But they didn't leave him alone. "Young man," the old woman said.

"Yesh, ma'am, that'ss me," Kirk agreed, nodding pleasantly.

"Young man, don't you think it's rather early in the day for this sort of behavior?" She looked coldly at Kirk while she ignored her husband's sleeve-pulling.

Kirk leered at her. "Thash okay, ma'am; me 'n my frien' here, we shtarted lash night. Hav'n't been to bed *yet*. Well, *he* hash." He giggled.

The elevator stopped at 14, and the old couple exited, she with a cold stare at Kirk, and the old man with an apologetic look his wife did not see. Kirk winked at him and did his best to smile hazily.

The doors closed and Kirk hit the button for the top floor. As the elevator rose, Sulu grunted. "Sulu?" Kirk called.

Sulu grunted again.

"Oh my God, Sulu. I hope you're not going to be sick."

The elevator stopped; Kirk emerged cautiously from it. No one around. Down the hallway, he spotted a door painted a different color from all the guest room doors; he decided that was the way to the roof. Kirk hefted his burden and began to walk weavingly toward it.

It *was* the roof accessway. Kirk gently eased Sulu off his shoulders and sat him against the wall. "I'll be right back," he told Sulu. "Stay put." The helmsman grunted solemnly; Kirk patted his cheek and drew his own phaser. Crouching, he eased open the door to the roof.

He saw a shadowy figure against the bright blue sky and fired blindly; he heard an object hit the roof, followed by the thud of a collapsing body. Kirk fished a pair of sunglasses out of his jacket pocket and put them on. He wasted no time in crashing through the accessway.

Two more! he thought, even as he fired. And they

were firing back, well wide of the mark. Kirk risked a glance up. *Damn flitters all over the place!* fumed Kirk. He didn't see one that was obviously Sam's, and did not know how he'd spot Cogley's flitter anyway.

But some of the ones above his head obviously belonged to the Ministry of Internal Security—and they were homing for Kirk's location.

And then Kirk saw a big, limousine-sized flitter zoom around a tall building opposite the hotel, and he knew that it was Sam Cogley manning the stick. Sam was rescuing *him*. Kirk ducked back inside, grabbed two handfuls of Sulu, and struggled back outside, even as the agents drew near.

Kirk now saw that one of the two men approaching him was Burke. He ignored him; the hovering flitter was blocking any possible stun shot, and a kill shot would take out the flitter first. Kirk didn't think Burke would do that to get him. As Kirk neared the flitter the passenger door popped open, and Cogley's voice was insistent: "Come *on*, Jim! The barn's burning down!"

"Coming, Mother," Kirk called; the captain was feeling fairly feisty by now. In three strides he was at the flitter door; he heaved Sulu inside—*Sorry for the rough stuff, my friend*—and jumped in after him. Cogley pressed a button, slamming the door shut. He yelled "Hang on!" and they got out of there well above the local speed limit.

Cogley spent the next several minutes at low altitude above the streets, whizzing in and out of likely looking hiding places, trying to muddy their trail.

"Where'd you learn to drive like this, Sam?" Kirk asked.

"Los Angeles."

Shortly thereafter, Cogley found a hole in heavy traffic above him. He eased into it; the guy behind him blared his airhorn in annoyance. Cogley said a nasty word.

"Up to our hips, Sam," Kirk agreed. "You have any idea what happened yet?"

Cogley shrugged; he was keeping one eye on the traffic and the other on the rear-view receptors. "Some. I figure our friend Nathaniel Burke was doing his job. He was certainly going to keep an eye on you, Jim; I didn't think he'd be so attentive where I was concerned. He must have assumed that the fugitive League members would try to get themselves somebody like me to represent them, and I happened to be the guy in town that day. Just lucky, I guess."

"So he had you followed to the hotel, found out that we were meeting, and put two and two together," Kirk guessed.

"That's probably it. He must have had Sulu drugged as a gambit, figuring it'd slow you up. I wonder how long he'll be out."

"You've got me," Kirk said. "I thought he might have been coming around before, but I suppose not. In fact, he's beginning to snore. Where are we headed now?"

"Gregory's Landing, for a rendezvous with a party of five, as per schedule."

"Let's hope Burke's heard about our meticulous planning and gives up right now." Kirk whistled tunelessly between his teeth; then he reached into his jacket pocket and produced one of the Internal Security men's phasers. "Take it, Sam. I've got plenty."

"No, thanks, Jim," Cogley grinned. "I only wear those things in court." He paused, sobering. "I'm glad you have one, though."

They sped north, safe for now in the mass of traffic.

Cogley dropped the flitter in back of a colonial-style house at the foot of a narrow street in the northernmost section of Gregory's Landing. It was a quiet neighborhood, with few neighbors. The lawyer cut the engine and sighed. "This is it."

"I see. Do we wait here all day, or does somebody have to go around front and ring the doorbell?"

"They'll be out; we're getting the once-over right now."

Kirk saw a curtain flutter in an upper window; whoever it was then backed away. Two minutes later the rear door of the house opened, and out came two men, muscly types in blue jeans and knockabout shirts.

"Max and Dave," Cogley said. "They're the ones who got in touch with me yesterday morning. They don't say anything they haven't memorized somewhere else. My prime client's changed his hideout at least twice that I know of; I guess he decided to bring these two out of the cold, after all."

Two more men came out. They were dressed as businessmen, albeit their clothes could have used a trip to the cleaners.

"I don't know these two," Cogley said. "Haven't met 'em. I know them only as 'Smith' and 'Jones.' Somehow, I don't believe it."

A fifth man emerged.

"Reuben Barclay," Cogley said. "The head man. I met him a long time ago on Earth. He had a big block of stock in one of my corporate clients, back when I had corporate clients."

Barclay was immaculately and stylishly dressed, even to a large diamond stickpin in his cravat. He appeared as unmussed as any man could be, even under the best of circumstances. He was heavy, balding, and looked vaguely threatening—and his aura of power was the greater for that.

"My turn now," Kirk said. He unlatched the flitter door and stood, appraising Barclay.

"Captain Kirk, I presume?" Barclay said. "Reuben Barclay—as, no doubt, Mr. Cogley has informed you. My associates." He gestured half-heartedly in the direction of the other four men. "I trust we're off to Government Field now?" He smiled.

"No," Kirk said. Barclay blinked, his smile fading.

"Change of plans, Barclay," Kirk continued. "The deal you cooked up and served to Cogley has been blown. No shuttle. We can't get to it."

Barclay's teeth were on edge. "Then what do you propose to do, Kirk?"

"First things first. You're all under arrest. You have the right to remain silent, and anything you say can and will be held against you in a court of law. You already have a lawyer, so I won't go into that part. You have a phone call coming. Want to make it?"

"No," Barclay said, fuming.

"Then stand there for a minute." Kirk came around and frisked Max and Dave, relieving each of several weapons. The business suits weren't carrying anything. Barclay had a penknife not good for anything but paring nails; Kirk confiscated it anyway. "In the flitter."

"Where are we going, Kirk?" Barclay demanded. "Do you have some idea about turning us over to the local authorities? Because if you do—"

"Save it, Barclay," Kirk snapped. "I'm under orders to deliver you to Earth for a trial. If Centaurus wants you, it can plead its case at your arraignment in Geneva."

"If any," Barclay smirked.

"Yeah." Kirk shot a glance at Sam Cogley, who did not return it. "In the car, *now.*"

Barclay stood still for a moment, and then shrugged. He sat in the back. "Who's this?" Barclay demanded, indicating the dozing Sulu.

"My best helmsman," Kirk said. "You touch him or

disturb him in any way, and I'll feed your heart to the pigs for breakfast." He turned. "That goes for the rest of you. Get in the car."

They got. Cogley sealed the doors, and they took off.

"Head due east," Kirk said. "I know where we're going."

"The valley you told me about?" Cogley asked.

"Yeah. The valley."

They sped at low altitude over the wild, untamed country that dominated the interior of New America. Under normal circumstances their flitter could have been picked out by one of the circling datasats orbiting any reasonably advanced Federation planet—but the Defense Center's insane computers had wiped the skies clean of satellites. They were safe from spying eyes.

No one was following, either, as least as far as Kirk could see. The flitter wasn't all that fast—the top speed on the indicator dial was eight hundred kilometers per hour, only two-thirds the speed of sound, and Cogley was coaxing every bit of speed he could out of the old bucket. It also drank fuel greedily. *Can this thing run thirty-two hundred klicks without a refill?* wondered Kirk. *I'd hate to have to stop for a loadup. The fewer people who see us, the better.*

After a couple of hours, Barclay spoke up. "Kirk?"

"Hmmm?"

"When do we arrive? I'm becoming a bit cramped in here."

Kirk shrugged. "We're about halfway there."

Barclay nodded. He reached into his inside pocket for a leather case; he opened it and produced a cigar. "Does anyone mind?"

"Yes," Kirk said. It was Barclay's turn to shrug; he put the cigar back in the case, and elaborately replaced the case in his jacket. The four with Barclay looked at Kirk as if to say, *Are you crazy? You don't say no to the Boss. If he wants to smoke, or slobber, or kill you, you do your level best to cooperate.*

Sulu, sprawled in the seat next to Barclay's, moaned. His eyes opened. "Oh, my aching head," he mumbled. The helmsman looked around. "Where are we? Captain?"

"Welcome back, Mr. Sulu," Kirk said, a little relieved. "Sam, got any aspirin for Sulu?"

"Look in the glove compartment. *I* didn't bring any."

Kirk opened it and found nothing.

"Allow me, Captain?" Barclay said. He snapped his fingers; "Smith" withdrew a small tin from his shirt pocket. *Damn!* Kirk thought. *I missed that when I searched him. Jim, boy, you're slipping.*

Barclay opened it and offered two of the tablets inside it to Sulu. "With your permission, of course, Captain," Barclay said, his voice lightly stressing the last word.

"Fine. Thank you, Barclay."

"Not at all."

Sulu took the tablets and dry-swallowed them. He rubbed his eyes and looked around. "What's going on, Captain?"

Kirk briefed him. Sulu was angry. "I fell for it," he said bitterly. "The oldest trick in the book."

"It's an old trick, all right," Kirk said, "but we weren't looking for tricks." The captain looked disgusted. "When he left the conference room yesterday, Burke as much as said he'd stop us if we try to enforce the Federation's interests in this matter." He glanced at Barclay and the others. "Burke knows what the rules are. He's breaking them."

Sulu considered it. "Captain, with all respect, if someone wiped out my home town and killed my family, I might not be in a mood to pay attention to due process, either."

Kirk nodded. What could he say? He agreed with Sulu. But he had orders, and he intended to follow them—to the letter.

They continued due east.

"This is it, isn't it, Jim?" Cogley asked.

Despite everything, Kirk smiled. "This is it, Sam. Garrovick Valley."

They had found the Farragut River and were following it north; it was like a highway into Kirk's valley. A few swift movements through mountain passes, and they were there. It was as beautiful as Kirk remembered it.

"Captain?" Sulu asked. "Do you have a place here, sir?"

"Yes, Sulu. Another dozen or so kilometers farther on."

Sulu was fascinated; so much open space! So *green!* "How much land, if you don't mind my asking?"

Kirk made an expansive gesture. "Everything you see."

"The *whole valley?"*

"Also the riverbanks back toward the source, the riverbanks south of here, and all rights attached thereto," Kirk answered, not without a hint of pride.

Barclay was looking out the window. "I commend you on your taste, Captain. This is quite nice. I envy you." There was a gleam of avarice in Barclay's eye.

In the pleasure he felt at coming home, Kirk had, for a moment, forgotten all about Barclay and his cohorts. It offended his hindbrain that a slug like Barclay should encroach on *his place,* but the captain knew better than to rail against their shared circumstances. *But if things weren't as they are, Barclay, and I found*

*you trespassing—well, they'd give me a medal for
what I'd do.*

"Right on up the river, Sam," Kirk said, instead of
what he wanted to say. "I'll tell you when to turn."

"There," Kirk said, pointing. "Off to starboard."

"You mean 'on the right,' " Cogley said. "Landing
area and everything. Great." Cogley whipped the flitter around and set her down gently behind Kirk's log
cabin.

So long ago, Kirk thought, *on this same spot, Bones
McCoy, Joanna and I set down, and I fell in love with
this place. Twelve years ago? Doesn't seem that long.
Joanna loved it so.* He noted his use of the past tense.
*Damn, I hate being out of touch with the ship! I wish
to hell I knew what was going on.*

Kirk popped the flitter door open and stepped out.
By touch, he selected his own communicator from the
one he'd purloined from the Internal Security agent
earlier, took it out of his jacket pocket, and flipped it
open. There was the familiar *errrkaerrrkaerrk* sound,
as the gadget found its frequency; then there was
nothing but a roar of static. *Upper atmospheric fallout
is still too high,* Kirk said to himself. He brought it
closer to his ear and listened carefully. Were there
voices there?

"Kirk to *Enterprise,* Kirk to *Enterprise,* come in,
please." He waited. Nothing. He tried again. The
ghostly voices on the comeback didn't seem to be
noticing him.

There was one more trick to try. Kirk thumbed the
emergency recall tab. Under normal circumstances,
the transporter room would receive this signal and
beam him up immediately; he could then coordinate a
pickup of the others. Kirk knew the transporter was
out of service, but the signal *might* get through and tip
the ship off to his position.

It didn't work; there was no answerback signal. Kirk shut the clamshell and returned it to his pocket. He looked at the others. "Nothing yet," he announced. "Let's get inside." Sulu, the closest to the door, entered first. One of the good things about Garrovick Valley was that Kirk never had to lock his cabin.

The place was rustic, but not primitive. The kitchen facilities were modern—microwave, quikfreez, stasis, full plumbing and recycling facilities—and the head was a navy man's dream. There was even a massage unit, built for two. So was the bed.

The log walls were covered with the traditional woodsman's trappings: gunpowder weapons (nonfireable trophies); artificial skins resembling those of the traditional raccoons, beavers and otters; and old, faded prints of woodsy scenes—hunters around a campfire, a group of men ice-fishing, and so forth. There was a bookcase filled with genuine antique volumes; Kirk kept them wrapped in plastic and read them frequently: Dickens, Hemingway, Asimov, Ross, and some others, none of them from later than, say, 2050.

Kirk pushed the bookcase out of the way—it rolled on hidden casters—and exposed a machined panel. He flipped a switch.

"What's that, Jim?" Cogley asked. The others looked on, interested.

"Starfleet radio. My commander's unit. More powerful than the communicators. Maybe I can punch a signal through to the ship." A small prompt box lit dully red: AUTHENTICATION.

"Kirk, James T., SC 937-0176 CEC."

VOICEPRINT MATCH CONFIRMED. That disappeared. DESTINATION.

"U.S.S. *Enterprise*, NCC-1701."

WORKING. Then, FREQUENCY INTERFERENCE. NEXT.

Kirk reached for the DEACTIVATE switch, but hesitated. He thought for a moment, and then pushed an unobtrusive yellow key in the lower right corner of the panel. Another cue bar lit dully red: EMERGENCY POWER OVERRIDE.

Kirk repeated his code and destination entries.

WORKING. Then, for a split-second, there was CONTACT ESTABLISHED; but it was quickly replaced by FREQUENCY INTERFERENCE. NEXT. Kirk sniffed; he smelled insulation burning. Then all the panel lights died. *I've really bunged it up now.* He sighed.

He wondered if his call had managed to get through. If it had—and the CONTACT ESTABLISHED indicator hadn't simply been a glitch in the overheated unit's circuitry—then Uhura might be able to run a trace on his position. Kirk was sure that if even the merest blip of a signal *had* gotten through, no matter how weak or brief, then Uhura could pin it down. Kirk was frankly and unashamedly baffled by the intricacies of subspace communications equipment and had a healthy respect for Uhura's skills.

17:82, the chronometer said. Kirk satisfied himself that the commander's unit wasn't on fire, unhooked it from the cabin's power supply to prevent its reactivation, and rolled the bookcase back against the wall. *I'll have to get the unit replaced, eventually,* he said to himself. *Not that it's done me much good. The first time I've ever used it, and look what happens.*

Kirk sighed. "Barclay," he said. "You can have that cigar now. It'll be a while." The captain turned and stepped outside.

Some flitters were capable of flight outside the atmosphere, capable of reaching destinations in near-orbit. Cogley's was a rented atmospheric-only, subsonic model that needed air around it to burn fuel. Kirk decided that staring at it wouldn't reconfigure its engines. The tanks were almost dry, anyway, and Kirk didn't maintain a fuel dump in the valley.

Night was falling; some of the brighter stars were coming out, now that it was a little past second sunset. Kirk soothed an old itch and spotted Sol in Cassiopeia; the sky was still too bright for Kirk's home sun to show its yellowish color, but the gleam of it was there. So were some of Kirk's other old friends: Vega, the Dipper, the three stars in Orion's belt. And there were some newer friends, the other planets circling Alpha Centauri. Centaurus didn't have a moon; Kirk missed one. The presence of a big, fat moon would have made it better, somehow.

Kirk went back inside the cabin. Sulu was handling K.P. tonight; he had rations going in the microwave and was frosting some beers in the quikfreez. Kirk hadn't been here in several years, but the stasis field had kept all the food as fresh as the day he'd bought it, years before. There was enough in the vault to keep everybody fed for weeks.

Cogley had, with Kirk's permission, warmed up the 3V. There was a small earth station hidden in the woods, but there were no broadcasting satellites for 3V anymore. Instead, Cogley had found one of Kirk's handful of omnitapes. Like his books, Kirk's films were antiques, although they were reproduced in modern media. Cogley, Barclay and the others were sitting on the cabin floor, more or less enchanted by the George Pal version of *The Time Machine*. It was reconstructed 3V, of course; the film had been made in 1960, well before they'd come up with the omnilens. It was early in the picture, and there was the three-dimensional illusion of an astonished and excited Rod Taylor, as the time traveler, talking excitedly to an elderly and half-daft Alan Young in his later incarnation as an air-raid warden, Young finally pulling away as the sirens of London screamed their last alert.

Then Taylor looked up in astonishment as the sky erupted in nuclear fire and the buildings began to crumble. "I'm not in the mood to see this," Cogley mumbled. He snapped the 3V off; the omnitape rolled to a halt and clicked out of its holder.

"I am," said Barclay.

"Leave it," snapped Kirk. "Sulu, is dinner ready yet?"

"Come and get it, Captain."

They gathered around the table, sat, and attacked the meal. No one said anything. They finished, and Cogley helped Sulu clean up; Barclay was content to sit in his chair, fold his hands and look at his thumbnails through hooded eyes.

Time passed slowly, but it was eventually time for bed. They didn't bother drawing straws for Kirk's double bed; Sulu and Cogley took that, and Kirk threw his spare bedroll in Barclay's direction. He knew that Barclay wouldn't draw straws with his men for that, either, and he was right.

Kirk picked a book off the shelf and settled into a comfortable chair for his watch. The rest of them slept surprisingly well.

Chapter Nineteen:
The Enterprise

THE BRIDGE WAS quiet with the hush of a routine watch.

Uhura was worried.

Captain Kirk had missed his morning check-in, and her efforts to reach him had not been successful. She had called President Erikkson's office over the shortwave transceiver several times and had been told repeatedly that the captain, Sulu and top government officials were in urgent meetings and could not be disturbed. Messages would be relayed, of course.

Uhura didn't like that. She thought the captain would call back, if he could . . . .

Now night was falling on the continent down below, and still she had heard nothing. She couldn't raise Erikkson's office at all on the shortwave. Communicator frequencies were still out. The transporters were not working yet, although Scotty had made their repair his top priority. Kirk and Sulu had taken *Galileo,* and Spock and Chekov still had *Columbus.* Right now *Columbus* was serving as a flying ambulance and cargo truck for the refugee camp Spock had found in New Athens.

If there'd been a third shuttle, Uhura would have torn down to the surface and taken a look for herself; Scotty would take the conn, whether he wanted to or not.

What galled Uhura was that things could be perfectly all right. Kirk *could* call on the president's transceiver, but was under no compulsion to do so; the *Enterprise* was no longer on alert. His only other way of talking to the ship would be to go out to the airfield and use the transceiver unit in *Galileo*. Kirk hadn't done that yet, but he had certainly been out of touch before under more pressing circumstances. The uncertainty of the situation gnawed at her.

So this is what command is like, Uhura thought.

She wished she could talk to Dr. McCoy about it, but he had assigned himself to detached duty at the New Athens camp, working with his daughter. Despite her worries, Uhura smiled. *I'd like to be able to tell the captain about that, too,* she thought.

She tentatively decided to raise hell if, in the morning, Kirk hadn't checked in and Erikkson's office continued to stall her. *And I can raise a lot of hell,* she said to herself, with a decisive and self-satisfied nod of her head.

Scott and MacPherson hadn't gotten much sleep in the past few days. It was becoming night aboard the ship as well, and the ship's two top engineers were still hard at work. Scotty had just finished uncrossing the last crossed circuit in the Jeffries tube, while MacPherson was still struggling with one of the Delaney valves that controlled the flow of coolant to the inboard port impulse engine.

"How's it goin', laddie?" Scotty asked him.

The big Celt snorted. "Balky as ever, Scotty. Th' upper-left quadrant is out o' phase, and I'm havin' t' shave th' lower-right quadrant t' fit. Tricky job, but I'll be done wi' it soon."

Scotty nodded tiredly. "I've got th' other lads cleanin' up th' last o' th' shorts in th' electrical system." He sighed. "I've ne'er seen th' poor girl hurtin' so badly."

MacPherson nodded. "You can be proud o' her, Scotty. Any other ship would have given up th' ghost an' just fallen apart if it'd gone through what this one has. This old girl o' yours ha' been fightin' like th' very devil, and she's come through it all in high style."

Scotty nodded again, but this time with more than a trace of pride. "I tell people o'er and o'er thot th' *Enterprise* is a special sort of ship wi' a life o' her own. She's got personality, this one does."

"I know. Th' *Gagarin* wasn't like her at all. No soul t' that bucket."

"Ah, lad, we did all right together when we served on her. But I know what ye mean, sure enough." Scotty paused. *"Gagarin* was like a hundred other ships I've set foot on. When I get t' Earth an' take the British Air flight from Heathrow to visit the old home places, I don't care about which plane I'm on; I couldn't e'en tell ye which one it was." Scotty patted a wall. "Planes ha' nae personality. Most ships don't, either. But this ol' girl is different. I'll be takin' a piece o' her soul wi' me wherever I happen t' be goin'. She's got style, laddie, and that style's served us all, includin' the captain himself."

"Hmmm." MacPherson tightened a connection on the Delaney valve and touched its coverplate here and there with a magnetic polarizer. "I think that'll do it," he said. "Let's try her out." The chief entered a series of codes onto a touchplate near the valve, and a green light winked on. MacPherson watched the valve carefully.

"Telltales all green, coolant flow nominal." MacPherson nodded, satisfied. "Now if th' valve doesn't blow, I'd say th' impulse engines are as good as they e'er were."

"Wish I could say th' same for the warp drive," Scotty replied. "But there's nae fixin' *thot* without a drydock and some new crystals. But th' impulse engines will get us t' Starbase Seven—not fast, but they'll get us there." He smiled. "An' when we get there, bucko, I'm goin' t' latch onto every gadget and gimcrack the latest catalog offers for a starship, and I'll be crammin' this darlin' t' th' overheads with th' best and most glitterin' things anyone ever saw."

Scotty patted the wall again, affectionately. "The ol' girl deserves th' best, don'tcha think?"

Dossie Flores was once again handling the helm and navigation stations; with the bridge roster stripped down for planetside duty, she and Peter Siderakis were working heel-and-toe watches. "Lieutenant Uhura?" she called. "Telltales indicate impulse engines are once again fully operational. Coolant circulation is nominal." She grinned. "If we have to beat it, we won't have to worry about springing a leak anymore."

Uhura smiled back. "Thanks, Deadeye." Boneweary, she got up and went over to the science officer's station, where Scotty had thoughtfully rigged a coffeemaker. The galley's delivery tubes had gone out when the computers had been wrecked, and so the usual goodies that came the bridge's way now had to be fetched by hand. The coffeemaker had been provided as a convenience, but Uhura now saw it as a necessity.

I don't know what I'd do without coffee, Uhura thought as she poured her sixth cup of the watch. *I think I've been up—what, thirty hours straight?* Her eyes were heavy with fatigue; she had grabbed a ten-minute doze in the command chair earlier, and that had helped for a while, but she could use another. *I don't think I've been this tired since I crammed for my Starfleet communicator's license exam.*

There wasn't any sugar left; Uhura didn't care. She added some whitener and sipped. *Good.*

A light winked on her communications board: IN-COMING TRAFFIC. *The Starfleet channel?* Uhura thought as she went over to answer it; she hadn't thought it necessary to man communications at all times, and Sergei Dominico had gratefully wobbled off to grab some sleep.

She put on her earphone and settled herself in her chair. *"Enterprise* here, Lieutenant Uhura."

Nothing. Just static.

"This is the U.S.S. *Enterprise,* in orbit around Alpha Centauri IV. We are not receiving you. Please boost your signal."

Did the static clear a tiny bit? Was there a voice in there somewhere? Uhura couldn't tell.

The INCOMING TRAFFIC indicator went out. Reluctantly Uhura cleared her board. Almost casually, she pressed the TRACE SIGNAL command, hoping that what was left of the ship's computer complex had remembered to log the call and its direction. *I hope it's not just a computer phantom,* she thought. *I don't think Scotty can cope with another repair, and Spock's not here to do it for him. God, I'm tired.* She yawned widely; the coffee wasn't helping much anymore.

An indicator panel lit. TRACE COMPLETE.

"Origin of call?" Uhura asked aloud.

COORDINATES 347 MARK 5. RANGE 3,210 KM. ERROR PLUS OR MINUS SIX PERCENT.

Huh? thought Uhura, confused. *That close aboard?* The sensors showed nothing approaching them, and there was no one and nothing else in this sky. *Just*

203

another computer glitch, I guess, she told herself, frustrated.

Then it hit her, and she came fully awake with the shock of it. *The coordinates!* she realized. *'Mark 5' is* straight down! *That call made it through the tachyonic blanket!*

A few minutes later, after Uhura and Flores had done some quick figuring, they found where 347 mark 5 was, relative to the *Enterprise:* It was somewhere in the middle of New America, one-third of the distance between New Athens (where Spock was) and McIverton (where Kirk was). That didn't help Uhura at all. *Who sent the call?* she wondered. *The captain, Mr. Spock, or somebody else? Or was it a computer phantom, after all? But the interference* could *be clearing a little; it's been days since the antimatter blast.*

What also didn't help was that the coordinates pinpointed a circle almost 630 kilometers around, or more than thirty thousand square kilometers in area. Uhura decided that *pinpointed* wasn't quite the word.

It was all very mysterious.

Chapter Twenty:
McIverton

THE CABINET HAD been up all night. If its members had been growing tired from their long and sometimes pointless discussions, the news of Kirk's successful escape that early morning had fully awakened them. They sat around the conference table. Some of the more brainless presidential appointees were still nattering uselessly about Centaurus's planetary rights and the pursuit of justice.

But Burke was bent on revenge. That involved justice, but only coincidentally. He had concealed his impatience well—but it was time to act. Kirk had flown the coop, and here these people were, still arguing over whose fault it was.

Perez, the defense minister, was at the table, silent as he usually was in Cabinet meetings. *He used to take his cues directly from the president,* thought Burke—referring to the deceased holder of that office, not the spineless idiot presently serving as chief executive—*and now he takes them from me. Good; I need him.*

Burke held Perez with his eyes for a moment; the defense minister nodded almost imperceptibly. Burke rose and cleared his throat in the middle of the statement by the minister of tourism.

"Mr. President?" Burke said. "May I humbly suggest that, while we all appreciate the thoughts of the distinguished minister of tourism on the subject of our legal rights in this matter—and I personally thank her for those valuable thoughts—we are faced with a pressing problem that demands action. I would like to talk about that."

The president sat impassively in his fine leather chair, looking at Burke. Erikkson, Burke's colleague in the old Cabinet, had always been impressed by Burke's single-minded approach to his work and had always respected him . . . and feared him a bit, too. Erikkson made no objection and gave no encouragement; that was enough for Burke, and he began. The minister of tourism, a large woman overdressed for an emergency Cabinet meeting, sat down, obviously miffed at being interrupted.

"Here's the logistical situation," Burke said. "Kirk and Sulu have escaped their hotel in the company of Samuel Cogley. We have to catch them. We are not at war with the Federation, we are not mad at the Federation; I think everyone in this room will agree that we do not wish to offend the Federation any more than can be helped. But we do not want to see the people who helped destroy New Athens escape justice—*and we will not allow it!*"

There was a murmur of approval in the room.

"We all know Cogley's record," Burke continued. "There's a good chance that Barclay and his bunch will walk out of a Federation court with a ticket to a nice, soft rehab colony. My guess is that—and I'm backed by some legal opinion on this—if we ask a Federation court for Barclay and company's return to Centaurus for trial, our application to the court would be turned down. Federation policy prohibits the death penalty for terrorist murder; Centaurian law demands it. The Federation says its interests in this case override ours because an annihilation weapon was used. I don't agree; we're the ones who lost the people."

The rumble of agreement was louder.

"And I don't see the Federation returning prisoners to face a capital charge. It's as simple as that. So my job is to see that Barclay and his friends never leave this planet.

"Let me be brief. We knew Reuben Barclay disappeared from his usual haunts in New Athens a week before Holtzman's deadline. With the other leaders of the League for a Pure Humanity still in the city, negotiating with the government, Barclay obviously figured *he'd* be the big man in the League if the worst happened. It did, and Barclay's the head of what's left of the League now; all the other leaders are dead. That, in fact, has led us to believe that the explosion was an accident—at least in its timing. It doesn't make sense that the top men in the League would hang around and wait to die; I think they were willing to postpone the deadline indefinitely—but something unexpected happened, and we'll probably never know just what it was.

"I guessed—correctly, as it turned out—that Samuel Cogley's presence in McIverton for a seminar would trigger an approach by Barclay. Cogley is a well-known lawyer with a bent for accepting 'impossible' cases—and winning them. That would attract Barclay. So I put two of my best men on Cogley's trail, and it paid off: We saw two of Barclay's henchmen approach Cogley yesterday morning. Unfortunately, we lost the two flunkies; they turned out to be pretty good at shaking a tail. But we stayed with Cogley, who went to see Kirk last evening at his hotel. He talked with Kirk for most of the night; I suppose they were planning Barclay's surrender. We couldn't plant a bug in Kirk's room because there wasn't a chance to do so, and like most luxury hotels, the Hilton Inn West proofs its windows against laserdropping; business types don't like the competition reading voice vibrations off windows.

"But one of my men noted that Kirk's shuttle pilot, Sulu, was out all night, presumably doing the town. On his own initiative, my man broke into Sulu's room, faked a note from Kirk, and left a packet of—well, it doesn't matter what. It's sufficient to say that Sulu was drugged in order to slow up Kirk, should Kirk decide to leave suddenly."

"Wasn't that a rather extreme thing to do?" asked the finance minister—a rather prissy type, Burke thought.

"I've already ordered a citation of merit issued to the agent involved," Burke said tersely. "To continue: Kirk overpowered the men I had watching him at the hotel, and Cogley picked him and Sulu off the roof in a flitter. They then disappeared into city traffic. Normally we'd run a trace through a spyeye using the flitter's transponder—but all the satellites were shot down by the defense system. We put out a radio alert, of course, but damn few police facilities have radios, and the normal communications bands are still swamped by tachyonic interference. Kirk, Sulu and Cogley got away, and they haven't been seen since. Their shuttle is still at the airfield, but it's useless to us."

"So what can we do?" asked the labor minister.

"It occurred to me," said Burke, "that the key to this whole situation was Kirk, but that we didn't know much about him at all. I ran his Starfleet records; the non-confidential stuff is all in the central databanks, and fortunately the New Athens 'banks were duplicated here as they were accumulated. Kirk's record is quite distinguished, but he's never had a job to do quite like this one. I doubt he likes it very much; the sense I get is that everything in him rebels against legal maneuvering—especially the possibility that guilty men might escape punishment for their crimes. Kirk is direct, a touch moralistic and, above all, ethical."

"So?" the minister of tourism asked coldly.

"So—I think that attitude will take the edge off Kirk's performance. His heart won't quite be in saving Barclay and his pals from us. Mind you, he has every intention of doing his duty, of bringing Barclay and the others to Earth for trial—but he's rebelling against that somewhere inside, where it counts. That gives *us* an edge.

"But there was something else, something I didn't expect to find," Burke continued. "I think I know where Kirk is."

Everyone in the room, except Perez, was startled. Finally the finance minister's voice rose above the others. "Well, where the hell *is* he, then?"

"Kirk is a registered landowner here," Burke said. "He's got a beautiful piece of land in the middle of this continent; there's a Ministry of Land Management file on it a meter thick, all consisting of prefiled offers to buy, should Kirk fall behind on his taxes. He's even got a cabin there. If I were Kirk and running, I'd head there. I wouldn't expect anyone to make the connection, at least not before my ship could pick me up. And it was just damn lucky I *did* make the connection."

"What do you need, Nathaniel?" Erikkson asked.

Burke told him; Perez nodded approval. "All right, then," Erikkson said. "A small force, lightly armed, to arrest Barclay and the other four. I won't authorize the arrests of Kirk, Sulu or Cogley; they're just doing their jobs, and they could probably make a case against *us*. We'll just let them leave."

Burke nodded; he was satisfied. "Thank you, Mr. President," he said. "Now, if you'll excuse us, Minister Perez and I have a lot to do."

"Of course," Erikkson said.

In the hallway outside, Perez said to Burke, "Nice job, Nat—but what would he have said if he'd known we sent that force out two hours ago? And that it's not so lightly armed?"

Burke smiled without humor. "What could he have done about it?" He paused. "I'm leaving for Garrovick Valley now. Flitter's on the roof. Want to come along?"

"Wouldn't miss it," said Perez.

Chapter Twenty-One:
New Athens

CHEKOV WOKE SHORTLY after second sunrise to the rising hubbub of the survivors' camp in Founders Park. Sleepily he looked around the small, darkened boathouse utility room in which he and Spock had spent the night, mixed in among Dr. Weinstein's small hoard of supplies. Spock was lying supine on his own bedroll against the opposite wall, his eyes open. *I vonder if he is avake yet,* thought Chekov.

Spock did not stir when Chekov sat up, which told Chekov that Spock was asleep—or was in a state of what passed for sleep—and whatever portion of his brain the Vulcan had put on sentry duty had been ordered not to pay attention to Chekov's movements. Chekov knew of a time once, during an emergency, when Spock had managed to stay awake for weeks without resting—something he had managed to do only through his iron control of supposedly involuntary bodily functions. But Chekov also knew it had been more weeks until Spock had fully recovered from the ordeal.

Chekov had slept in his uniform, and its fabric did not wrinkle. He grabbed his personal kit and quietly left the room. He wished his body were as resilient as his Starfleet clothes; he ached all over from sleeping on the floor. The day before had been busy—in all, he'd flown four round trips between Weinstein's camp and the *Enterprise* for supplies, plus hours of ambulance and reconnaissance work—and three hours of sleep had not been enough. *A shower is too much to ask, I know, but perhaps there is coffee,* Chekov told himself hopefully. *Perhaps there is ewen a lump or two of sugar for it. I vill not dare hope for a Danish to go vith it.*

There was a breakfast line just outside the boathouse. Some two thousand of the refugees in Founders Park had been detailed by Weinstein for food roundup duty. Working together, the food teams had virtually cleared the northern section of New Athens of supplies and were working their way south. The park did not have stasis fields—broadcast power was out for the duration—so all supplies had to be nonperishable.

Sanitary arrangements were less formal and involved a series of long trenches dug in a soccer field next to the main camp. Modesty was up to the user; generally, modesty was ignored. Chekov was glad there was a small head aboard *Columbus;* there was even a sink.

The breakfast line wasn't very long this soon after second sunrise; Chekov soon made it to the big coffee urns a team had salvaged from a Sears, Roebuck in the southern part of the city. There wasn't any Danish or sugar, but there *were* tubs of reconstituted scrambled eggs. Chekov thought they would go down well.

The middle-aged woman serving the eggs smiled toothily at Chekov as she ladled some onto his plate. Chekov thanked her and, looking around, found a big tree to sit under; the old veteran had somehow managed to keep most of its leaves through all the troubles that had beset the city. Chekov grabbed a plastic fork from a bin with a sign that read DON'T THROW ANYTHING AWAY! and ambled over to the tree, taking care not to disturb the sleeping people he walked past and sometimes over.

He sat and relaxed, looking up into the sky. It was going to be another heavily overcast day, and that was a good thing. Chekov doubted that very many of these people had managed to bring their sunglasses with them as they fled their homes, and the overcast would save Weinstein and his people from treating thousands of cases of sunglare.

Such things led Chekov to think of Connie Iziharry. She was somewhere around here, Chekov knew, but it wouldn't be easy to find her—and Chekov was not sure he wanted to. Well, yes, he did . . . but he did not want to part from her again, and it would be easier not meeting her in the first place. Chekov stared into his coffee cup. *I thought it might have been for real,* he mused. *I really thought so, this time. I am indeed— what is Sulu's English word?—a yerk.*

"Hi, Pavel," came a voice.

"Hello, Connie," Chekov said, rising. "You look tired."

"Thanks," Connie Iziharry said. "So do you."

Chekov was embarrassed. "I did not mean to be rude, Connie. I vas concerned. Please forgive me."

Iziharry sighed. "No, *I'm* sorry, Pavel. I *am* tired, and it's beginning to get to me. Where's the coffee?"

"Over there." They walked back to the breakfast line together; Connie's status as a camp nurse allowed her to go to the head of the line without waiting. She refilled Chekov's cup and got one for herself.

They went back to the tree and sat silently for a while. Then Connie said, "Lucky I found you."

"I haven't been around the camp much," Chekov

said. "Ve—myself and Mr. Spock—vere flying most of the night. He is still inside. I am staying close to the boathouse until I find out vhat he vants to do today."

"More of the same, I suppose."

"I imagine. But when Captain Kirk and Mr. Sulu return from McIverton, ve vill have another shuttle for recon and supply duty. I vill velcome that."

"I'll bet you will," Connie said. She paused. "Pavel, I wanted you to know. I'm planning to stay here, even after the *Enterprise* leaves."

Pain lanced through Chekov, but he kept his face impassive.

"I've been talking to Dr. Weinstein and a few other people. This city—the whole planet—will take years to come back from this, this disaster. They need all the help they can get. And I'm *from* here, Pavel—oh, not from New Athens, but it's my world—and I have to help. My blood is here."

She laughed self-consciously. "I joined Starfleet to get the hell away from here. I guess I thought they didn't need me . . . oh, I don't know *what* I thought. But I'm a good nurse, Pavel, and Saul Weinstein needs a good nurse even more than Bones McCoy."

"Have you talked to Dr. McCoy?" Chekov asked.

"Yes. He'll approve my resignation request, and he says he's sure the captain will, too." Connie paused. "Pavel, what I wanted to ask you . . ."

Chekov waited.

"Well," Iziharry continued, "it's like this: Navigators can quit the service, too, you know."

Chekov blinked. "Resign? Me? And do vhat?"

"*Stay* with me, you goof!" She was smiling . . . but her eyes appeared frightened of something.

Oh my dear sweet God, Chekov thought. *I cannot do this, stay on vone vorld only. Not even for her. Oh, no. Vhy did this have to happen?*

Connie's hopeful smile faded as she watched Chekov's face. She nodded slowly. "You won't," she said flatly. "You're a wanderer. You belong out there, among the stars. I thought I did too, once, but it took all this to prove I was wrong."

She paused. "I hoped that . . . maybe . . . you'd find the same thing was true of yourself." A tear rolled down her cheek; she wiped at it. "Sorry. Anyway . . . I'm sorry I wasn't enough to make you stay."

"No, Connie," Chekov said quickly. "Please! You do *not* understand—I cannot do this thing you ask. I ask you, in return, just to think about it for a vhile. Ve only arrived yesterday, Connie, and you have decided today to stay? Is that fair to yourself? To *me?*"

"You don't know the nightmares I had, Pavel. I'd wake up in the middle of the night aboard the ship while we were on our way here. Death, destruction, my parents suffering; everyone I loved, horribly gone. Maybe I was screaming; I don't know. You thought I was being shy about—certain things—but I just couldn't have anybody see me like that. And when I got here, Pavel, and started working . . . well, all the fear and the sorrow stopped. I felt like I was doing something useful and worthwhile, maybe for the first time in my life."

Chekov at last nodded slowly.

"And you would be looking at the stars every night if you stayed here with me," Connie said. "I know I couldn't bear that." She paused. "If you ever change your mind, Pavel, you know where to find me."

She kissed him quickly. "I have to run. I love you."

And she did. Chekov watched her go, even after he could no longer see her in the gathering crowds of morning.

He stood there, silent and still, for several minutes until Spock approached. "Good morning, Ensign," the Vulcan said briskly. "I trust you are adequately rested? It is time for our check-in with the ship."

"Coming, Mr. Spock."

Not long after that, *Columbus* was back in the air over New Athens, on an approach course for the *Enterprise*.

Uhura had decided to raise hell. Her calls to McIverton over the shortwave had finally roused the night duty officer at the presidential offices, and her persistent demands that Captain Kirk speak to her had finally brought President Erikkson to the microphone. Uhura soon satisfied herself that there was trouble; Erikkson seemed—unfriendly.

And there was that mysterious trace from the middle of the continent.

Uhura put two and two together. She had seen people do that in the past and get an answer of five, but her instincts told her she was right.

And she *always* trusted her instincts.

It was time for Spock to take hold of things.

Chapter Twenty-Two:
Garrovick Valley

KIRK COULD EASILY remember standing watches more unpleasant than this one.

The captain was actually rather content. Here he was in his favorite place, sitting in an utterly comfortable, custom-contoured chair, a steaming coffeepot to his left and a thick, good book in his lap. The spotlamp he was using did not disturb those sleeping in the room.

It was the middle of a beautifully mild and quiet Centaurian night, and Kirk was home, for the first time in quite a while. The hell with the circumstances; he was enjoying it.

Kirk glanced at the luminous chronometer on the far wall. It read 02:77, and that meant just about twenty-five Centaurian minutes to the end of his watch. Kirk yawned.

He glanced over at the bed. Sulu—like Kirk, still dressed in civilian clothing—was dead to the world. *Let him sleep*, Kirk decided. *Another hour or two of this won't kill me—and Sulu's still got a good dose of that drug, whatever it was, in him. He should sleep it off.* Kirk walked back to his chair, poured himself a fifth cup of coffee, and picked up his book. It was one of his oldest: Asimov's *Foundation Trilogy,* a timeless piece of work Kirk had read twice before.

He got lost in it again, and the next time he looked at the chronometer it read 05:52. *Good God,* Kirk thought ruefully. *The night's almost gone. Well, Sulu, you owe me a couple of hours' sack time, I think.* With a little regret, Kirk folded the dustcover flap into the book to hold his place, and put it down next to the now-empty coffeepot. His eyes felt gritty; his mouth tasted worse.

Kirk switched off the spotlamp and stood. The sky was beginning to lighten as firstdawn approached his mountains. Soon the birds would greet the day with song; Kirk decided he wanted to be outside for that. He grabbed his jacket and put it on against the early-morning chill. He opened the cabin door quietly and stepped outside.

ZZZZZSSSSssssss! went past his ear.

Instinctively Kirk crouched and flung himself back inside, slamming the door shut with his booted foot. "Everybody *up!*" he ordered. "Sulu! Weapons case. Fast!"

The helmsman had risen quickly at the slam of the door. Now he ducked under the bed and retrieved a suitcase-sized black case with an *Enterprise* insigne on it: a standard-issue shuttlecraft portable weapons case. It looked like leather but was much tougher than that, and any attempt to force it open would result in its destruction—and the destruction of everything else within a radius of fifty meters. Sulu pressed his thumb against a touchplate on the lock; the case decided it was allowed to open, and it did.

Sulu passed phasers, pistol grips and extra power packs to Kirk and Cogley, and kept a set for himself. He relocked the case, slamming it shut.

Barclay and his four associates were awake, now.

"Smith" and "Jones" were sitting on the floor, watching Kirk and Sulu examine their weapons. Cogley was looking at his own phaser, a bit mystified; he had never held one before. Max and Dave were looking warily out the front window. Barclay was reclining comfortably on his bedroll, his arms folded underneath his head; he didn't seem to have a care in the world.

"What's happening, Captain?" asked "Jones." He looked a little mussed.

"We've been shot at," Kirk said shortly. "High-energy-level weapon. We must have a nice char mark on the front of the cabin now." Kirk did not mention that the beam had passed his head no farther away than ten centimeters; otherwise, he would not have heard it. He tagged it as a focused phaser blast, invisible and silent—and deadly.

It was not as efficient as a standard phaser blast, so it didn't have as great a range—which only meant that whoever it was outside was too damned close to the cabin to suit Kirk.

Barclay's eyebrows went up. "So. We've been followed," he drawled. "I don't think much of your hiding place, Captain."

"You can't afford to sneer, Barclay," Kirk said. "You're too close to being dead right now. So shut that hole in your face and stay down on the floor."

"Who fired that shot?" Burke raged, not far away.

"Dunno, sir," a lieutenant colonel in the Security Service replied. "Coulda been anyone in that stand of trees over there." He pointed; about fifteen troops in camouflage gear had taken shelter there, preparatory to raiding Kirk's cabin.

"When this is over, Colonel, I want a full investigation," Burke said through gritted teeth. "Your man has blown the element of surprise in this mission. Now we have to capture alive a number of men who don't want to be taken—and they're backed up by one of the toughest men in Starfleet!"

"We'll get 'em, Minister Burke," the lieutenant colonel said, a touch nervously.

"Oh, you'd better," Burke returned, too quietly. *Those bastards in there killed my wife and kids, and if you think they're getting a chance to get away because some damn fool punk squeezed off a shot, you're crazier than they are. Who the hell did you lose in New Athens, Colonel?*

"And let me remind you of your orders, Colonel," Burke continued, scathingly. "You are not to take any, repeat, *any* offensive action against Captain Kirk or Lieutenant Sulu. I don't care what they're wearing—Starfleet uniforms, civilian suits, or your Aunt Mabel's kitchen apron—you know what those two men look like; I showed you the pictures myself. I'm warning you, Colonel: Be more careful. Your force may defend itself if Kirk and Sulu resist—but Kirk and Sulu are Federation officers and will be treated as such. They are *not* the enemy! Your men will *not* take potshots at them, as if this were some Thanksgiving Day turkey shoot! *Got that?*"

"Yessir!" the lieutenant colonel said, his jaw clenched. "Permission to proceed, sir?"

"Go." The man saluted and went.

Perez strolled over and stood beside Burke. "Sorry for the foul-up, Nat. Deerfield's a good man, though; I think you were a little hard on him."

"Oh, really?" Burke said coldly, still looking toward the cabin. "He may be *your* man, Dan, but it's *my* operation. Take some advice: Don't forget it."

After a moment Perez went away, too, leaving Burke alone with his vengeance. Nobody dared bother Burke again after that.

* * *

Crouching below the front windowsill, Kirk watched the hills. Once in a while he thought he could see some movement of the foliage against the wind. The presence of a few infiltrators indicated the presence of many; from what Kirk knew of standard encirclement tactics, he guessed there must be a force of seventy or eighty in the area. *Well, we can eliminate the notion of running for it,* he thought. *We're surrounded.*

"Well, Kirk?" Barclay demanded. "Just what are you going to do to ensure our safety?"

Kirk ignored him.

"I'm talking to you, Captain. I demand the courtesy of an answer."

"I'd advise you to be a little more quiet, Mr. Barclay," Sam Cogley said from his position at the other window. "The captain is rather busy."

"When I want your advice, Cogley, I'll tell you," Barclay snapped. "Kirk, if you're thinking of surrendering us, let me tell you this: Don't do it. You wouldn't like the consequences." Barclay smiled nastily.

"Keep your client quiet, Sam," Kirk advised. His mind was on other things. Tactically, their situation was desperate. Kirk had two men to protect five other men, none of whom could be trusted with a weapon. Kirk knew these woods far better than the members of the invading force, but that knowledge was useless as long as Kirk was confined to the cabin. The cabin had no secret exits, no arms cache, no transporter pad, not even a flying carpet.

All that the infiltrators had to do was storm the cabin; three men could not hold off nearly a hundred—not for long, anyway. An infantry combat phaser on heavy stun would do the job. That assumed, of course, that Burke—Kirk knew it had to be Burke out there, and maybe Perez, too—was interested in taking them alive. He wasn't sure about that, but the fact that the cabin and those in it still existed was a good sign. If Burke wanted them all dead, then one plane dropping one "smart" bomb could have done the job during the night. The assumption that Burke wanted them alive severely limited what Burke could do to capture them—as long as Barclay and his boys didn't try to leave the valley.

That meant they had time—a little, anyway. "Watch the window, Sulu," Kirk ordered as he took his communicator from his belt. He flipped it open; the initiating signal went out, but there was no answerback. Communications were still out.

Kirk's only alternative to voice communication would have been a ground-to-space laser signaler—and *Galileo* didn't have one aboard; a signaler wasn't standard equipment, according to the book. That was an oversight Kirk would remedy within one minute of his return to the *Enterprise* . . . assuming he *did* return. Under these conditions Kirk could have simply poked a hole in the roof, stuck the nozzle of the signaler through it and fired a beam of coherent light into space. Visible light would pass through the tachyonic interference barrier as if it were glass; the *Enterprise*'s sensors would then quickly find the laser beam and trace it back to its source. They *did* have phasers, but the weapons could not fire a powerful enough beam to be detected from orbit.

Thinking of his ship again, Kirk looked up—and saw a swarm of jeeplike military flitters and, above them, several fixed-wing jet aircraft. *They've got the sky covered, too,* Kirk thought. He discarded his half-formed plan of creating a diversion while Sulu hustled everyone else into Cogley's flitter and took off. No matter what Kirk did, the sky forces would easily target Cogley's civilian clunker and bring it down—

possibly gently, with tractor beams . . . but perhaps not so gently, with a pair of air-to-air missiles.

Kirk ran it through his mind again. *We're relatively safe as long as we stay in here, as long as Burke knows where we are and feels he's in control. If we leave, Burke will think he's losing control, and we're dead. But we've got to leave. Now just how the hell are you going to pull* this *one off, Jim?*

Kirk was frank enough with himself to admit he could see no way out, short of abject surrender to Burke—and the surrender of his prisoners to planetary authority. That was strictly against his orders . . . not to mention Federation law. Kirk was more stubborn than to give in. He had arrested these weasels; he was responsible for them. He'd see this thing through, and he'd beat Burke.

But he was damned if he knew how.

Chapter Twenty-Three:
The *Enterprise*

THE TURBOLIFT DOORS squeaked open, and the returning party from the *Columbus*—Spock, Chekov, and both McCoys—stepped quickly onto the bridge.

Joanna McCoy had never been aboard a ship of the line before; her experience was limited to small impulse-only craft on the rare occasions she had gone to Starbase 7 as a child. She looked around curiously. Those on the bridge, realizing who she must be, grinned and waved quickly before turning back to their duties. A bit self-consciously, she smiled and waved back. *I wish I didn't look like something the ocelot dragged in,* she thought.

She would not be aboard the *Enterprise* now if her Uncle Jim weren't in trouble. She liked Uncle Jim a lot, and she had never allowed herself to wonder just why. She had also not yet been willing to be separated from her father, now having been with him and worked with him as a colleague for several days—but her sense of duty would have prevented her from leaving with Bones McCoy for that reason alone. However, once her father had told her why he was leaving Dr. Weinstein's camp, Joanna had quickly asked to come along. Both Spock and Weinstein had okayed it.

"I have the conn, Miss Uhura," Spock said. "Mr.

Chekov, please take the science officer's station; I will be needed in the command chair. Miss Flores, I realize you have been on duty for some hours, but I ask that you remain in the navigator's position."

"Of course, sir," Dossie Flores said as Chekov slid into Spock's usual seat.

"Miss Uhura, is there anything I need to know before I determine a course of action?" Spock asked.

"I don't think so, sir," Uhura said from her communications station. "While you were all on your way back up here, I attempted sensor readings of the area from which we received the subspace communications blip, but interference is still swamping most sensor frequencies. Those that still work are useless to us in the search."

Spock thought for a moment. "Since you have not heard from the captain or Mr. Sulu, you have rightly assumed that there has been trouble. Your second assumption—that the communications blip was a signal from Captain Kirk—is actually two assumptions: one, that the blip was not an anomaly and, two, that the captain was responsible for it. It might have been Mr. Sulu, or a third party unknown to us."

"Oh, stop the lesson in logic, Spock!" Bones McCoy said, exasperated. "Where the hell is Jim?"

Spock was unperturbed. "I was about to say that Chief MacPherson has checked the communications system for anomalies in the tracer subassemblies and has found none—"

"Aye, thot's correct," boomed MacPherson from his engineering station.

"—and so I believe Miss Uhura's assumptions were warranted. As for the precise origin of the signal . . ." The science officer held out a computer-generated map of the hemisphere below them; it showed a standard projection of New America. A large circular area was shaded.

"The signal came from somewhere inside the shadowed area," Spock finished. He handed it to McCoy, who looked at it briefly. Joanna glanced at it, and then looked more closely.

"I believe we will have to perform a visual search of the entire area, since we cannot do better with the sensors under present conditions," Spock said. "A random pattern will suit us best—"

"Mr. Spock? Excuse me," Joanna interrupted. "Daddy, the valley's on this map. Right here." She indicated it with a finger; it was on the eastern edge of the shaded area. McCoy nodded, then *hmmm'd* as he realized what his daughter was implying.

"The valley?" Spock inquired. "Which valley, Miss McCoy?"

"Garrovick Valley, Mr. Spock," Joanna answered. "Captain Kirk might have gone there."

"I think she's right, Spock," McCoy said. "I should have seen it myself."

"Garrovick Valley?" Spock said, curious. "Named after the captain's former commander aboard the *Farragut?*" The Vulcan took the map back. "I see the valley is not named on this map, but there is a Farragut River running through it. I infer the captain had something to do with bestowing names on these geological features?"

"Very good, Spock," Bones McCoy said. "Jim owns most of the land you have right there under your finger." He paused. "I'm surprised he's never told you about it."

"He has obviously never felt the need to do so," Spock said. "Miss McCoy, do you have any reason to believe the captain would have gone there, as opposed to another place in the search area?"

"He loves it there, Mr. Spock. He has a cabin with full facilities. He keeps it well-stocked with supplies. If he had to hide, I think he'd do it there. I know I would."

Spock nodded. "Would the cabin happen to have a commander's communications unit installed in it?" he asked.

"What's that?"

Bones interrupted. "Yes, it does. It was put in when Jim got the *Enterprise*. He hid it behind a bookcase—"

"Thank you, Doctor," Spock said, cutting him off. "Mr. Chekov, since our sensors are virtually useless to us in this instance, I'll need a visual inspection of the area immediately surrounding the captain's cabin. Miss Uhura, I believe you can guide Mr. Chekov in the use of the long-range cameras?"

"Of course, sir." Uhura moved behind Chekov and began punching buttons. The main bridge viewscreen began to swim with colors. "Thank goodness visible light frequencies aren't affected by tachyonic fallout," she said.

A picture formed. "That is the walley in qvestion from an apparent height of two hundred kilometers," Chekov said. No one could see anything out of the ordinary; at that apparent altitude, they might have missed the Great Wall of China if it had been in the valley. "Going to extreme magnification now."

The picture swam again. "Apparent height now, uh, five kilometers—look there!" Chekov pointed; there seemed to be a swarm of motes circling and careening in the air over the valley. "Aircraft, many of them!" Chekov said excitedly.

"There does seem to be something in the valley attracting them," Spock said dryly. "Miss McCoy, your intuition has served us well. Mr. Chekov, the magnification is insufficient to see if our people are in the valley, but I think we can assume such to be the case."

"Well, I sure would," Bones McCoy said. "Spock, what are we going to do about this?"

Spock paused. "If the captain is under attack, then this ship will, of course, go to his aid. Mr. Siderakis?"

"Yes, Mr. Spock?" the helmsman replied.

"Phaser status, please."

"Charged and ready, sir. Manual aiming and firing mode only; computer guidance is out."

"Have phasers standing by," Spock said. He stroked his chin thoughtfully. "I am reluctant to go in shooting. I saw no evidence of armed force being used against the captain's postulated position; I was looking for fire, smoke and other indications of violence. I also do not intend to take the *Enterprise* into battle against a friendly power."

"They're not being so damn friendly, Spock," McCoy grated. "It looks like the invasion of Altair VI down there."

"I realize that, Doctor—but there may be another way to accomplish our goal." Spock took out his communicator and flipped it open. "Spock to Mr. Scott."

"Aye, Scott here."

"Mr. Scott, I require your presence on the bridge."

"Verra well, Mr. Spock. I'll be right up. Scott out."

A few minutes later Scott was on the bridge—and he was talking very loudly indeed.

"Ye want t' do *what* with ma ship?" he was saying. "Are ye daft, sir?"

"My mental functions are unimpaired, Mr. Scott," Spock said patiently. "I suggest that you calm yourself. I have asked you a question; I need an answer."

"Aye, sir, then here's one," Scott said. "Ye canna take a starship inta atmosphere and expect her t' perform with anything approachin' precision. Ye may remember th' time we hit th' black hole and got bounced through spacetime, right inta old Earth's atmosphere. We had th' devil's own trouble makin' standard orbit from there—and th' ship was in far better condition then than now."

"I do not require any great degree of precision, Mr. Scott. I simply wish to prevent the *Enterprise* from crashing into the surface. Can that be done?"

Scott shook his head. "Mr. Spock, with all respect, this ship is not a glider. She canna handle high-altitude winds—or low-altitude ones, either. Our drift compensators are nae workin' right, and they're nae built to handle winds anyhow. I canna say wha' outside weather conditions might do t' th' impulse engines; th' outside weather might bother them, since they were nae designed for planetary conditions. Th' *Enterprise* is nae a landing craft and shares none o' th' abilities with same."

"Thank you for the information, Mr. Scott," Spock said. "I am now aware of the reasons why an approach to the surface would be difficult. My question, however, concerned whether such an approach is possible or impossible under present ship's conditions."

Scott blew out a breath. "The ol' girl's hurtin' too much, Mr. Spock. It pains me to say it's nae possible."

There was a moment of silence. Then Alec Mac-Pherson rose from his chair and cleared his throat.

"Scotty, if ye will pardon me?" the big Scot began. He cleared his throat again. "I beg t' differ wi' me boss on this matter, wi' all respect t' him."

Scotty looked surprised. So did some others on the bridge. This was the first instance in which the "twins" had publicly disagreed.

"'Tis true thot th' warp engines are out for th' duration, until we haul ourselves t' a starbase for crystal replacement and a major rewirin' job." Mac-Pherson paused. "But I think I see a way t' route impulse engine control through th' warp-drive governors—and as ye know, Scotty, th' warp governors are many times more precise than those for th' impulse engines."

Scotty blinked. "How d'ye propose t' do that, lad?"

"The impulse engines require but three dimensions o' governance," MacPherson explained. "Hyperspace and pseudotime guidance—all that can be ignored. I can channel those navigation centers inta compensatin' for atmospheric conditions, such as wind. Scotty, d'ye see my approach yet?"

The chief engineer was nodding slowly. "Aye, thot I do, laddie. Damn, I wish I'd thought o' it ma'self. We'll do it. Mr. Spock, ma apologies; the lad's approach ought t' work. We'll see if th' ol' lassie's truly got th' right stuff or no."

"Thank you both, gentlemen. I suggest you begin your work; I do not believe we have very much time. Mr. Siderakis, prepare a course and stand by."

"Aye, aye, sir."

Spock turned his attention back to the viewscreen, and waited.

Chapter Twenty-Four:
Garrovick Valley

SECOND SUNRISE HAD come; Kirk and the others had been forced to don sunglasses against the glare from outside. The almost painful brightness was far from helpful in keeping track of the subtle movements of shrub and brush—movements that revealed to Kirk just where Burke had disposed his forces.

Kirk was sure the troops outside had much better eye protection than sunglasses.

Barclay and his fellow Leaguers sat huddled in the middle of the cabin floor; Kirk wanted them as far away as possible from any window. Barclay seemed content; the four others appeared nervous. Kirk wished he could open a window—but the shatterproof windows had turned out to be his cabin's main defensive mechanism. If Burke decided to lob a gas grenade into the cabin, he'd have to blow a hole in one of the walls first; Kirk's windows were dynaplast, not glass, and wouldn't break under anything less than the force of a good, dense mass traveling at supersonic speed.

Unfortunately, Kirk thought as he rubbed his tired eyes, the windows weren't *hyperpolarized* duraplast.

Kirk used blackout shades against glare—more primitive and cabinlike, he'd thought—and the shades had to be up so he could see out.

Not for the first time, Kirk wished he had grabbed some sleep. His every muscle ached, particularly the ones in his back; no amount of toner isometrics seemed to relieve the stiffness. He rubbed the back of his neck.

"Attention inside the cabin!" came a voice on a loudspeaker. Burke's voice.

"This is Minister of Internal Security Burke. Captain Kirk, your cabin is surrounded, as you undoubtedly realize. I require that the suspects in the New Athens bombing be turned over to Centaurian custody. We do not acknowledge that the Federation has any authority in this matter. Your arrival and subsequent actions on this planet constitute a violation of our government's sovereignty, under relevant sections of the Federation Charter.

"No one has any intention of harming Federation personnel in the course of their duties—but Federation interference in this matter cannot be tolerated. We do not intend to allow the suspects in your custody to leave this planet without all jurisdictional disputes settled."

Sam Cogley snorted. "He has no intention of settling any 'jurisdictional disputes,' " he said. "There aren't any, and he knows that."

"I know it, too, Sam," Kirk said. "It doesn't make any difference anyway. Sulu, keep a sharp eye out; Burke may be counting on his monologue to distract us a little, take our edge off."

"Aye, aye, Captain."

"We demand the immediate surrender of the suspects now in your custody," Burke continued. "You, your aide and Samuel Cogley will be free to go. You have ten minutes to consider these terms. At the end of that time, Captain, we shall be forced to take the suspects by force of arms. I await your reply."

Silence fell—but it was soon interrupted by Barclay. "I hope you realize, Kirk, that I will not tolerate a surrender," he said.

Kirk was interested. "Why not, Barclay? What can you do about it? I raise the white flag, and that's it, as far as you and your friends are concerned. No skin off my nose, just a couple of thousand words of explanation to Starfleet."

"And, no doubt, Starfleet would not mind very much—if the only consequence of your surrender was the loss of our freedom. But there is far more at stake." Barclay looked cool; he was operating now.

"Such as what?" Kirk asked, drawing him out.

Barclay was willing to be led. "Let me tell you a little story, Captain. Let's take a . . . *hypothetical* . . . planet, much like this one. Astonishingly like this one." Barclay grinned humorlessly. He had everyone's attention.

"There's a political movement on this planet we're considering," Barclay continued. "It starts with a few forward-looking citizens, who see what a debilitating effect membership in the Federation has had on a once-vibrant culture. Human and natural resources have been diverted from domestic use. Aliens have entered the local economy and have returned nothing, except for their noxious influences on a formerly pure human culture. Members of lesser human races have been allowed to persist in their ceaseless disrespect for an advanced human culture they did not and could not have attained on their own—"

"Mr. Barclay," Cogley said, "I advise you to stop. Anything you say can be held against you in court—"

"Shut up, Cogley," Barclay said. "I'm speaking

hypothetically here; the captain knows that. Don't you, Captain?"

Kirk nodded. "Go on, Barclay. I'm fascinated."

"Certainly. The struggle begins, as it must, in the old, outmoded political arenas. The small group of advanced thinkers in the movement know their program will benefit all humans; its attractions are undeniable, yet the political system will not tolerate the vast and sweeping changes being proposed. After years of struggle, it comes to pass on our hypothetical world that a brilliant but unappreciated scientist, long a member of this *hypothetical* movement, stumbles on something truly amazing, Kirk. Can you imagine what it might be?"

"Haven't the faintest idea."

"I thought not," Barclay smirked. "Strange—I would have thought that someone of your racial makeup and obvious intelligence would have worked it out long ago." *Sulu's a patient man,* thought Kirk. *I would have slugged this maggot five minutes ago.*

"I'm afraid I haven't hit on it yet, Barclay," Kirk said. "What was it—hypothetically?"

"Merely a breakthrough that, for once, gave our fictional movement the political and social power it had so long merited but been denied. Captain, what do you know of antimatter?"

"A lot."

"Then you know it is both difficult and quite costly to produce. The technique and expense are beyond the means of any organization but a multiplanetary government—or a galaxy-spanning military force, such as Starfleet." Barclay paused. "Or, I should say, it used to be."

"Go on," Kirk prompted.

"This scientist hit upon a new theory of subnuclear manipulation, Kirk. It was so simple, and so easily put into practice, that for relatively little money—and with the approval of the leaders of his movement—he himself, with no help, manufactured several hundred grams of antimatter in a basement laboratory. No heavy shielding, Kirk; no big equipment. He had little more than a simple pressor-tractor array to manipulate things the way he wanted them. He also had several simple cardboard boxes. Do you know what our imaginary friend did then, Captain?"

"I think I do, Barclay," Kirk answered, his teeth set. "He constructed several annihilation devices out of, God save us, cardboard boxes; the antimatter in each was held safely in a magnetic field, until it could be triggered by canceling the field and bringing the antimatter into contact with the surface of the box."

"Correct!" Barclay exclaimed, sarcastically clapping his hands. He was enjoying this. "In fact, he built four such devices. At once this political movement I'm talking about became the second most powerful military force in the Federation, right after the vaunted Starfleet. Three annihilation bombs were taken to different cities on our made-up planet, watched over by the most trusted people of the movement. Each was ready to detonate his or hers, and die, should circumstances require it.

"So on a certain day," Barclay continued, "this scientist visits the president of his planet and demands a political role for himself and his followers. Without revealing the specific nature of the power now backing his words, the scientist tells the president that if the movement's terms are not met, the capital of our hypothetical planet will be reduced to ruins. The old fool assumes this is a nuclear threat, similar to ones made time and again by simple-minded political activists of all stripes since the twentieth century. A thorough search for a nuclear device is made, and of course it is unsuccessful. No such device exists.

"The government does not agree to the movement's

terms. The heroic scientist at the heart of our little fiction decides that the burden is his, and his alone, to carry. He volunteers to sit somewhere in the capital area, waiting, with a harmless-looking cardboard box in his lap. Where better than a spaceport, say, to pass the time?"

Barclay stopped to light a cigar. He puffed as everyone in the room silently watched him; Kirk noticed that Max, Dave and "Jones" seemed as drawn in by Barclay's tale as Kirk himself was; "Smith," on the other hand, looked only vaguely interested.

Barclay built a finger's worth of ash, and then continued. "The deadline passes. The scientist awaits a message from the leaders of the movement, who have heroically remained in the capital to the last moment—and beyond it—in an effort to come to terms with the government. The scientist is out of touch with his comrades; he waits for some word to be brought to him."

"And then what, Barclay?" Kirk prompted.

Barclay shrugged and gestured with his cigar; a small roll of ash fell to the cabin floor. "Unknown, I'm afraid. Something rather unexpected must have happened. The word was not given, yet the device was detonated—with the promised devastating effect."

"And a million people died," Kirk said.

"Couldn't be helped," Barclay returned. He drew on his cigar and exhaled blue smoke. "But one leader of this *hypothetical* movement remains—to carry on the struggle. And there are three annihilation devices remaining to help him do so, Kirk . . . which is why I don't think you'll surrender me to the local authorities. After all, Captain, you don't want to be responsible for another million—or two million, or three million—deaths, now, do you?" Barclay smiled cynically.

"You son of a bitch," Dave snarled, rising. He leapt

at Barclay—who withdrew something quickly from somewhere inside his jacket. Kirk saw a flash of steel, and then Dave cried out with pain as he collapsed on top of Barclay. There was blood.

Dave's move had been too quick for Kirk to do anything to cover him—but he fired a stun charge at Barclay, who collapsed backward to the floor from his sitting position. His cigar rolled toward Kirk's feet; the captain pitched it into the fireplace and wiped his hand on his shirt.

"Keep those three covered, Sulu," Kirk snapped as he went to see what he could do for Dave. He rolled the man over; he had a stab wound in his gut, just under the solar plexus. Kirk didn't have a Starfleet medikit, and had only a hazy idea of what to do with one—but there was a woodsman's first-aid box in the cabin head, and Kirk fetched it. He used a compression bandage and bellyband on Dave and administered a shot of something the label said was designed to slow his metabolism. *It's for snakebite,* Kirk said to himself, reading the label on the injector, *but it may help slow the bleeding by reducing his heart rate.* Kirk wondered whether a shot for pain was contraindicated, and decided that it was; it might, he thought, slow Dave's system to the point of death.

Kirk threw a bedcover on Dave and adjusted it. The bloodstained knife had fallen near Barclay's hand; Kirk saw it was one of his own dinner knives. *The bastard must have palmed it last night,* Kirk thought. *I wish to God I'd seen this coming.*

Kirk got to his feet and turned to the three Leaguers. "Max, you didn't know about the New Athens plot." It was a statement, not a question.

Max shook his head numbly.

"But you two did," Kirk said to "Smith" and "Jones."

"Not me!" the latter said quickly. "I didn't know a damn thing about this, Captain!"

"Quiet!" ordered "Smith."

"Jones" rolled quickly away from "Smith." "Going to stab me, too, you louse? Look, Captain, my real name is Teodor Vladsilovich. I live in McIverton. I was a chapter head in the League, sort of a noncommissioned officer. God help me now, but I swallowed most of what the League stands for and tolerated the rest."

"What did you know about the plot?" Kirk demanded. He looked at Cogley. "Don't say it, Sam."

"Mr. Vladsilovich is aware of his rights under the law," Cogley said mildly. "I need not remind him of them."

"I don't care about that," Vladsilovich said. "Look, Captain, I was minding my own business, holding meetings and rallies and fund-raisers when Barclay and this guy 'Smith' show up and demand a place to stay, one where they won't be seen."

"When was that?" Kirk asked.

"Three days before New Athens went up," Vladsilovich said. "I found a house for them in Gregory's Landing. They told me they'd come west because the cops back east were after them for incitement to riot. I believed it; after all, it's a sucker charge, and the police frequently harassed our members at rallies.

"The house I got them was owned by a League member who was in New Athens on business. Uh, he never came back. You understand?"

"I think I do. Go on."

"Then New Athens happened, and I finally put two and two together. Everybody scattered. I went and hid in the Gregory's Landing house with Barclay and his friend, here; I thought the government would be looking for me, too, and I didn't have anywhere else safe to go. Max, here, came with me."

"Who *is* Max, anyway?" asked Kirk.

"Both Max and Dave were sergeants at arms at our meetings. Dave met us later."

"And who's 'Smith'?"

"I'm warning you, Vladsilovich," hissed "Smith"—but Sulu had him covered. "I'm warning *you*, creep," the helmsman said. "Smith" turned, saw the phaser pointed straight at him, and settled back, glaring at Vladsilovich.

"His real name is Holtzman," Vladsilovich said.

Kirk was startled. He turned to face the other man. "You're *not* the scientist—"

"His son," Holtzman said proudly.

Barclay was still out. Kirk first tied Holtzman's hands and feet together, and then tethered him on a short line to the base of the heavy kitchen table. He then trussed the unconscious Barclay. The captain then conducted a quick search of the two bound men and found nothing.

"Vladsilovich, Max, I'm accepting your parole," Kirk decided. "Sulu, arm them. We need another couple of phasers on our side. Burke's ten minutes are almost up." Kirk had decided that Max and Vladsilovich might be fools, but they were not mass murderers and had had no prior knowledge of the New Athens plot. Besides, he *had* to trust them; he needed their help.

Sulu issued weapons to the two of them. "Traitors," Holtzman snarled from the floor. "Traitors to my father's memory, traitors to your race, traitors to humanity." He spat.

"I ought to wipe that up with your face," Kirk said. Holtzman shrugged as best he could in his bonds.

Kirk looked out the window. Now he could see a line of troops, at least the eighty he'd expected and probably more, openly forming at the edge of the clearing in which Kirk's cabin sat. *Yeah, there's a combat phaser, too,* Kirk thought resignedly. *Well, Burke, you're still not getting Barclay—or the Boy Wonder, either. And I'm not going to sacrifice these other three to your appetite for revenge. You want a fight, you'll get one.*

Kirk and the others waited.

"The ten minutes are up, Captain Kirk," came Burke's voice over the loudspeaker. "Use a white flag at the window to signal your intent to surrender."

Kirk stepped closer to the window, where he could be seen plainly, and gave a signal of an entirely different kind . . . but one even more ancient.

"Very well, Captain," Burke said. "On my order, the force will advance." There was a moment of silence . . . but in it, Kirk heard a distant rumbling. It grew louder by the second. He wondered what it was; it seemed to come from the sky.

Kirk craned his neck upward; he couldn't see anything. *Wait a minute!* he thought. *There's nothing up there—the flitters and jets are gone!*

And the rumbling noise was becoming a vibrating, almost tangible thing. *It's like a slow-motion earthquake,* wondered Kirk. Small objects began to dance on the cabin's shelves as the entire structure began to shake slightly.

Kirk looked outside. Some of the troops were running away! Others had dropped their arms and were holding their hands against their ears; combat helmets had been discarded and were lying on the ground, forgotten.

Even inside Kirk's insulated cabin, the noise was fierce. Objects were now dancing right off the shelves and crashing to the floor, but Kirk could no longer hear the breakage. The duraplast windows were ringing in their frames, but they were holding.

What the hell is it? Kirk wondered. He looked outside again—and gasped.

The *Enterprise* was sailing slowly and majestically toward his cabin, over the gentle land, at an altitude of not more than one hundred meters.

Burke saw her, too, and cursed. He watched the troops drop their arms and run. *Who wouldn't run from that damn thing?* he thought.

It was over; Burke could not and would not risk his men against a starship. Of all the things Kirk might have done, could have possibly done, he had not imagined this. It was undefeatable; he was checkmated.

He turned to Perez, tears in his eyes. The defense minister nodded mournfully, understandingly; he put a hand on Burke's shoulder. *A good try,* Perez was saying. *A very good try. But, Nat, they were just too big for you.*

Burke turned and walked to his command flitter. Perez followed, covering his ears against the sheer wall of noise from the mighty impulse engines of the *Enterprise*. Burke didn't bother.

Kirk had never seen her like this before; he felt the sting of tears. His lady was coming to the rescue once more, and he was grateful again to the depths of his soul. *God, she looks magnificent!* he thought. She shone a brilliant white in the light of the suns as she effortlessly cruised the cobalt-blue sky.

And she was *big!* Kirk had last seen her close-up from the outside—only the day before?—yet that had been in space, where anything built by man was made less by the vast scale of the cosmos. But here, against only the smallest piece of that cosmos, she dominated all, becoming an *Enterprise* triumphant.

She had finally come to his valley. Here, in close proximity, were the two things Kirk loved the most in his life. He could never remember being so happy, of having such a sense of *rightness* about things. *Spock, you're right,* he thought dizzily. *Humans* can *overdose on joy, after all.* Kirk was buzzed on rapture . . . but not so much that he did not notice the appearance of a shuttlecraft from the stern of the *Enterprise* . . . a craft that would take him up to his other home.

Chapter Twenty-Five:
The Final Frontier

Captain's log, stardate 7520.7:

Lieutenant Uhura reports a hail from U.S.S. Hood, due to arrive in Centaurian standard orbit at stardate 7521.5. The Hood will assume our central role in New Athens relief operations, freeing us at last to go to Starbase Seven for ship's repairs.

The dissipation of the tachyonic interference blanket around Centaurus is accelerating, now that nearly two weeks have passed since the New Athens disaster. Today is the first day subspace communications frequencies in this sector have been clear enough to reach Starfleet easily, so I have had Uhura package all recent log entries and transmit them to Starfleet Command. Those logs include commendations for ship's officers Spock, Sulu, Chekov, Scott, MacPherson, and Flores. I am also proud to note that this ship and its crew have earned a "Well done" from Admiral Buchinsky.

It had been seven days since Kirk's return to the *Enterprise*, a week of refit, repair and redoubled efforts to bring additional aid to the population of New Athens.

Once Starbase 7 had passed the word that the Centaurian defense system had been deactivated, all manner of aid had been dispatched from virtually every important member of the Federation. Earth's nations mourned the destruction of the hospital ships *Dooley*, *Cavell* and *Sakharov*—but had quickly sent the *Tutu*, *Barnard* and *Semmelweiss* to replace them. They, and more than twenty other ships, were now in orbit around Centaurus, and the thousands of doctors and nurses aboard them—as well as desperately needed medical equipment and supplies—were now at work treating the injured. And more such ships were on the way. It was becoming a crowded sky again.

Saul Weinstein was still handling things at Founders Park, but now with all the help he had always needed. With the authority of his Starfleet command rank, Kirk had declared martial law in the New Athens area and installed Weinstein as the area's surgeon general. He had also appointed Thaddeus Hayes—the chief of protocol who'd greeted him and Sulu in McIverton— as administrative head of the martial law district; that saved Kirk from doing the job himself. The captain figured that anyone who had started out as a labor mediator could handle the minor chore of running a disaster zone. Kirk had been right; Hayes was performing splendidly in the job. *Wouldn't be surprised if that man has a future in planetary politics,* Kirk thought.

Kirk also hadn't minded the thumb-in-the-eye that his declaration of martial law had given to the government of President Erikkson. Kirk had as much as said the government was incompetent to handle the emergency. It was true enough, though. According to Spock's report, no evidence that the government had ever dispatched a repair mission to the Defense Center had been found, and there had been no effective government presence at Founders Park—except for the presence of some local cops who had shown up anyway. Kirk wondered what Erikkson had been waiting for. The captain assumed that there would be some changes made in the next elections; Kirk might even send in his landowner's absentee ballot, for once.

Kirk had been briefly tempted to accompany *Columbus* down to McIverton to collect *Galileo* from Government Field—but he assumed that Sulu and Chekov would enjoy the trip even more without him . . . especially with six Security men at their side, each toting a number-two phaser and hoping for trouble. However, the pickup had been made without incident.

Bones and Joanna McCoy were still working in Founders Park, although they spent their nights aboard the *Enterprise,* now that there were doctors and nurses aplenty to cover for them and the transporters were working again. Dr. M'Benga was serving as the *Enterprise*'s chief medical officer pro tem; Kirk was carrying Bones on his lists as temporarily detached from duty.

Kirk smiled as he recalled again that last landing of the *Columbus,* and how he'd emerged from his cabin to see Joanna McCoy stepping from the shuttle gangway, the first out. Bones had followed her out, medikit in hand; Kirk had gestured with a thumb toward the cabin and said, "Stab wound, Bones; he's on the floor. The other one's got phaser stun." McCoy had nodded quickly, mumbling a greeting to Kirk as he flashed by.

But Kirk hadn't noticed. He was looking at the living Joanna McCoy. No one had yet told him she was alive and safe; no one had had the chance. After standing still for a moment, Kirk had grinned sheepishly; he could not find the words of greeting and relief and joy he wanted.

But words hadn't been necessary. Joanna squealed, "Uncle *Jim!!!*" and ran to him and hugged him until he thought his spine would crack.

Kirk hadn't minded that a bit.

Scotty and MacPherson, working as closely together as always, had completed repairs to the ship's badly abused internal communications systems and patched the impulse control centers enough to permit a safe trip to Starbase 7, where drydock personnel would shortly be swarming all over and through Kirk's ship. Spock was estimating a repair time of six weeks, five for the work itself and an extra week "to allow for human inefficiency." That was one of the things Kirk liked about Spock: With him, you always knew exactly where you stood.

Two days before, a Federation scout ship—U.S.S. *Conrad*—had pulled alongside. Her captain had taken formal custody of the five suspects in the New Athens bombing for transport to Earth. Kirk had sent along a sworn statement outlining Barclay's recitation of the "hypothetical" circumstances of the blast.

Sam Cogley had gone with them. Kirk had talked with the lawyer just before departure.

"Are you going to see this thing through to the end, Sam?" Kirk had asked. "Seems to be just your kind of case."

Cogley had stared into his coffee cup. "No, Jim, I'm dropping the case once my clients secure legal representation on Earth," he'd said. "I wouldn't mind defending the other three, but I can't do that without prejudicing the case against the first two. So I'm bowing out . . . but I'll suggest a few names to my clients."

"Why are you pulling out?" Kirk had asked.

Cogley'd nodded slowly. "A fair question. I owe you an answer, and I'll give it to you—as long as it never leaves this room."

"Understood."

"I'm an old lawyer, Jim. I've seen it all. You do what I do for a living, and you get an instinct for what the truth is in a case. I felt all along that Barclay was lying to me about his role in the conspiracy. My gut told me he and Holtzman's son, at least, had known about the plan to bomb New Athens all along."

"He must have," Kirk had said. "Once tachyonic interference from below cleared up enough, we sensor-scanned the surface of Centaurus for antimatter and easily found the three annihilation weapons Barclay boasted about back in the cabin. Security disarmed them, and I gave them to the *Conrad*'s captain for evidence. I wonder why Barclay showed his hand like that?"

Cogley had taken a sip of his cooling coffee. "Because he's fundamentally *stupid,* Jim. He couldn't resist boasting about his 'power,' and he must have figured, somehow, that a starship couldn't detect the presence of antimatter from orbit. Ridiculous! But a smart man—even a not-so-smart one—would never swallow the League's political program. It's just warmed-over national socialism, with an unhealthy chunk of racial hatred thrown in for flavoring."

"Delusions of grandeur?" Kirk had asked. "Sounds likely, anyway. Barclay figured he was so damn good that no one could stop him. He must have figured he'd get off Centaurus, courtesy of the Federation, and then stop the Federation from taking action against him by threatening to use his three remaining bombs."

Cogley had nodded. "The secret of cheap antimatter production was lost with Isidore Holtzman. His son doesn't know how to do it; Barclay certainly doesn't, and Holtzman didn't work with assistants. Of course, given the hint, some bright boy will figure it out all over again, and there might be another problem someday. But at least Barclay's run is at an end."

Kirk had nodded, agreeing. "But how did you know he was guilty, Sam?"

Cogley had paused. "I always trust my gut, Jim. It's like when, a couple of years ago, I took on the job of defending a starship captain in a case involving airtight, indisputable evidence that he was guilty of gross negligence and perjury, and maybe murder, in the death of a fellow officer. Open and shut—but my gut told me then that you were innocent, Jim, despite how things looked for you . . . just as my gut's now telling me that Barclay and Holtzman are guilty as hell of conspiracy. They may be guilty of far more than that. But guilty or innocent, Jim, those two deserve the best defense they can get; that's the way it works. And I can't deliver that; I've seen New Athens. They'll have to hire somebody who hasn't."

"What will you do next?" Kirk had asked.

Cogley had come up with the ghost of a grin. "After the *Conrad* drops my soon-to-be-former clients on Earth and their representation is set, I'm coming back here. The Federation's decided to charge Nathaniel Burke and Daniel Perez with gross obstruction of justice. Seems they used their government posts to try to keep a starship captain from securing custody of five suspects wanted by the Federation."

Kirk had stared at Cogley, and then burst out laughing.

Cogley had smiled. "It'd be a conflict for me if it ever got to trial, Jim, because I was so involved—but it'll never get that far. I've already put out feelers, and the Federation prosecutor will be satisfied if the two of them simply resign their offices and drop out of government for keeps."

"Somehow, I don't mind that much," Kirk had admitted. "Burke and Perez lost their families in New Athens. That affects a man."

"It surely does," Cogley had said, finishing his coffee. . . .

"Call from Mr. Spock," Uhura called out from the communications station, interrupting Kirk's reverie.

"Thank you, Lieutenant." Kirk thumbed the ACCEPT pad on the arm of his chair. "Yes, Mr. Spock?"

"Captain, I am down in the computer room. I have something you may be interested in. Are you able to come down here? You will not need a 'clean suit'; I have sealed all working computer banks."

"Certainly. Be right down. Kirk out." The captain rose. "Mr. Sulu, you have the conn. I'll be down in the brain room."

"Aye, aye, Captain."

The turbolift doors squeaked open for Kirk, and he stepped inside. "Computer room," he said, and the idiot circuits Spock and Scott had installed to substitute for the computers' much more complicated vocal-response processors shut the doors and sent the 'lift on its way. *God, it's nice to have things working again,* Kirk told himself.

The 'lift doors opened, and Kirk saw that the entrance to the computer room, usually sealed shut, was wide open. "Spock?" he called.

"In here, Captain," the Vulcan said.

Kirk entered. Things were all right. As Spock had said, the intact banks of the computer room had been sealed behind shields of acrylic to preserve the utter cleanliness they required; the rest of the banks had been ruined and, for them, cleanliness no longer mattered. Spock had spent a morning completing the shielding so that he could enter the computer room without having to go through the lengthy personal cleansing process each time. *Logical,* thought Kirk.

"Greetings, Captain," Spock said politely. "I believe I have an answer to the question of why most of our computer banks were destroyed."

"Oh. From your tone, I take it that it wasn't an act of sabotage, after all?"

"Not that, nor was it the fault of anyone's carelessness. We were the victims of a freak accident—but it may turn out to be a fortuitous one."

"An 'accident.' What do you mean, Spock?"

"Quite simply, Captain, we went through a black hole—or we could say quite as easily that a black hole went through *us*. It left its mark behind it: the perfectly circular and regular holes drilled through the dead computer banks. Look here." Spock walked to bank 15, counting from the left; he touched it with an inertial screwdriver, and it rolled out from the wall.

"Observe, Captain," Spock said, pointing at the hole in the bank. "Bank fourteen, the one to the left of this, is intact. You see that the hole in bank fifteen does not *quite* penetrate it entirely. Now bank sixteen"—Spock withdrew it from its bulkhead—"was completely penetrated. This is also true of banks seventeen through two twenty-four. I found that bank two twenty-five was intact, so I withdrew number two twenty-four entirely from the bulkhead and found the other end of the hole, perhaps a centimeter deep inside."

"So a black hole did it? How do you know?"

"I inferred that from the tricorder readings I took soon after the computer banks were rendered nonoperational," Spock said. "However, I did not credit my initial assumption, because not all facts fit. Simply put, a black hole should not do what this one did."

"What did this one *do,* Spock?"

"Look at this, Captain." Spock handed Kirk a computer printout. It read:

TIME 0.0000000087 SEC
DISTANCE 20.8655928 METERS
RADIUS 6.5800255222685 X 10^{-22} CM
MASS 4431.0476216943 KG (STD)
TEMP 4.4310476216943 X 10^{32} K

"That is really all there is to it, Captain," Spock said. "The Hawking equations concerning black holes apply here. We have known since the twentieth century that small black holes—those massing less than planetary size—are not eternal. Very small ones die very quickly. However, until now, no black hole is known to have come into spontaneous existence since the Big Bang. Such have been theorized, but none has ever been found.

"At the time the hole damaged our computers, the *Enterprise* was making warp two. At that speed the ship travels nearly twenty-one meters in just under nine billionths of a second. The hole was not moving; rather, we traveled through where the hole was, and that is what did the damage. The length of the track the hole left in our computer banks is the amount of distance the ship traveled in the time the hole existed. Further, allowing for massive tidal and thermal forces, and the fractive quotient of the material used in casting the banks, the diameter of the hole's track is consistent with the diameter of the black hole, as conjectured."

"But wait a minute, Spock," Kirk said. "If I'm reading this printout right, you say the black hole massed nearly four and a half tons."

"Correct, Captain."

"That means we were hit by the equivalent of a

good-sized boulder traveling at eight times the speed of light. Why aren't we dead?"

"I do not know yet," Spock said. "Theoretically, the energy released by such a collision should have utterly destroyed the *Enterprise*. That it did not is both fortunate and mysterious. It may be that we are talking about two different kinds of qualities of mass, one of which may only partially affect the other. The situation challenges everything I know of physics, Captain, and I have been studying it for most of this past week with only limited success."

"You'll get another academic paper out of it, anyway," said Kirk.

"Several, undoubtedly," Spock said. "However, I wish I had more data with which to write them. But at least there is this: We have a unique artifact here before us, Captain—a complete, unbroken life history of a black hole, from beginning to end. A close inspection of the track of the black hole may some day yield discoveries that have eluded us for some time."

Kirk rubbed his chin. "Keep after it, Spock. We'll have five—or six—weeks at Starbase Seven; you have that much leave time coming to you, at least. Use it to the fullest."

"Thank you, Captain. I appreciate it."

"Uh, one more thing. I'd been hoping you might find the time to go with me to Centaurus for a stay in Garrovick Valley. The ship will be in the hands of the repair crews for some weeks, and we've all got some R and R coming, but I don't suppose . . . ?"

"On the contrary, Captain. I would be pleased to join you. I found the valley pleasant and restful in the brief time I was there with *Columbus* for your pickup. The valley agreed with my sense of the aesthetic."

"Oh. Well, fine, Spock! Come by when you care to, stay as long as you want. There's no schedule and no calendar at my place."

"I think I might like it by the riverbank, Captain," Spock said musingly. "It looked quite peaceful there." The Vulcan paused. "Captain, may I be permitted a question?"

"Of course, Spock."

"Why have you never told me of the valley? Its purchase seems quite an achievement."

Kirk thought for a moment, and then shook his head. "I don't know, Spock. I never talk about my place. The only person aboard the ship who knew about it was Dr. McCoy, and that only because he was with me when I found it, many years ago. I suppose I may be jealously guarding my privacy somehow."

"I understand 'private matters,' Captain," Spock said. "And I understand that a starship captain has many demands on him. A Vulcan has deep and unshakable notions of privacy." He paused. "I was—disturbed—that you perhaps thought I would not recognize the valley's importance to you, or that I would not respect any confidence concerning it."

"No. Never that."

"I am relieved. Later, then, Captain?"

"Of course." Kirk turned to leave.

"Go well, Jim," Spock said to his back.

Captain's log, stardate 7521.6:
> *The U.S.S.* Hood *has arrived, and her captain has relieved this ship of duty at this station. Starfleet has cut our orders for drydock work at Starbase Seven, and Mr. Scott assures me the ship is ready to go.*
>
> *Iziharry, Constance, a nurse in the medical section and a native of Centaurus, has reconfirmed her desire to stay home and assist in rescue and reclamation efforts. I have accepted her resignation from the service with regret. Three other personnel—McHenry,*

Thomas; Garibaldi, Mona; and Siderakis, Peter—have submitted separation requests for the same reason, and I have approved these as well. Iziharry will continue working with Dr. Weinstein; the other three will take jobs in the Reclamation and Reconstruction Agency being set up by Thad Hayes. Each of the three will be a worthy addition to the RRA.

Dr. McCoy will remain behind as well, but only temporarily. He will rejoin the Enterprise *at Starbase Seven when our repairs have been completed. In the meantime he will work with his daughter, Joanna, under Dr. Weinstein. I have offered Joanna McCoy an appointment to the Medical School Division of Starfleet Academy, and she is considering acceptance. Her father heartily approves of the notion. So, for that matter, do I; Joanna McCoy would make a splendid addition to Starfleet's medical roster.*

And so, at last, it was all as it should be, with Mr. Spock at his science station and Captain Kirk in the command chair, seated behind Sulu and Chekov manning the positions at the helm. "Mr. Chekov, lay in a course for Starbase Seven," Kirk ordered.

"Computed and laid in, sir," Chekov responded smartly.

Kirk was feeling that familiar thrill again—the one he felt every time he was about to say *this:* "Helmsman, take us out."

"Aye, aye, sir," Sulu answered.

The hum of the impulse engines rose high as the *Enterprise* set out once more to soar among the stars that lined her never-ending road.